LEGENDARY

BOOK 3

CHRISTINE POPE

TRIAL BY FIRE

ISBN: 978-1-946435-91-0

Published by Dark Valentine Press

Cover design by Indie Author Services

Ebook formatting by Indie Author Services

CHAPTER ONE

The electromagnetic pulse hit at a little after three in the morning, yanking me from sleep as effectively as though someone had grabbed me by the arm and thrown me to the floor.

The digital clock went dark, while across the room, my phone gave a single panicked flash before it, too, went black. The table fan on the dresser died at the same moment, its faint hum stopping so abruptly that the resulting silence pressed against my eardrums, a heavy, unnatural pressure that made my panicked breath sound like a roar.

But that silence lasted only a heartbeat before my electromagnetic sense—the strange gift I'd apparently inherited from generations of similarly talented women—erupted in a burst of agony.

I sat upright in bed and pressed both hands to my temples as wave after wave of distorted energy crashed through my body. This wasn't the familiar background hum of Silver Hollow's portal or the gentle pulse of the forest's natural electromagnetic field. I'd gotten mostly used to those over the past few weeks, even though I knew it would take much longer than a few short weeks to truly accept them as part of myself.

No, whatever I was sensing now was chaotic and desperate. Dying.

Something in the forest was screaming.

For a moment, I sat in the utter darkness of my bedroom—a room without even the faint glow from the digital clock to illuminate the void—and tried to process what I was feeling, even as my brain shrieked at me to go take some ibuprofen or something, anything that might dull the agony even for a few minutes.

The terrible, shredded sensation was unlike anything I'd experienced before. It had texture and depth, layers of meaning my mind struggled to interpret, something that felt completely foreign. There was pain, yes, and desperation, absolutely. But underneath those surface emotions, I sensed something older and far more complex. I wasn't picking up on a rabbit entangled in a snare or even a bear caught in an illegal trap. This was something ancient, something that had existed long before human civilization and was now crying out for help in a language my abilities could barely comprehend.

My nose began to bleed, an unwelcome warmth dripping down onto my upper lip.

I grabbed a tissue from the nightstand and held it to my face as I stumbled through the dark hallway. The big Craftsman house felt far too empty at night, even though I'd been living here alone since February, and now it was the middle of August. For my entire life, this house had been filled with my grandmother's presence—the way she hummed in the kitchen as she prepared that evening's meal, the cheery sound of her voice as she asked how my day had gone, the soft rustle of journal pages as she recorded her observations about the portal and the incredible creatures that sometimes crossed through from the other side.

Now she and my mother were both gone, trapped on the other side of an interdimensional crossing, lost in a realm I could barely comprehend and couldn't reach. The house was mine by default, filled with furniture and memories but empty of the people who'd made it a home.

I forced myself to shake off the melancholy, even as I made my way down the dark stairs to the first floor, the Kleenex still pressed against my nose. No time for brooding now. Whatever was screaming in the forest needed help, and the distress call felt as if it was getting weaker by the second. Every instinct in my body screamed that if I didn't reach the source soon, I'd be too late.

When I opened the front door, the night air that greeted me was cold and damp, chilly enough to make me pull in a shocked breath. Stars wheeled overhead in an unusually clear sky, and the new moon meant the darkness was absolute beyond the pale illumination the porch light sent out into the yard. I went back inside long enough to jam my feet into my hiking boots—which I'd left near the coat rack in the entry—and grab the heavy-duty flashlight from the entry table.

The pull in my chest was like a fishhook lodged behind my sternum, tugging me toward the forest with increasing urgency. I'd never felt anything like this before. Sure, I could always sense when the unicorn was near, and I'd also been able to feel it when the griffin stranded temporarily in Silver Hollow needed my help, but this was utterly different.

I paused on the porch, one hand on the railing, and tried to center myself. Lately, I'd been doing my best to teach myself techniques for managing electromagnetic overload—grounding exercises, visualization methods, ways to filter the constant barrage of electronic noise that plagued modern life. But those techniques were designed for everyday interference, not for whatever was happening now. I might as well have been using a garden hose to fight a forest fire.

The distress call pulsed again, stronger this time, and my knees buckled. I grabbed the porch railing with both hands, and the flashlight clattered to the wooden planks. Blood dripped from my nose onto the floor, missing the toes of my hiking boots by less than an inch. It looked black in the starlight.

"Come on, Sidney," I muttered to myself. "Pull it together. Whatever's out there needs you."

I forced myself to breathe slowly, counting to four on the inhale, holding for four, exhaling for four. The technique didn't stop the electromagnetic assault, but it gave me enough control to function…sort of. I pressed the Kleenex I held against my nose and was relieved to see that at least the bleeding seemed to have stopped, so I bent and retrieved the flashlight and made my way down the porch steps.

The gravel driveway crunched under my boots as I hurried toward the closest trailhead, about a quarter-mile from the property. My mother's old Subaru sat in its usual spot in front of the garage, and for a moment, I considered taking it. The forest roads were rough, but I could get to the portal site much faster by car than on foot.

But no—the electromagnetic pulse had killed the power in my house, which meant it had probably fried every electronic device within a significant radius. The car wouldn't start even if I tried. Sure, the thing was almost twenty years old, but it still had an electronic ignition.

I was maybe fifteen yards down the street when headlights swept across me, and Ben Sanders' truck came skidding to a stop only a few feet away.

Relief flooded through me so intensely that my eyes burned. I hadn't realized until that moment how much I'd dreaded facing this alone. Ben was here, the man who'd seen me at my worst over the past few months and who'd watched me develop these strange abilities without running screaming in the other direction…the man who'd somehow become the most important person in my life without either of us quite meaning for it to happen.

He was out of the driver's seat before the engine stopped, his hair sticking up at odd angles and his battered old field jacket thrown on over what looked like pajama pants and a T-shirt that read "Bigfoot Doesn't Believe in You, Either." The laptop bag slung over his shoulder bounced against his hip as he jogged toward me, and I could see the glow of active equipment through the mesh side pocket.

"Tell me you felt that," he said, slightly breathless. His hazel eyes were wide with the same mixture of worry and excitement I recognized from every other supernatural crisis we'd faced together this crazy summer. "My equipment went insane. Every sensor I have just registered a spike that shouldn't be possible. I'm talking about magnitude readings that would require a solar flare or a nuclear detonation, but somehow localized to maybe a two-mile radius. Sidney, what the hell is happening?"

"I felt it." My nose had started dripping again. I lifted my abused Kleenex and wiped blood from my upper lip. "Something's dying out there, Ben. Something big."

His expression shifted when he saw the blood, his excitement at this new phenomenon immediately replaced by concern. He closed the distance between us and gently tilted my chin up so he could examine my face in the beam of his flashlight. "You're bleeding. How bad is the overload?"

I didn't see much point in lying to him, so I simply said, "Bad."

There was an understatement. The electromagnetic ebbs and flows of the forest had affected me before now, but my body had never reacted in such a viscerally physical way until this point. "But I can function. We need to move. Whatever's out there, it's connected to the portal. I can feel it. If it dies...."

I didn't finish the sentence. I didn't need to.

Ben's jaw tightened. We both understood what might happen if the delicate magical ecosystem around Silver Hollow's interdimensional crossing collapsed. The portal seemed to have stabilized somewhat over the past few weeks, now that the griffin had returned to its world and the shadow stalkers had been banished, but my mother and grandmother were still trapped on the other side. If something happened to destabilize the current delicate balance, they might be cut off forever. And that was assuming the dimensional barriers didn't rupture completely, which could unleash God-knows-what into our world.

"How far?" he asked, his gaze moving toward the trailhead.

"Maybe two miles northeast. The old-growth section near the portal." I had to stop and lean against the wooden trail marker post as another wave of electromagnetic distress moved through me. This time it carried images with it, fragments of sensation that didn't translate cleanly into human experience. Fire that wasn't fire. Wings that caught starlight. A cycle interrupted, broken.

Wrong.

Ben's hand was warm and steady on my elbow, and I could sense his electromagnetic signature as clearly as I felt my own heartbeat. That was new, or at least more pronounced than it had been. Over the past few weeks, I'd become increasingly aware of the way Ben's bioelectric field resonated with mine, creating a kind of harmony that amplified my abilities when he was close. It should have felt invasive, having someone else's electromagnetic presence so intertwined with my own. Instead, it felt like finding the other half of a circuit I hadn't even realized was incomplete.

Was that why I'd had an almost immediate connection to him, even when common sense had told me the last thing I needed right now was a relationship?

"Sidney, if you're already bleeding, maybe we should—"

"I don't have a choice." I straightened and met his gaze, trying to project far more confidence than I felt. "Whatever's out there, it's calling for me specifically. I can feel it reaching toward my abilities, trying to guide me. If I don't respond…." I shook my head. "I don't know what will happen if I don't answer it, but I can feel how wrong this is. Whatever's going on, this isn't supposed to be happening."

He studied my face for a long moment, and I could see him weighing the risks, calculating odds the way he always did. At last, he nodded. "Okay. But we're doing this smart. I'll monitor your vitals and the electromagnetic readings. If things start going sideways, we'll head for home immediately. Agreed?"

"Agreed," I lied. No matter how much this might mess me up, I knew I had to find the source of pain in the woods and do whatever I could to make it right.

We moved faster after that, following game trails I knew by heart even in the dark. The forest pressed close on both sides—Douglas firs and coast redwoods that had stood here for centuries, their presence solid and reassuring in the chaos of the electromagnetic storm battering my senses. Under normal circumstances, I would have been able to hear the trees' slow conversation through their root networks, the gentle electromagnetic dialogue that connected every plant in the forest. Tonight, however, that background symphony was drowned out completely by the dying creature's distress call.

Ben kept pace beside me, his flashlight beam cutting through the darkness while he periodically checked the EMF reader clipped to his belt. The device beeped urgently every few seconds, its readings spiking with each pulse of electromagnetic energy. I could feel his concern like something physical against my skin, but he didn't try to slow me down or suggest we turn back. He trusted my judgment, even when I wasn't sure I trusted it myself.

"The frequency patterns aren't like anything I've seen so far," he said after we'd been walking for maybe ten minutes, his breathing only slightly labored despite the steep terrain. "It's not random interference. There's structure to it. Almost like some kind of communication."

"It's calling for help." I had to stop again as my nose started to bleed more profusely. The tissue I had clutched in one hand was already soaked through, so I shoved it into a pocket and pressed my sleeve to my face instead. The nylon fabric came away dark with blood, and I wondered absently if I'd ruined it forever. "Whatever is out there, it knows I'm coming. It's trying to guide me."

Ben pulled a clean bandana from one of his many jacket pockets—the man was like a walking camping supply store—and handed it to me. "Here. Save your sleeve."

Probably too late for that, but I pressed the bandana to my nose anyway and kept moving. The electromagnetic pull was getting stronger, which meant we were close. But it also felt as if it was getting more chaotic with each step we took. I didn't know what was out there, but I could tell it was losing its ability to maintain the signal.

Losing strength. Dying.

"We need to move faster," I said, and broke into a jog despite the rough terrain.

"Sidney, wait—"

But I was already running, bandana still

pressed against my nose as I followed the invisible thread that connected my abilities to the source of the distress call. Tree branches whipped at my face and arms, and roots tried to trip me. I didn't care, though. The creature's pain was my pain now, resonating through every nerve in my body, and the only way to make it stop was to reach it.

Behind me, I heard Ben curse and then the sound of his boots pounding on the trail as he ran to catch up. His flashlight beam bounced crazily through the trees, creating shadows that seemed to leap and writhe.

The forest around us grew denser as we pushed deeper into the old-growth section. Some of the trunks of the trees around us were so wide that you could drive a car through them, their bark deeply furrowed and scarred by centuries of fires and storms. The canopy overhead was thick enough that even my powerful flashlight barely penetrated more than a few yards ahead.

I'd been in this section of forest before, but never at night, and never while running at full speed through the darkness. Back then, I'd only wanted to explore as much of the woods as I possibly could, to let myself be alone with the trees. I'd had no idea that one day, my strange abilities would be able to sense the way those trees communicated with one another, how their bioelectric network was as strong as anything we humans could build.

"Sidney!" Ben's voice was sharp with alarm. "Your hands—look at your hands!"

I glanced down and immediately saw what he was talking about. My fingers were trembling uncontrollably, and even in the dim light, I could see how they'd gone fish-belly white, almost gray. The electromagnetic overload was affecting my entire nervous system now, disrupting the signals that controlled muscle coordination and blood flow.

This was bad. This was worse than any overload I'd experienced before. If I pushed much harder, I'd risk permanent neurological damage.

But the creature's distress call pulsed again, weaker this time, and I knew I didn't have a choice. I could deal with the consequences later. Right now, someone—some*thing*—needed help.

"I'm okay," I said, which was such an obvious lie that Ben didn't even bother to respond. "We're close. I can feel it."

The terrain leveled out as we reached a section of forest I didn't immediately recognize. The trees here stood in an almost perfect circle around a clearing, their branches creating a natural cathedral overhead. Starlight managed to penetrate the canopy here in a way it didn't anywhere else, creating a pool of silver illumination in the center of the clearing.

And in that pool of light, something glowed with a fitful orange fire, a large bird with its head drooping against the ground.

The color was wrong. I'd read enough in my grandmother's journals to know that phoenix fire was supposed to burn white-gold, pure and clean as starlight, even though I'd never seen one myself —well, not before now, anyway.

This color was wrong. Corrupted.

"Oh, my God," Ben whispered beside me, and I felt his hand find mine, our fingers interlacing automatically. "Is that—"

"A phoenix." The word came out as a harsh breath.

We stood at the edge of the clearing for a long moment, both of us too stunned to move. I'd known, intellectually, that phoenixes existed. My grandmother's journals had documented several sightings over the decades, always brief glimpses around the time of the portal's opening. But knowing something existed and actually seeing it were two very different things.

The creature lay in the center of the clearing, its wings spread across the moss and ferns like a broken fan of living flame. Even dying, even contaminated, it was the most magnificent thing I'd ever seen. Its body was roughly the size of a large eagle, but the resemblance ended there. Its feathers seemed to be made of actual fire, flickering and dancing even though the creature lay motionless. But the fire was wrong, tainted with shadows that writhed through the golden light like infection spreading through a wound.

The electromagnetic signature I'd been following emanated from the phoenix like heat from a bonfire, but it was fractured and chaotic. Where it should have been a pure, clean pulse, instead it stuttered and sparked, fighting against some kind of interference that corrupted the natural rhythm.

"Sidney." Ben's voice was tight with a mixture of awe and scientific fascination as his gaze moved from the EMF meter he held in one hand to the enormous bird lying so limp and helpless in the center of the clearing. "I'm picking up two distinct electromagnetic signatures. One is the phoenix itself—that's the clean pulse you're probably sensing. But there's another signal overlaying it. It's artificial. Mechanical, I think."

My blood went cold despite the heat radiating from the dying creature. "Someone did this," I said, even though I had no idea how such a thing was even possible. "Someone's been interfering with the phoenix's fire."

"More than interfering." Ben's gaze was now fixed on the EMF meter, his expression growing grimmer by the second. "Whatever this artificial signal is, it looks like it's actively corrupting the phoenix's natural pattern. Sort of like a computer virus, but for magic."

As we approached, the phoenix lifted its head. Its eyes were ancient and intelligent and filled with such profound pain that sympathetic tears began to stream down my face to mix with the blood still dripping from my nose.

Help me, it seemed to say, although no sound emerged from its beak. The plea resonated directly in my electromagnetic senses, bypassing language entirely. *The cycle breaks. The fire corrupts. Help me, guardian's daughter.*

I was on my knees next to the creature before I'd even consciously decided to move. Up close, I could see the true extent of the damage. The shadow corruption wasn't only in its fire—it had spread through the phoenix's entire being, dark veins that pulsed with an energy that made my head ache.

"What happened to you?" I whispered, reaching out with a tentative hand. It hovered inches from the phoenix's wing, and I could feel the heat radiating from its corrupted fire.

The creature's response came as a flood of images and sensations. A natural cycle of death and rebirth, repeated countless times over the centuries. The portal's energy sustaining the process, providing the dimensional stability the phoenix needed to complete its resurrection. But recently, something had changed—electromagnetic interference that disrupted the natural rhythms, equipment in the forest that shouldn't be there. And when the phoenix had tried to begin its latest rebirth cycle, that interference had corrupted the process.

The fire that should have consumed and renewed had instead been poisoned, trapped in a state between death and life, unable to complete the transformation.

"How long?" Ben asked quietly. He'd knelt beside me, his equipment already out and recording data. "How long has it been like this?"

Another wave of sensation answered him. Weeks. The phoenix had been suffering for weeks, growing weaker as the corruption spread, unable to complete its rebirth but also unable to fully die.

"This isn't natural," I said, anger burning through the electromagnetic fog in my head. "Someone did this. Someone's been interfering with the portal's magic."

Ben's fingers tightened on the EMF meter, and his expression was grim as he spoke. "The surveillance devices Dr. Rosenthal and DAPI left behind. I think there are more than what we found. A lot more."

We'd stumbled across various bits of equipment in the woods over the past few weeks during our usual hikes—sensing equipment I didn't recognize, cameras, motion sensors. Everything we located, we took back with us, since Ben could use some of the items. However, it seemed clear now that there were still more of Dr. Rosenthal's devices hiding in the trees than we knew.

Before I could respond, the phoenix convulsed. Its fire flared brighter for a moment, and a surge of desperate energy pulsed through the clearing. The trees around us groaned and creaked, and somewhere in the distance, I heard branches snapping.

"It's destabilizing," Ben said urgently, his gaze moving back to the EMF meter. "Whatever's keeping it in this state, the energy is starting to cascade. Sidney, if this continues—"

I finished his thought for him. "The portal. If the phoenix's fire is connected to the portal's stability, and the corruption spreads…."

We both understood what that meant. The portal was the anchor point for countless magical beings—including my mother and grandmother, who were trapped on the other side. If it collapsed, they would be cut off forever. Silver Hollow's entire supernatural ecosystem would collapse.

And the way the phoenix's fire was guttering

told me that we had a couple of days at best. Maybe far less.

Please. The phoenix's voice was weaker now, fading. *The fire remembers. Help it remember what it should be.*

"I don't know how," I said, desperation making my voice crack. "I don't know how to heal you. I don't know how to cleanse corruption. My grandmother's journals never mentioned anything like this."

The phoenix shifted one wing, and I saw that underneath, close to its chest, was a section different from the rest of its body, a place where its fire burned clean and bright, pure gold without a trace of shadow. From that spot, a single gold feather drifted to the ground.

You carry family's gift, it seemed to say. *You sing the electric song. Let the clean fire guide you. Help me remember.*

I looked at Ben and saw my own uncertainty reflected in his eyes. But I also saw trust. He believed I could do this. He believed I could figure out how to save this ancient, suffering creature.

"Okay," I said, then took a deep breath and immediately regretted it when that gulp of cold air made my head swim. "Okay. Ben, I need you to monitor everything. If something goes wrong

—if I start channeling too much energy—you have to pull me back."

"Sidney—"

"Promise me."

He hesitated, then nodded. "I promise. But we're doing this together. I'm not going anywhere."

I bent and picked up the clean feather, and the moment my fingers touched it, I understood what the phoenix wanted. The fire had memory. It had pattern. And somewhere inside this corrupted, dying creature, that clean pattern still existed—buried, but not destroyed.

If I could reach it with my electromagnetic abilities, if I could resonate with the clean fire and help it remember its true nature, then maybe I could start to burn away the corruption.

It was a long shot. It might not work. And even if it did, it might kill me in the process.

But looking into the phoenix's ancient, pain-filled eyes, I knew I had to try.

"All right," I said quietly. "Let's see if the guardian's daughter can sing the electric song loud enough."

I pressed both hands to the phoenix's wing and closed my eyes, then reached deep into those strange abilities that had surfaced over the past few months. The clean feather's pattern became my guide, showing me what the fire was supposed to be. And slowly, carefully, I began to sing it back to the dying creature.

At once, its fire surged toward my touch like a drowning person reaching for rescue, and the clearing erupted in light.

Behind my closed eyelids, I felt Ben's hand grip my shoulder, anchoring me, keeping me connected to the physical world even as my consciousness merged with otherworldly fire.

And then black flame swept over me.

CHAPTER TWO

The phoenix's corrupted fire cast shadows across Sidney's unconscious face, and Ben didn't know what scared him more—that she wasn't waking up, or that his EMF reader had just risen past levels that shouldn't exist outside a nuclear reactor.

"Come on." He shook her shoulder again, harder this time. At first, he'd touched her almost timidly, but now his desperation made him rougher than he'd intended. "Sidney, *please.*"

Nothing. Her pulse was steady under his fingers, but her skin had gone clammy, and the blood from her nose had dried in dark tracks down to her chin. When he'd pulled her away from the phoenix ten minutes ago, she'd been convulsing. Now she was completely still.

The phoenix stirred, and the orange-black fire

surrounding it pulsed brighter. Every time it moved, the corruption spread a little farther through those magnificent wings. Ben watched another feather succumb—pure gold transforming to sick amber threaded with shadow.

Definitely halfway contaminated now. Maybe a whole lot more.

Waiting hadn't done a bit of good. Now he had no choice but to reach out for help. His fingers began to scrabble for his phone, buried somewhere in the satchel he'd brought with him, and then he remembered that the EMP must have fried every electronic device within a two-mile radius. Except, somehow, his equipment. The sensors he'd pulled from his laptop bag—some of which were pieces left behind by Dr. Rosenthal's team—were all working, all screaming warnings about energy levels and electromagnetic interference patterns that violated every law of physics he understood. Which, he had to admit, wasn't a whole lot. He'd been teaching himself as best he could, but his background was in archaeology and cryptozoology, not quantum electrodynamics.

What he needed right now wasn't working sensors, though. He needed a hospital. He needed some kind of assistance, although he wasn't sure whether modern medicine could even help Sidney.

He needed—

"Ben Sanders."

He spun toward the voice, one hand already going to the knife on his belt before his brain caught up and recognized Agent Rebecca Morse as she stepped into the clearing. She wore cargo pants and a long-sleeved thermal shirt instead of the severe suits that had been her uniform when she was conducting her investigations in Silver Hollow, although her blonde hair was pulled back as tight as ever. Behind her, the forest was starting to show hints of approaching dawn, the black sky softening to charcoal gray along the eastern horizon.

"Agent Morse." Ben didn't lower his hand from the knife. After everything that had happened over the past few weeks—DAPI surveillance, government interference, Sidney nearly hauled away for "enhanced interrogation" —his trust in federal agents had worn pretty thin. He knew that Rebecca Morse had been disgusted by Sonya Rosenthal's methods and had even taken a leave of absence after Rosenthal was safely relegated to a desk job three thousand miles away, but knowing and trusting were two very different things.

Rebecca Morse's gaze moved from him to Sidney, then to the phoenix, and he watched her face cycle through several expressions too quickly for him to read. Shock, for sure. Maybe calculation.

Awe.

"Rebecca," she said briefly, although Ben wasn't sure he'd ever be able to think of her as anything except "Agent Morse." She went on, "My equipment picked up an electromagnetic pulse three hours ago. I've been tracking the source since then." She took two steps closer and kept her hands visible in an obvious attempt to soothe his jittery nerves. "Is she alive?"

"Sidney? Yes. But she won't wake up, and I can't—" His voice cracked, and he cleared his throat and forced himself to try again. "The phoenix is dying. When she tried to cleanse the corruption, it overwhelmed her nervous system."

Rebecca Morse knelt beside Sidney and checked her pulse, then pulled a small flashlight from her belt and examined her eyes, all her movements professional and efficient, like someone who'd administered field first aid plenty of times before. When she straightened, her expression was sober but determined.

"We need to move her—both of them, actually." She gestured at the phoenix. "There's a facility fifteen miles north of here. A man named Daniel Jessop had a research station there—it's been abandoned since the sixties, but the structure's intact. More importantly, it's off DAPI's official grid."

"'Off the grid'?" Ben stared at her, trying to process her words and have them make sense. "But you're with DAPI."

"I *used* to be with DAPI," Rebecca corrected him. "I'm on leave right now, and when I come back, I'm being reassigned to the Sacramento field office. That doesn't mean I agreed with everything Dr. Rosenthal wanted—wants—to do."

"'Wants to do'?" Ben repeated. He didn't like the sound of that at all. "I thought she was finished. I thought the government washed its hands of her and stuck her in a desk job somewhere."

Rebecca's expression was almost pitying, as if she wasn't sure she wanted to destroy any illusions he might have been harboring about how those sorts of things actually worked in the real world. "You know what they say—whenever a door closes, a window opens."

Meaning, he supposed, that Rosenthal had found a way to continue her work, probably backed by a completely different department. That was the problem with something as big as the U.S. government—the right hand often didn't know what the left was doing.

Rebecca Morse continued to gaze at him

steadily, and the frankness he saw in her stern but not unattractive features made him lower the knife. "Ben, I can help you," she went on. "But we have maybe twenty minutes before Rosenthal's tactical team arrives. The EMP knocked out most of their communications, but they'll have backup systems restored soon. When that happens, they'll come here in force, tracking the source of that pulse."

The phoenix made a sound—not quite a cry, more like wind through a dying fire. Another wave of corruption spread through its wings.

Ben gazed down at Sidney's unconscious face, then looked over at Rebecca Morse.

He wanted to believe her, but….

"How do I know this isn't a trap?"

"You don't." Her voice was flat. "But if you stay here, Sonya Rosenthal will take Sidney into custody, dissect that phoenix to understand its biology, and use everything she learns to weaponize dimensional anomalies. So you can trust me, or you can watch that happen."

The clearing went quiet except for the phoenix's labored breathing and the distant sound of tree branches moving in the pre-dawn wind. From inside his satchel, Ben's equipment beeped softly, recording data he'd probably never have time to analyze.

"Fine," he said. "But I'm carrying Sidney."

"I'll handle the phoenix." Agent Morse pulled

a thermal metallic blanket from her pack. "This is woven with electromagnetic shielding. It should contain enough of the fire signature to keep us off Rosenthal's sensors."

Ben gathered Sidney into his arms, and her head lolled against his shoulder. She weighed less than he'd expected—or maybe adrenaline was making him stronger. Either way, he held her close and waited while Rebecca wrapped up the phoenix.

It lay there without resistance as she gathered it in the shielded blanket. That worried Ben more than anything. A healthy magical creature should have fought, should have refused to be handled by strangers. This one just lay there, fire guttering like a candle in the wind.

They moved fast through the trees, Morse navigating with the confidence of someone who'd studied these woods extensively. Ben kept checking Sidney's breathing, counting each rise and fall of her chest. Still alive, thank God. Still with him.

"How long have you been watching us?" he asked after several minutes of silence.

"DAPI's had surveillance on Silver Hollow for six months, maybe more. It's hard for me to say, since Sonya Rosenthal didn't exactly confide in me. I might have been assigned to this project, but we weren't best buddies." She ducked under a low branch and adjusted her grip on the wrapped phoenix. "But after I went on leave, I thought it a good idea to monitor your town as best I could. I couldn't shake the feeling that things weren't over."

No. They definitely weren't. Not by a long shot.

However, he decided to focus on something else Rebecca Morse had said.

"'Six months,'" he repeated. It was a lot longer than he'd thought. "So…long before I even arrived in town."

Her shoulders tensed, but she kept walking.

"The unicorn brought me to Silver Hollow," Ben continued. Anger had begun to build inside him, hot and sharp. "And what about the symbols Sidney and I found all over the forest? Was the guy we saw on the trail cam one of yours?"

Rebecca stopped walking and turned to face him. In the growing light, he could see the conflict in her expression.

"One of Sonya Rosenthal's," she corrected him. "DAPI had one of their agents carve those symbols not too long after you arrived. Dr. Rosenthal wanted to see what it would do to Sidney's abilities to have conflicting energies in the forest, whether unbalancing the portal would cause her gifts to go into overdrive. But beyond that, she wanted someone with your expertise, your background, and your...." Rebecca hesitated there before adding, "Your specific electromagnetic signature."

Ben stared at her. Sidney's weight in his arms felt heavier now, more real. "What the hell does my electromagnetic signature have to do with anything?"

"Keep moving," Rebecca said, and turned away. "I'll explain at the facility. We're running out of time."

He followed because he didn't have a choice. Sidney needed medical attention, and the phoenix needed help he couldn't provide. Rebecca Morse was right about one thing—if they stayed in that clearing, DAPI would find them.

But he made a mental note to get answers. All of them.

The abandoned research facility looked like something from a Cold War nightmare—a concrete bunker half-buried in a hillside, covered with decades of moss and vine growth. Agent Morse produced a key card from her pocket, and the exterior door opened with a hiss of hydraulics that suggested someone had been maintaining the place all along despite its abandoned appearance.

"Down here." She led him into a stairwell lit

by battery-powered emergency lights. The air smelled like metal and must and something else Ben couldn't identify. Probably just age.

Three flights down, they emerged into a corridor lined with doors. Agent Morse headed straight for one marked "MEDICAL" and pushed it open.

The room inside was cleaner than Ben had expected—an examination table, medical supplies in glass cabinets, monitoring equipment that looked like it had been installed within the past year.

"How did you even know about this place?" he asked as he carefully laid Sidney on the examination table. One arm dropped over the edge, but she didn't stir as he gently took hold of it and placed it at her side.

"Some drug runners were using it for a while, but they were rounded up a while back, and it's sat empty since then." Rebecca set the wrapped phoenix on a secondary table along the far wall. "Let's just say that a friend of mine let me know about it when I mentioned I might need a place to go to ground. He sent me the key card a few weeks ago."

Ben supposed it was a good thing to have friends in high places. And it also seemed she'd been planning contingencies for a while, maybe as soon as she realized that Sonya Rosenthal hadn't been as safely sidelined as they all thought.

"And DAPI won't be able to find us here?"

Rebecca's shoulders lifted. "I doubt it. The place hasn't been used in any kind of official capacity for years. I suppose at some point, someone might come around to check on the property, but we'll make sure to be long gone by then."

Her answer wasn't exactly definitive, but it sounded to him as if they should be safe here, especially since they didn't plan to take up permanent residence. They just needed to use the facility long enough to be sure their two patients had stabilized enough to be moved again.

He pulled the remaining sensors from his bag and started setting them up around Sidney and the phoenix. They needed EMF readings, electromagnetic field mapping, bioelectric monitoring—anything that might tell him what was happening to Sidney's nervous system.

"Her vitals are stable," Rebecca said as she checked Sidney's pulse and pupil response again. "But there's something else going on. Look at her hands."

Ben glanced down at Sidney's hands where they lay flat on the table. Her fingers were trembling in unconsciousness, tiny involuntary movements, as though some kind of electrical current was still firing through her nerves. When he held his EMF reader near her skin, the display went haywire.

"She's still channeling," he said. "Even unconscious, she's connected to the phoenix somehow."

Agent Morse pulled up a chair and sat down, her expression now strangely weary. "I need to explain some things before we go any further. Things that are probably going to make you angry. But you need to hear them."

That didn't sound good at all. However, Sidney was his first priority, so Ben positioned his laptop where he could monitor all the sensor feeds before he turned to face Rebecca Morse. "I'm listening."

A faint breath escaped her lips. However, her tone was steady and brisk as she said, "Six months ago, DAPI detected unusual electromagnetic patterns emanating from the Pacific Northwest. The readings were consistent with what we call a stable dimensional anomaly—a permanent tear between our reality and somewhere else." She pulled off the exam gloves she'd been wearing and rubbed her hands together, as if to warm them. "Dr. Rosenthal established a surveillance network across forty-seven sites where the signal was strongest. Silver Hollow was site seventeen."

Forty-seven sites. Ben wasn't sure he wanted to acknowledge how big the operation had been, but he knew that burying his head in the sand wouldn't help any of them. "And you've been watching all of those sites?"

"Watching and recording and analyzing." Rebecca Morse looked over at Sidney's unconscious form and pulled in a breath. "But Silver Hollow was different. The energy readings here were off the charts, and they seemed to be centered on one person. Sidney's grandmother first, then Sidney herself after her grandmother disappeared."

"You knew about the portal," Ben said, his tone flat.

A lift of Rebecca Morse's slim shoulders. "Dr. Rosenthal's team theorized, at any rate. The evidence suggested that something was allowing creatures from another dimension to cross into ours. But they couldn't prove it without human testimony, without someone who'd actually witnessed the phenomenon." She met his gaze. "That's where you came in."

The anger Ben had been doing his best to suppress flared hot within him. "So you used me."

"Dr. Rosenthal used you," Rebecca said, still sounding brisk, as if she thought being matter-of-fact was the best way to handle this unpleasant subject. "She realized that you had the academic background and the technical skills, and—this is the most important part—

you had an electromagnetic signature that resonated with Sidney's at a very specific frequency."

Ben thought about every moment he and Sidney had spent together, the way her abilities seemed stronger when he was close. How he'd felt drawn to her almost immediately in a way that wasn't entirely about her outer beauty.

Trying to sound as dispassionate as possible, he asked, "What kind of frequency?"

"The kind that creates a ten to twenty percent amplification effect." Agent Morse pulled a tablet from her pack and brought up a graph covered in colored lines. "Your bioelectric field and Sidney's synchronize for some reason. When you're in close proximity, her abilities are enhanced."

The graph showed two waveforms—one in blue, one in red—oscillating in near-perfect harmony. Where they overlapped, the amplitude spiked.

Ben wasn't sure he wanted to believe what he was seeing. "So…you're telling me I'm some kind of battery for her?"

"No. You're more like a tuning fork. Your presence helps her abilities resonate more clearly, more powerfully." Agent Morse's voice softened, and she went on, "Sonya Rosenthal specifically wanted someone with your electromagnetic profile in Silver Hollow. She wanted Sidney's abilities pushed to their maximum so she could study what happened."

Ben glanced at Sidney again, his gaze focusing on the way her hands still trembled.

The rage inside him burned as hot orange and streaked with black as the phoenix itself.

"She engineered this," he said, his voice flat. "Rosenthal wanted Sidney stressed, wanted her abilities strained. That's why there's been so much interference in the forest. She's been deliberately destabilizing things."

"Yes." Agent Morse returned the tablet to her bag, her expression almost resigned. "The surveillance equipment DAPI hid in the forest isn't just passive monitoring. It generates electromagnetic interference designed to disrupt the natural flow of energy through the portal network. Dr. Rosenthal hypothesized that increased instability would force Sidney to use more power more frequently, giving us better data on her capabilities."

The phoenix stirred in its electromagnetic blanket, and a pulse of heat spread through the room. One of Ben's sensors started beeping urgently.

"It's destabilizing," he said as he checked the readout. "The corruption's at seventy-three percent now."

Rebecca Morse stood at once and moved to

the phoenix's table. She pulled back part of the blanket, revealing one wing. In the harsh fluorescent light, the corruption looked even worse—shadows crawling through living flame like infection through a wound.

"The interference equipment has been running for two weeks," she said quietly. "This phoenix has been trying to complete its rebirth cycle for those two weeks, and every time it gets close, the interference corrupts the process."

"Jesus Christ." Ben stared at the suffering creature, and his mouth tightened. "Rosenthal did this deliberately."

"After her defeat when the griffin was here, she needed a crisis, something that would prove her theories were accurate. Something that would force Sidney to use extreme power, that would push her abilities past their normal limits." Rebecca shook her head. "What better crisis than a dying phoenix? An ancient creature connected to the portal's fundamental stability, slowly being killed by artificial interference?"

Every moment since he'd arrived in Silver Hollow—the strange occurrences, the increasing instability, Sidney's growing powers—all of it had been engineered, orchestrated by people who saw him and Sidney not as human beings but as test subjects to be poked and prodded as necessary.

"The night Sidney fought off the shadow

stalkers, when she was trying to send the griffin home," he said. "Rosenthal was recording that."

A nod. "Every second of it. She has footage of Sidney channeling enough electromagnetic energy to burn shadow magic out of a dimensional predator. She has readings that show Sidney's nervous system adapting in real-time to handle power that should have killed her." Now Rebecca Morse's voice was flat with disgust. "Dr. Rosenthal called it the 'forced evolution protocol.' Put someone under enough pressure, and their abilities will expand to meet the threat."

His eyes narrowed. "That's torture."

"No, that's science. According to her, anyway."

Sidney made a small sound, and Ben was beside her in an instant. Her eyes moved under their lids, rapid and distressed. The trembling in her hands had spread to her arms.

"She's still trying to cleanse the phoenix," he said, checking the sensors once again. "Her bioelectric field is reaching toward it even now."

"The connection between them is strong." Rebecca retrieved her tablet and pulled up another graph. "Look at this. These are the electromagnetic signatures from both Sidney and the phoenix. See how they're synchronized?"

Ben studied the overlapping waveforms. Sidney's pattern was chaotic, jumping and spiking, but underneath the chaos was a steady pulse that matched the phoenix's dying rhythm exactly.

"They're entangled," he said. "On a quantum level, maybe. Or something analogous to it in whatever physics governs magic."

"Which means if the phoenix dies while they're connected…." Rebecca didn't finish the sentence.

She didn't have to. Ben understood the implication all too well. Sidney's consciousness was partially merged with the phoenix's. If that ancient creature died while they were still linked, the psychic backlash could shatter Sidney's mind.

Or worse.

"How long does it have?" he asked.

"Based on the current rate of corruption?" A small shrug, as if Rebecca knew this was something far beyond her control. "Maybe thirty-six hours. Less if the interference continues."

"Then we'll shut down the interference."

She shook her head at once. "The equipment is distributed across the entire forest. There are more than fifty individual units, each one hardened against tampering and equipped with anti-removal protocols. Even if we could locate all of them, we'd need specialized tools and a lot of time that we don't have."

Maybe she was being too pessimistic. "How much time?" Ben asked.

Rebecca sent him a very direct look then, as if to tell him he was grasping at straws. "Days. Probably more like weeks."

Ben glanced at Sidney, then at the phoenix, and then back at Rebecca Morse. "That's not acceptable."

"I know." She met his gaze steadily. "But there's another option. A more dangerous one."

Of course it was more dangerous. Voice even, he replied, "I'm listening."

She set her tablet on top of her bag. "Rosenthal's interest isn't in the phoenix itself. It's in the process of rebirth, the way phoenix fire can consume and remake matter. She believes that if she can understand the mechanism, she can weaponize it. She wants to create devices that can disintegrate anything, then reconstruct it according to different specifications."

Ben stared at her, not sure he wanted to have heard any of this. "You're talking about dimensional warfare."

"Exactly," Rebecca replied calmly. "If DAPI can control phoenix fire, they can potentially reshape matter at the molecular level. Destroy enemy installations and rebuild them as allied bases. Turn soldiers into something else entirely." She paused there before adding, "It would be the ultimate weapon."

"And you're opposed to this?"

Not even a blink. "I became a federal agent to protect people, not to help the government weaponize things it doesn't understand." Her voice was hard as she continued. "What I saw in the surveillance footage, what Dr. Rosenthal wants to do with that information—it's wrong."

Ben studied her face, looking for any signs of deception he might be able to find there. The problem with people who were trained in interrogation was that they were also trained in how to lie convincingly. But Rebecca Morse's electromagnetic signature—he could feel it now, could sense the subtle bioelectric patterns that accompanied genuine emotion—seemed sincere.

"What are you proposing?" he asked.

Without hesitation, she replied, "We let the rebirth happen. Here, in this facility, with Sidney guiding the process. If she can help the phoenix complete its cycle cleanly, without corruption, then the interference equipment becomes irrelevant. The phoenix will have already transformed."

"And Rosenthal?"

"Will lose her primary experimental subject," Rebecca replied calmly. "She'll still have the surveillance data, but without an active phoenix to study, her research becomes theoretical. That will make it much harder to sell to the military."

Ben looked down at Sidney again. Her face was pale except for the dried blood caked beneath her nose, and her breathing had gotten shallower. "That assumes Sidney can actually help the phoenix. She nearly died trying to cleanse five percent of the corruption. There's much more than that left."

"I know," Rebecca said, still almost preternaturally calm. "Which is why we need time. And why we need you."

"Me?" he asked, not sure what she meant.

She reached for her tablet and pulled up another graph. This one showed three waveforms instead of two—Sidney's chaotic pattern, the phoenix's steady pulse, and a third one Ben recognized as his own bioelectric signature.

"Your electromagnetic field stabilizes Sidney's," Rebecca explained. "When you're close to her, her power becomes more focused, more controlled. That amplification effect I mentioned earlier? It doesn't just make her stronger. It also makes her more efficient."

The three waveforms on the screen moved in synchronization, creating a pattern that was more stable than any of them individually.

"So you're saying I can help her control the cleansing process." The logical part of his mind didn't want to believe any of this, but it was hard to ignore what his own eyes were telling him.

"I'm saying you're essential to it. Without you, she'll burn herself out trying to purify the phoenix. With you, she has a chance." Rebecca closed her tablet, adding, "But it will be dangerous…for both of you."

Ben thought about all the insane things that had happened since he'd arrived in Silver Hollow—the appearance of the unicorn and the arrival of the phoenix, the way he and Sidney had worked together to save the town from shadow stalkers, and how her abilities seemed to have grown stronger when he was near.

How he'd started to feel her presence like another sense, as natural as sight or hearing.

Dr. Rosenthal had engineered their meeting. She'd manipulated events to bring them together. But what he and Sidney had built since then—the trust, the partnership, the connection that went deeper than either of them had expected—that was real.

That was theirs, and theirs alone.

"What do you need me to do?" he asked.

Something about the set of Rebecca Morse's shoulders seemed to relax a little. "First, we wait for Sidney to wake up. She needs to understand what's happening, what's at stake. This has to be her choice."

"And second?"

"We hope no one finds us before we're ready."

Ben looked at Sidney, still lying unconscious on the examination table. On the other side of the room, the phoenix was similarly immobile, its fire guttering lower with each passing minute. Then his gaze moved to the medical equipment and their jury-rigged sensors and everything they'd need if they were going to attempt something as insane as guiding a phoenix through its rebirth cycle.

He had no idea how long that might take. He could only hope that no one on Rosenthal's teams would choose that precise moment to monitor the readings from a research station that supposedly had been defunct for longer than he'd been alive.

The phoenix stirred again, and this time, it managed to lift its head. Those ancient eyes fixed on him, and he felt something brush against his consciousness. It wasn't words or even images. Just a sense of profound urgency mixed with something that might have been hope.

Help her. Help us both.

"I'm trying," Ben whispered.

Rebecca Morse touched his shoulder. "You need to understand something else. Something about why Dr. Rosenthal wanted you here specifically."

He turned to face her. Rebecca's dark eyes—such a contrast to her pale blonde hair—showed a strange sort of compassion.

"Your electromagnetic compatibility with Sidney isn't random. It's genetic." She was still holding her tablet, and she swiped a finger over its screen, pulling up another file. "DAPI has been tracking hereditary patterns in bioelectric signatures for twenty years. Your family tree intersects with Sidney's six generations back."

"You're saying we're related?" he demanded.

"Distantly. Genetically, you're more like seventh cousins. But electromagnetically?" She showed him a chart that appeared to compare two sets of DNA. "You share specific genetic markers that govern how your nervous systems process electrical signals. That's why your bioelectric fields resonate."

Magical ability seemed to run in Sidney's bloodline, so he'd already halfway guessed that there had to be a genetic component to all this. "Rosenthal knew about our connection when she recruited me."

A nod. "She specifically searched for someone with your combination of traits—technical expertise, electromagnetic compatibility, and professional credibility that would make your documentation believable." Rebecca Morse sounded almost bitter. "You weren't chosen randomly. You were targeted."

The phoenix made another sound, weaker this time. Seventy-four percent corrupted now.

Sidney's hand twitched, her fingers curling as if reaching for something.

"We need to set up a perimeter," Ben said. "Security cameras, motion sensors, whatever you have. If Rosenthal's people somehow manage to figure out that we're here, I want a warning."

"Already on it." Rebecca turned away from him and began to pull equipment from her pack, what appeared to be compact surveillance devices that she started placing around the room's entrance. "These will give us five minutes' warning if anyone approaches down the main corridor."

"What about the other entrances?"

"There are three. I'll lock them down after I finish here." She paused. "Ben, if this facility is breached, I won't be able to protect both of you. You need to be prepared to run."

"I'm not leaving Sidney."

"Even if staying means getting captured?"

He looked at Sidney's unconscious form, at the blood on her face and the way her body trembled with exhausted effort. "Especially then."

Rebecca Morse studied him for a long moment, then nodded. "Fair enough. But let's try to avoid that scenario." She finished placing the last sensor and headed for the door. "There's food and water in the cabinets. Medical supplies if you need them. If something happens to me, you have to get Sidney and that phoenix out of here. Use the maintenance tunnel. It exits three miles north of here in an old lumber yard."

"Where will you be?"

"Creating enough noise to draw their attention away from you." She offered him a grim smile. "I'm good at creating noise."

Then she was gone, and Ben was alone with Sidney and the dying phoenix—and two hours that felt like two minutes.

He pulled his chair close to Sidney's examination table and took her hand. It was still trembling, still channeling electricity that made the hairs on his arm stand up. But it was warm and solid…and here.

For now, anyway.

"I need you to wake up," he said quietly. "I need you to wake up and tell me what to do, because I'm a scientist, not a miracle worker, and what you're attempting here is definitely in the miracle category."

The phoenix's fire pulsed weakly, and his sensors registered another spike in the corruption level.

Maybe thirty-six hours wouldn't be enough.

Especially since Sidney still wasn't waking up.

He checked her vital signs again—pulse steady, breathing regular, but no response to stimuli. Her brain activity was normal on the monitors Agent Morse had set up, but there was something else showing on his electromagnetic sensors. A feedback loop between Sidney and the phoenix, growing stronger and more synchronized with each passing minute.

They weren't just entangled. They were merging.

"Damn it, Sidney." He squeezed her hand gently. "What did you do?"

The phoenix answered with another pulse of corrupted fire, and this time Ben felt it, a wave of heat and pain and desperate need that crashed into him like a breaker on the shore. The creature was suffering, had been suffering for weeks while DAPI's interference equipment slowly poisoned its rebirth.

And Sidney, in her compassion and power and stubborn refusal to let something die on her watch, had connected herself to its pain.

If he couldn't wake her up soon, if he couldn't help her complete what she'd started, the corruption would spread to her, too. If that happened, it would destroy her from the inside out.

The phoenix's fire guttered lower.

Sidney's hand twitched in his, and her eyes moved again under their closed lids, faster now. The trembling in her hands had spread to her whole body, and the electromagnetic readings from his sensors were spiking erratically.

"Come on," Ben whispered. "Come back. Please."

The phoenix lifted its head and looked at him

with those ancient, knowing eyes. And he understood what it was trying to tell him.

Sidney wasn't unconscious. She was elsewhere, following the connection between her consciousness and the phoenix's fire, diving deeper into magic that no human was meant to touch.

He couldn't wake her up.

He could only wait and hope that when she finally surfaced, there was still enough of Sidney left to come back to.

CHAPTER THREE

I woke to the smell of disinfectant and the steady beep of medical equipment, and for a confused moment, I thought I was in a hospital. Then memory came flooding back—the phoenix, the contamination, the way I'd tried to cleanse its fire and felt my entire nervous system overload in response.

"Sidney." Ben's voice, rough with exhaustion and relief. "Thank God."

I opened my eyes. Harsh fluorescent lights made me squint, and when I tried to sit up, every muscle in my body screamed at me to stay put. Ben's hand was warm on my shoulder, steadying me.

"Easy," he said. "You've been unconscious for more than six hours."

Six hours. I looked around the sterile room,

taking in the equipment that surrounded me—both medical and scientific, which I guessed must be monitoring the active electromagnetism all around—and a wrapped bundle on another table across from me that could only be the phoenix.

"Where are we?"

"An old research facility that used to be run by a scientist named Daniel Jessop. Rebecca Morse brought us here." Ben pulled his chair closer. His hair was so mussed that it looked as if he'd stuck his head inside a wind tunnel, and dark circles shadowed his eyes. "How do you feel?"

A very good question. As much as I would have preferred to avoid doing so, I made myself take inventory. My head throbbed, and my nose seemed oddly sore, although I noticed that the blood had been wiped away. When I lifted them from the exam table where I lay, my hands trembled, and I could still sense the phoenix's electromagnetic signature like a second heartbeat underneath my own.

"Like I got hit by a truck," I said. "A very big truck. How's the phoenix?"

For a second, Ben didn't say anything. But then he took a breath and replied, "The corruption won't stop spreading. It's passed seventy-five percent. It seems stable for now, but…."

He didn't finish the sentence.

He didn't have to.

I closed my eyes and, shaky as I knew I was, did my best to reach out with those strange abilities that had awakened over the past month, following the connection between my consciousness and the phoenix's fire. The corruption was worse than I'd feared—it had gone past the physical into something at its very core, eating away at whatever magic made the creature what it was. And underneath the contamination, I could feel the phoenix's pain and exhaustion and desperate need to complete its rebirth cycle before it was too late.

"Sidney." Ben wrapped his fingers around my nearest hand. It felt so good to have him hold me like that, his skin warm against my icy flesh. "I have something I need to tell you. It's about DAPI and why all this is happening."

The way he said those words made me feel shakier than ever, but I knew I had to ask anyway. "What about DAPI?"

"The electromagnetic interference that's been killing the phoenix? DAPI did it deliberately. They've had surveillance equipment all over the forest for the past six months, and it's not just recording data. It's actively generating interference to destabilize the portal."

I stared up at him, at the dark stubble on his chin, at the shadows under his eyes. "They did all this *on purpose?*"

A single nod. "Rosenthal wanted a crisis, something that would force you to use your abilities at maximum power so she could study what happened." His jaw tightened with anger as he added, "The phoenix has been suffering for weeks because of DAPI's equipment."

While I'd been trying to get on with my life, running the family pet shop and attempting to come to terms with my abilities—and falling for Ben at the same time—this ancient creature had been slowly dying. It had been tortured by artificial interference designed to push me into exactly this situation.

"That's not all," Ben continued, as though he knew he needed to get everything out before he lost his nerve. One finger moved over the back of my hand, and I realized he was trying to comfort himself as much as me. "The reason I came to Silver Hollow in the first place—the unicorn sighting—DAPI fabricated it. And then they carved those letters in the trees to further destabilize you."

The room tilted even though I was still lying down, and I gripped the edge of the examination table to try to steady myself. "*What?*"

"Rosenthal recruited me specifically. She knew about my research, my background, and...." The words trailed away there, and he drew in a breath, seeming to gather himself. "And my electromagnetic signature. Apparently, I resonate with your abilities in a way that amplifies them by ten to twenty percent. That's why they wanted me in Silver Hollow. That's why they engineered our meeting."

I thought about every moment Ben and I had shared since he'd arrived in town, how we'd worked together to save Silver Hollow from the shadow stalkers. The way my abilities had grown stronger after we'd spent time together.

And I thought of how I'd started to trust him, to care about him, to let myself feel things I hadn't felt since losing my mother and grandmother to the portal and the world beyond it.

Everything orchestrated. They'd manipulated us.

"So none of it was real," I said.

"No." Ben's hand tightened on mine, and he leaned in a little closer, his eyes imploring me to believe him. "Sidney, no. What DAPI did—bringing me here, setting up the circumstances—that really did happen. But what we built? That's ours. They can't engineer feelings. They can't manipulate the kind of connection we share."

I wanted to believe him. But how could I trust my own emotions when everything that led to them had been a lie?

"They've been watching me for months, ever since I came back here after my mother and grandmother disappeared," I said, knowing how bitter I sounded. "Recording everything. Studying me like a lab rat."

He didn't bother to deny it. "Yes," he replied. "And it gets worse. From what Rebecca Morse told me, DAPI is tracking forty-seven different sites that have some kind of electromagnetic anomalies occurring there. Silver Hollow is just one of them. Rosenthal has a massive surveillance network tracking every dimensional anomaly in the Pacific Northwest."

Jesus. How many times had I used my abilities over the past couple of months? DAPI had been there the whole time, recording and analyzing and using me as an experimental subject without my knowledge or consent.

The thought of that violation made me glad I hadn't eaten anything recently. Otherwise, I was pretty sure I would have leaned over the side of the exam table and thrown it all up.

"I'm going to kill her," I whispered, a rage utterly unlike me taking hold, burning and fierce as phoenix fire. "I'm going to find her, and I'm going to make her—"

"Sidney." Ben cut me off there, his voice gentle but firm. "I know you're angry. I'm angry, too. But right now, we need to focus on the phoenix. If it dies while you're still connected to it, the psychic backlash could shatter your mind."

I looked at the wrapped bundle across the room. Even through the electromagnetic shielding of the metallic blanket that surrounded it, I could feel the phoenix's pain. It had become part of me during that brief moment of connection in the forest, and now I couldn't separate my consciousness from its suffering.

"How long does it have?" I asked.

His mouth thinned for a second, but his tone was even enough as he replied, "Maybe thirty hours. Less if the interference continues."

It could have been worse. On the other hand, it could have been a lot better, too. "Then we have to shut down the interference."

He shook his head at once. "According to Rebecca Morse, there are more than fifty units scattered across the entire forest. Even if we managed to locate them all, we'd still need days or weeks to disable them."

Well, that was just great. "So what are we supposed to do?"

He didn't hesitate, only said, "We let the rebirth happen. Here, where the interference can't reach. Rebecca thinks if you can guide the phoenix through its cycle cleanly, then the corruption will burn away during the transformation."

I thought about how I'd felt when I'd tried to cleanse just five percent of the corruption surging inside the phoenix. My nervous system had overloaded, and I guessed I must have come close to death, or they wouldn't have brought me here to recover, would have instead just taken me home.

"There's so much left," I said. Tears of frustration burned my eyes, and I angrily blinked them away. "I can't—"

"You won't be doing it alone." Ben's fingers tightened on mine again. "My electromagnetic field stabilizes yours. When I'm close, your abilities become more focused and efficient. That amplification effect Rosenthal wanted to study? It works both ways. You make me stronger, and I make you more controlled."

I looked at our joined hands and sensed the subtle resonance between our bioelectric fields. He was right. When Ben was near, my abilities didn't merely get stronger—they also got clearer. The constant electromagnetic noise that usually plagued me faded into something manageable.

"They engineered this, too," I told him. "You and me working together. That's what Rosenthal wanted all along."

His shoulders lifted slightly. "Maybe. But that doesn't make it any less real." Gaze focused on my face, he went on, "Sidney, I came to Silver Hollow because I wanted to study cryptids, to understand the intersection between magic and science. But finding you? Learning about your abilities? Falling for you? That wasn't in any of Rosenthal's plans."

No, probably not. All she wanted was data. I had a hard time believing that she'd ever been in love, had ever felt this sort of connection to another person. She wouldn't have been counting on any of that.

And I so wanted to trust that what Ben and I had built together was genuine despite the manipulation that had brought us together. But every time I thought about DAPI watching us, recording us, using our connection as an experimental variable, I felt violated all over again.

"I need to see the surveillance equipment," I said then. "I need to understand what they did."

Ben hesitated for a moment before giving a reluctant nod. "Rebecca left us her tablet. I can try to pull up the schematics."

He retrieved the device and brought up a map of Silver Hollow overlaid with dozens of small red dots. Each one represented a surveillance unit—cameras, EMF sensors, and the insidious interference generators that had been slowly killing the phoenix.

"They're everywhere," I said, heart sinking as I scrolled through the data. "The forest, the town, even in the Carmichaels' backyard right behind my house."

"I know," Ben said simply, although I detected a trace of bitterness underneath his calm tone. "Rosenthal wanted comprehensive coverage. She's been tracking every electromagnetic anomaly, every time you used your abilities. We have to assume that she has months of detailed recordings."

I zoomed in on one of the units near the portal site and pulled up its specifications. I didn't understand everything I was seeing, but I understood enough to make my anger burn that much brighter.

"These seem like they're something more than recording devices," I said. "Look at the power output. They're generating pulses at specific frequencies, aren't they?"

Ben leaned closer, eyes narrowing slightly as he absorbed the data displayed on the screen. "Those look like frequencies that match the phoenix's natural bioelectric signature. So they're not just disrupting the rebirth cycle. As far as I can tell, they're actively corrupting it."

"Weaponized magic," I said. Only a few weeks ago, I wouldn't have even understood what that meant. Unfortunately, DAPI's interference had opened my eyes to a whole lot of things I would have preferred never to have known. "That's what Rosenthal wants, isn't it? She's figured out how to turn dimensional energy into something that can be controlled and deployed."

I didn't want to think about what that meant. If DAPI could weaponize phoenix fire, if they could learn to corrupt and control dimensional magic, then creatures like the phoenix would become military assets, nothing more than targets for capture and experimentation.

My grandmother had spent her entire life protecting the portal and the creatures that crossed through it. My mother had followed in her footsteps, sacrificing everything to keep Silver Hollow's secrets safe. And now the U.S. government wanted to turn all of it into weapons.

"We have to stop her," I said, my tone fierce.

"We will," Ben said. "But first, we have to save the phoenix. Without it, the portal destabilizes. Your mother and grandmother could be cut off forever."

He was right. I couldn't let my anger at Rosenthal distract me from what mattered most. The phoenix was dying, and I was the only one who could help it.

"How do we do this?" I asked. "The cleansing process, I mean. What does Rebecca Morse think will work?"

"She thinks you need to guide the phoenix through its natural rebirth cycle and let the fire consume the corrupted parts and rebuild from clean energy." He pulled up another graph on the tablet. "But you'll need to maintain the connection the entire time. For hours, maybe. And if the corruption spreads to you during the process…."

"I could end up corrupted, too," I finished for him, since he didn't seem eager to complete the sentence. "Or dead."

He didn't blink. "Yes."

Once again, I glanced over at the phoenix's oddly bundled form. Even through the shielding that surrounded it, I could feel its desperation. This ancient creature had been suffering for weeks because of human interference, and now it was asking me—a mortal woman who'd only discovered her abilities a few weeks ago—to save it.

"I don't know if I can do this," I said, and my voice trembled on the last syllable.

"You can." Ben sounded very certain. "I've watched you face down shadow stalkers and negotiate with griffins and channel enough electromagnetic energy to overload government surveillance equipment. You're stronger than you think."

When he put it that way, he made me sound like Wonder Woman. Inside, though, I felt like a quivering mound of Jell-O. "That was different," I protested. "I was only reacting to what was happening. I wasn't thinking about what I was doing. And what I need to do for the phoenix requires the kind of control I simply don't have."

"Then we'll figure it out together." He laid down the tablet so he could press his other hand against mine, surrounding my cold fingers with warmth. "That's what we do, Sidney. We face impossible things and find a way through them."

I stared up at him—at the exhaustion in his face and the determination in his eyes and the way he held my hand like he could anchor me to this reality through sheer force of will. DAPI might have engineered our meeting, but they couldn't have predicted this. They couldn't have known that Ben would become the person I trusted more than anyone in the world.

"Okay," I said. "We'll do this together."

The smallest lift at the corner of his mouth as he replied, "Always."

The word hung in the air between us, so much more than those two simple syllables. Something shifted within me, some barrier I'd been maintaining crumbling under the weight of everything we'd been through together.

He must have felt it, too, because his expression softened. He let go of my hand so he could reach over and cup my face, his thumb brushing across my cheekbone.

"Sidney," he said, his voice quiet but intense. "I need you to know something. Everything DAPI did—bringing me here, setting up the surveillance—none of that matters. Because what I feel for you is real."

My breath caught. "Ben—"

"I know the timing is terrible. I know we're in the middle of a crisis, and you must be furious about the way Rosenthal manipulated us. But I need you to hear it again." His hazel eyes seemed to darken as he stared down at me. "I love you. I've loved you since almost the moment I met you. And whatever happens with the phoenix, whatever happens with DAPI, that's not going to change."

For a moment, I couldn't breathe, couldn't think. All I could feel was the warmth of his hand on my face, the way my abilities resonated with his electromagnetic field, and the truth of his words settling into my bones.

"I love you, too," I whispered.

A moment of silence, and then he bent down and kissed me. Nothing gentle or tentative about it, but desperate and claiming and real. I kissed him back with everything I had, pouring the past few weeks of denial and fear and longing into the connection between us.

His hand slid into my tangled hair. My fingers curled into his shirt and pulled him down toward me. And between us, our bioelectric fields began to resonate in harmony.

I felt it the moment the resonance became visible—a spark of blue-white light jumping between our skin where we touched, followed by another. Then it turned into a cascade of tiny electrical discharges that made the air around us crackle with energy.

Ben pulled back just enough to look at me, his eyes wide. "Is that…?"

"Our electromagnetic fields synchronizing," I said, the words coming out in a breathless whisper. "I've never seen it happen before."

Another spark jumped between us, and my abilities surged in response. They didn't seem as overwhelming as they usually were, but instead were focused, almost contained, as though Ben's presence was tuning my power to exactly the right frequency.

"This is what Rosenthal wanted to study," Ben said. His voice was rough, although I wasn't sure whether that was from suppressed passion or anger. "The amplification effect. The way we enhance each other."

"Screw Rosenthal." I pulled him back down toward me and kissed him harder, my tongue finding his. "This is ours," I whispered fiercely. "Not hers. Not DAPI's. Ours."

He made a sound of agreement and deepened the kiss, one hand sliding down to my waist. More sparks danced across our skin, blue-white energy that painted shadows on the concrete walls. I could feel our bioelectric fields merging, creating something stronger and more stable than either of us could generate alone.

Ben's hand slipped under the hem of my shirt, his touch sending cascades of electricity across my skin. I gasped against his mouth, and he froze.

"Is this okay?" he asked. "We don't have to—"

"I want to," I said. "I need to. After everything DAPI did, all the ways they violated my privacy and my choices, I need this to be mine. I need to choose something for myself."

Understanding dawned in his eyes, followed by a rush of heat that warmed his hazel eyes to almost gold. "Sidney—"

"Please," I whispered. "Help me reclaim this. Help me feel like I have control over something."

He kissed me again, more slowly this time, but no less intense. His hand moved higher under my shirt, fingertips tracing patterns across my ribs that made electricity dance in their wake. I arched into his touch, and more sparks jumped between us.

We should have been worried about the phoenix and the impossible task ahead of us. But right then, in that moment, all I cared about was Ben's hands on my skin and the way our electromagnetic fields sang together and the proof that, despite everything DAPI had done, this connection was ours.

His lips moved to my neck, and I tilted my head back, giving him access. One hand caught in his hair while the other traced the line of his spine through his shirt. He shuddered against me, and I felt his electromagnetic field pulse in response to my touch.

"We're putting on quite a show for the security cameras," he murmured against my throat.

I hadn't realized there were cameras, but then, I didn't know much about this facility except that it had been built decades ago and abandoned for a long time.

The thought should have killed the moment, made me self-conscious. Instead, it made something fierce and defiant rise within me.

"I don't care about the cameras," I told him. "Screw them. Screw everyone."

Ben lifted his head to look at me, and the expression on his face was somewhere between awe and desire. "You're amazing."

I kissed him again and put every ounce of defiance and determination into our embrace. His hands moved to the button of my jeans, and I reached for his belt, and—

The door burst open.

We pulled apart, the exam table squeaking as Ben slid off so he could stand, while I sat upright for the first time since I'd awakened. Rebecca

Morse stood in the doorway, her expression somewhere between apologetic and urgent.

"I'm sorry to interrupt," she said. "But we have a problem."

Ben's hand found mine automatically, our fingers interlacing. The sparks had faded, but I could still feel the resonance between our electromagnetic fields.

"What kind of problem?" he asked.

"I just found out that DAPI is mobilizing military units. They've decided to treat the EMP as a potential terrorist attack, so they're preparing for tactical deployment." She came farther into the room, a frown pulling at her dark brows. "I have to believe they're scanning the area for any possible places we could have used to hide, and that means sooner or later, they'll figure out where we've gone to ground. I estimate we've got twenty-four hours, maybe less, before Rosenthal's troops storm this facility."

Twenty-four hours. I looked at the phoenix, still wrapped in its electromagnetic blanket, still slowly dying.

"That's not enough time," I said. "None of us knows how long the phoenix's rebirth cycle might take."

"Then we'll have to accelerate the process somehow." Rebecca Morse moved to the phoenix's table and began carefully unwrapping the shielding that had sheltered the creature all this time. “Dr. Rosenthal wants to weaponize phoenix fire. We need to understand how the rebirth mechanism works if we’re going to counter her.”

The phoenix stirred as the blanket came away, and I felt its consciousness brush against mine. It was still suffering, still desperate, but also hopeful now that I was awake and aware.

“We need expertise,” Ben said. “Someone who understands phoenix mythology and the mechanics of rebirth cycles.”

I lifted an eyebrow. “Well, someone like that shouldn’t be too hard to find.”

Ben gave me a faint smile in response to that remark, but then his expression grew serious again as he continued, “There’s a man I know. Lewis Webb. He’s a cryptozoologist who specializes in dimensional creatures and their life cycles. He might have some information we could use about phoenix rebirth.”

I frowned. “Can we trust him?”

“He’s spent his career documenting supernatural phenomena without trying to weaponize them. That’s more than I can say for most researchers in this field.” Ben squeezed my hand. “And right now, we need all the help we can get.”

Agent Morse nodded. “I can arrange a secure meeting. But it has to be soon. DAPI’s surveillance net is tightening.”

Twenty-four hours to save an ancient creature, stop a government conspiracy, and prevent the weaponization of dimensional magic. Twenty-four hours to do the impossible.

Again.

"Set up the meeting," I said. "But it has to be somewhere remote. Somewhere DAPI won't expect." I paused for a moment and thought furiously, mentally ticking through every obscure place in the area that might suit our purposes. "There's an old fire lookout tower about ten miles east of here," I went on. "It's been abandoned for years, but it has a clear view of the surrounding forest. We'd see anyone approaching long before they reached us."

"That could work." Agent Morse had pulled a tablet out of her field jacket and was already typing coordinates into it. "I'll contact Lewis Webb and arrange the meeting for this evening. That will give us a few hours to prepare."

A few hours. I wasn't sure if we could afford that much time, but we needed to know everything about the phoenix's rebirth cycle before we embarked on such a dangerous experiment. An impossible situation, just like everything else I'd faced recently.

"We can do this," I said. "And it'll be on our terms, not Rosenthal's."

Rebecca Morse smiled grimly. In her cargo

pants and hiking boots and thermal Henley-style shirt, she didn't look much like the polished FBI agent who'd confronted me only a month earlier. That was all right, though. Now I understood that she was an ally. A friend.

And we needed all the friends we could get.

CHAPTER FOUR

The fire lookout tower rose above the pine canopy like a skeletal finger pointing at the sky. Ben pulled Rebecca's big black SUV onto the overgrown access road and killed the engine, then studied the structure through the windshield. The tower had been abandoned for decades, its wooden stairs weathered to gray, its windows dark and empty. But it would give them a clear view of anyone approaching, which was exactly what they needed.

"You're sure Lewis will come?" Sidney asked from the passenger seat. She'd been quiet during the drive, her electromagnetic senses stretched thin as she monitored the area for any possible DAPI surveillance. Her face was still tight with effort, and he noticed how her fingers were white-knuckled on the door handle.

"He'll come." Ben paused to look down at his watch. Four-thirty. They had half an hour to go before the scheduled meeting. "Lewis doesn't trust government agencies any more than we do. When I told him what was happening, he said he'd been waiting years for someone to finally stand up to DAPI."

Rebecca emerged from the back seat, her dark gaze already scanning the tree line with the air of someone who'd done this same sort of thing hundreds of times before. "I'll set up a perimeter. If anyone approaches, we should have about five minutes' warning."

She pulled some surveillance equipment from her pack and disappeared into the forest. Ben watched her go, then turned to Sidney.

"How are you holding up?"

She didn't answer immediately. When she did, her voice was careful, not betraying much beyond a quiet determination. "I can function. That's what matters right now."

That wasn't what he'd asked, but Ben knew better than to push. Sidney had been running on fumes ever since the phoenix incident in the forest, and the six hours of unconsciousness that had followed hadn't been nearly enough recovery time. Her nose had started bleeding again during the drive, and she'd tried to hide it by pressing tissues against her face and turning toward the window.

He'd pretended not to notice. It wasn't as if they could turn back.

No, they had to see this through, no matter what happened.

"Come on," he said as he opened the Suburban's door. "Let's get up there before Lewis arrives. I want to check the tower's structural integrity."

They both got out of the vehicle and headed over to the watchtower. The stairs groaned under their weight as they started to make the climb, but they held. The whole way, Ben kept one hand on the railing and the other ready to grab Sidney if she stumbled. To his relief, she made it to the top platform without incident, although he noticed she was breathing harder than the climb would have normally warranted.

The view from the lookout was worth the effort. Evergreen forest stretched in every direction, broken only by the occasional logging road or stand of aspens and oaks. Ben pulled his binoculars from his pack and scanned the horizon. Everything seemed utterly calm—no vehicles, no obvious movement except the wind through the trees.

"Looks clear," he said.

Sidney leaned against the railing and closed her eyes. Ben felt a subtle pulse that he thought was her electromagnetic field reaching outward, searching the same area he'd just studied with the binoculars. After a moment, she opened her eyes.

"Nothing within three miles except Rebecca," she said. "If DAPI's tracking us, they're not anywhere close yet."

"Good." Ben checked his watch again. Four-forty. "Lewis should be here soon."

They waited in silence, watching the sun angle lower through the pines. Ben found himself hyperaware of Sidney's presence beside him—the way she favored her left leg slightly, the tremor in her hands that she couldn't quite hide, the traces of dried blood that remained under her nose despite all her attempts to clean it.

The kiss in the medical facility felt like it had happened in another lifetime, even though it had been only a few hours ago. He wanted to reach for her hand, wanted to pull her close and feel that resonance between their electromagnetic fields again. But they were exposed up here, visible to anyone with a good scope, and physical contact would only make Sidney's abilities flare.

Later, he promised himself. When this was over, when the phoenix was saved and DAPI was dealt with, they'd have time for more than stolen moments between crises.

A vehicle was approaching from the south. Ben raised his binoculars at once and tracked its progress. An ancient Jeep Wrangler, mud-spattered and dented, with Oregon plates. The driver was alone.

"That's Lewis," he said.

The Jeep parked next to Rebecca Morse's SUV, and a man climbed out. He appeared to be in his early seventies, with a gray beard and weathered skin that spoke of decades spent outdoors. He wore cargo pants and a field vest covered in pockets, and he moved easily despite his age, telling Ben that he'd probably spent a lot more time tracking cryptids in the woods than he had behind a desk.

As soon as he emerged from the Jeep, Rebecca materialized from the trees, her hand hovering near her sidearm until Lewis raised both hands in a peaceful gesture. They exchanged words Ben couldn't hear, and then she gestured toward the tower.

"He's coming up," Sidney said.

Sure enough, Lewis was already moving toward the base of the tower. Once he got there, he took the stairs two at a time despite his age, making the climb pass much more quickly than theirs had. When he reached the platform, he studied Sidney and Ben with sharp brown eyes that missed nothing.

"Ben Sanders," he said, extending a hand. "Good to finally meet you in person. Your research on chupacabra migrations in the Sonoran Desert was groundbreaking."

Ben shook his hand, an embarrassed smile touching his lips. He hadn't thought anyone had read that paper except a few other diehard chupacabra enthusiasts. "Lewis, this is Sidney Lowell. She's—"

"The guardian's daughter," Lewis cut in before he turned to Sidney with something like reverence in his expression. "Your grandmother's journals are legendary in cryptozoology circles. I've spent twenty years trying to verify half of what she documented."

Sidney frowned at once. Her tone guarded, she asked, "How do you know about my grandmother's journals?"

"I don't. Not directly, at any rate." Lewis pulled a battered-looking canvas messenger bag from his shoulder and set it down on the platform's dusty floor. "But I've spent forty years documenting phoenix sightings across the Pacific Northwest, and there's a pattern. Every documented sighting within a hundred miles of Silver Hollow has been notably more detailed, more accurate, more informed than sightings elsewhere. Clearly, someone in the area has been observing phoenixes for generations and keeping meticulous records."

Ben saw Sidney's posture shift slightly, becoming even more wary.

"That's speculation," she said, her arms crossed.

Lewis didn't appear too put off by her vaguely hostile tone. "It is," he said, sounding cheerful. "But it's informed speculation." He knelt and opened his bag so he could pull out a bunch of file folders thick with documents. Ben wasn't sure how they'd even all fit in there, and he wondered if the satchel was the real-life equivalent of the "bag of holding" he'd come across when he played a little Dungeons and Dragons back in junior high. "I never met your grandmother, of course," Lewis continued. "Everything I've found has only said that Emily Lowell ran a pet shop, lived quietly, kept to herself. On paper, she was ordinary. But the pattern of sightings, the quality of the few cryptid reports that did manage to come out of Silver Hollow, the way certain researchers were subtly steered away from this area...." He let the words trail off before adding, his brown eyes now twinkling, "It sure looks to me like someone was protecting something. I've always suspected the Lowell family knew far more than they let on."

Sidney's stony expression didn't flicker. "Is that a fact."

Lewis met her gaze directly, still with that

cheerful glint in his eyes. "I'm not asking you to confirm or deny anything. I'm just saying that if there were journals, if there were generations of careful observation and documentation, then they would be invaluable. And they would need to be protected from agencies like DAPI."

"DAPI," Ben repeated. The agency itself wasn't a secret, or he wouldn't have been able to look it up online after Rosenthal and her goons first appeared in Silver Hollow, but it wasn't common knowledge, either.

"Among others," Lewis said. "The Dimensional Anomaly Protection Initiative is just the public face of the organization. At least three other agencies are running parallel programs, all competing for the same data." He spread his files across the platform's floor, making Ben and Sidney back up a little to give him more room. "I've been documenting their activities for fifteen years, ever since I heard about them and thought something wasn't adding up. So I've been tracking patterns, recording incidents, and collecting testimony from researchers who've had encounters with them."

Ben knelt so he could get a closer look at Lewis Webb's files. Each folder was labeled with a location and date: *Nevada Test Site, 2018. Olympic National Forest, 2020. Crater Lake, 2022.*

Dozens of them.

"These are all dimensional sites?" he asked.

A nod. "Confirmed or suspected. DAPI has surveillance networks at every location where the dimensional barriers are thin." Lewis pulled out a specific file and handed it to Ben. "This is what you need to see."

The file was labeled "RESEARCHER DISAPPEARANCES - PATTERN ANALYSIS." Ben opened it, and his stomach clenched as he scanned the contents.

Twenty-three names. Twenty-three cryptozoologists, physicists, and paranormal researchers who'd gone missing over the past decade. Each one had been investigating dimensional phenomena.

And each one had been contacted by DAPI shortly before they disappeared.

"Jesus," Ben breathed.

"Read the dates," Lewis said.

Ben took a second look at the list. The disappearances had accelerated over the past three years. One in 2022. Three in 2023. Eight in 2024. And already five in 2025.

"DAPI is eliminating anyone who knows too much," Sidney said. She'd moved closer so she could read over Ben's shoulder, and there was something reassuring about having her next to him like that, her long hair just touching his shoulder as she bent to look at the files.

"Or recruiting them into programs so classified that their old lives have to be erased," Lewis said grimly. "I don't know which is worse."

Ben's thoughts went immediately to the cold calculation in Sonya Rosenthal's eyes when she'd tried to take Sidney into custody. As far as he'd been able to tell, DAPI operated without oversight or accountability, making them very dangerous.

He had to ask the question. "How close are you to making this list?"

"Very close," Lewis replied, and now the cheerful glint in his eyes was gone as if it had never been. "I've had three separate visits from DAPI agents in the past year, each one more aggressive than the last. They want my research, my contacts, my documentation of every cryptid sighting I've ever recorded." He paused there, meeting Ben's gaze squarely. "They offered me a position on Rosenthal's team. When I refused, they made it clear that refusal might not be an option for much longer."

"That's why you're here," Sidney said, her earlier hostility evaporating even as she spoke. "You're burning bridges by helping us."

"I'm picking a side," he said. "There's a difference." He pulled out another file, this one much thicker. "This contains everything I know about

DAPI's facility network. Locations, security protocols, research priorities. If you're going to fight them, you need to understand how they operate."

Ben took the file and flipped through it. It contained satellite imagery, floor plans, guard rotation schedules, and much more. Lewis had been thorough, although God only knew how he'd gotten access to all this information.

"There's a facility thirty miles to the northwest of here," Lewis continued. "An old military base, supposedly decommissioned in the nineties. DAPI has been using it for high-security research for about five years. If Rosenthal is planning something big, that's where she'll do it."

Sidney's hand found Ben's arm, her fingers digging in hard enough to bruise. "Ben," she said, her voice a harsh whisper. "We're not alone."

He followed her gaze. At first, he saw nothing but trees and sky. Then he caught it—a dark shape moving against the clouds, too steady to be a bird.

"Drone," Agent Morse called out from the stairs. Where she'd come from, Ben had no idea, but he assumed some of her scanning equipment must have picked up the drone and she'd sprinted back here to tell them to take cover. She made it inside the space and immediately flattened herself. "Get down, all of you!"

They dropped to the dusty floor. Ben pulled his EMF reader from his pocket, and the readings confirmed what Sidney had already sensed—an artificial electromagnetic signature, probably military-grade surveillance equipment.

"How did they find us so fast?" Lewis asked, his lean form pressed against the weathered wood of the platform.

"They didn't," Sidney said. Her voice had gone tight, although Ben wasn't sure whether it was from worry or the simple pain of forcing herself to the rough floor after being unconscious only a few hours earlier. "It's on a patrol pattern. We just got unlucky."

Ben watched the drone through a window that probably hadn't had glass in it for decades. The drone was maybe two hundred yards out, moving in a careful grid. Military hardware, he thought, probably equipped with thermal imaging and electromagnetic sensors.

If it got much closer, it would detect their body heat and electronic devices, and then it would be game over.

"Sidney," Rebecca Morse said in a near-whisper. "Can you jam its signal?"

"I'm already depleted," Sidney replied in a similar undertone. "If I try to—"

"I know what I'm asking. But if that drone reports our position, we'll have tactical teams here in minutes." Rebecca's voice was steady but urgent. "I need you to knock it out of the sky."

Ben felt Sidney's hand tighten on his arm. Through their connection, he sensed her electromagnetic field—already strained, already pushed past safe limits. What Rebecca was asking could kill her.

"There has to be another way," he said.

"There isn't." Sidney pushed herself up to a crouch and pressed one hand to her temple. "Ben, get ready to catch me if this goes wrong."

"Sidney—"

But she was already reaching out with her abilities as he spoke. He felt a surge of electromagnetic energy and watched as Sidney's entire body went rigid with effort. Blood started flowing from her nose again, faster this time, dripping onto the dirty wood floor.

The drone stuttered in the air. Its smooth flight pattern became erratic, and Ben could hear the whine of its motors struggling against the unseen interference. Sidney's hand shot out, fingers curling like she was physically grasping the device, and then she pulled.

The drone's electromagnetic signature surged, then flatlined. It dropped from the sky like a stone, disappearing into the trees with a distant crash.

Sidney swayed. Ben caught her before she hit the floor, her body dead weight in his arms. Her eyes had rolled back, showing only whites, and blood poured from both nostrils now.

He lowered her gently and checked her pulse. It was still there, but rapid and thready. "Sidney, come on. Stay with me."

Her eyes fluttered. When they focused on his face, he saw that one pupil was larger than the other—a sure sign of serious neurological distress.

"Did I get it?" she whispered.

"You got it. You got it, but you pushed too hard. Your pupils are uneven, you're bleeding, and —" His voice cracked, and he paused for a second so he could gather himself. "Why do you keep doing this to yourself?"

"Because someone has to," she replied. Her palms went flat against the dusty floor, and he could tell she was trying to sit up.

"Oh, hell no," he told her, holding her firmly but gently so she had no choice but to let herself relax against the floor again. "Not right now, you don't. Just lie still for a minute."

For a second, her mouth pursed, and he worried she was going to argue with him. The weakness of her body must have told her this was no time for protests, though, because she settled back down and closed her eyes, as if realizing that the best thing she could do now was conserve as much energy as possible.

Rebecca knelt beside them and was already

pulling medical supplies from her pack. "This isn't quite the same as a concussion, but let's follow the same protocols. Keep her still, monitor her responsiveness, and watch for any sign of a seizure."

Lewis Webb had moved toward the window so he could be safely out of the way while they worked. Now his gaze was fixed on the approximate place in the forest from where the drone had gone down. "That was amazing. I've never seen anyone with that level of electromagnetic control before."

"At what cost, though?" Ben snapped. He kept his hand on Sidney's shoulder, feeling the fine tremors that continued to run through her body. "She's killing herself by degrees."

Rebecca Morse's mouth compressed for a moment. Then she said, "But she's alive. And we're not surrounded by DAPI tactical teams." She held a wad of gauze against Sidney's nose as she added, "Sometimes the only good choice is the least terrible one."

Ben wanted to argue with her, wanted to rage at the impossibility of their situation. But Rebecca was right. They were alive, the drone was down, and they'd bought themselves time. That had to be enough.

For now, anyway.

"How long before DAPI realizes the drone is offline?" he asked.

"Minutes," she replied briefly. "We need to move." A pause as she glanced over at Lewis, who still stood by the window. "Is there anything else we need to know?"

Lewis knelt at once and rifled through his files, then pulled out a specific document. "Phoenix resurrection. Ben said you're trying to help one complete its rebirth cycle."

"That's the plan, anyway," he said.

"Then you need to understand something crucial." Lewis handed him the document. A brief look told Ben that it appeared to be an academic paper, decades old and written in dense, technical language. "Phoenix fire doesn't merely consume and remake. It requires a witness. Someone who can anchor the phoenix to reality during the transformation, or it becomes lost between dimensions."

Ben scanned the paper, a sinking sensation beginning somewhere in the pit of his stomach. None of this sounded very good. "Define 'anchor.'"

"An anchor is someone with electromagnetic sensitivity who can maintain a psychic connection with the phoenix throughout the entire rebirth process. Someone who can hold the pattern of what the phoenix is supposed to be while its physical form dissolves and reconstructs." Lewis's expression was grave, and his gaze shifted toward Sidney, who still lay motionless on the floor. "Your grandmother tried it once, Sidney. That's in her journals. She maintained the connection for eight hours before she had to break it, and even then, she spent three days unconscious afterward."

Sidney pushed herself up to a sitting position despite Ben's protests. Blood still leaked from her nose, and her vision was clearly affected by the way she squinted, but her voice was sharp. "I've been through my grandmother's journals multiple times. I never saw an entry about anchoring a phoenix."

Lewis studied her for a moment, his gaze considering. "The 1978 entries. August, specifically. Did you read those?"

"I...." Sidney made a frustrated motion with one hand and then winced, as if even that small gesture had been enough to make her head ache. "I digitized the journals that dealt with recent portal activity and current threats. Shadow stalkers, dimensional barriers, electromagnetic anomalies from the last ten years. The older journals...." Her words faded away there, and Ben could see realization dawning in her worried, crystal-gray eyes. "I was doing triage. Focusing on what seemed immediately relevant."

"Phoenix entries from almost fifty years ago

wouldn't have seemed urgent," Lewis said, and he gave her an encouraging smile. "Not when you had shadow stalkers manifesting in your forest."

"How did you even know about the phoenix anchoring?" Ben asked. "If Sidney hasn't read those sections yet, and Emily Thompson was so secretive—"

"She was secretive, yes, but she was also something of a scientist," Lewis broke in. "Or at least, someone who'd trained herself like one, even if she didn't have a diploma to prove it. In 1979, an anonymous paper appeared in the *Journal of Cryptozoological Studies.* It described phoenix rebirth mechanics in extraordinary detail, far too much detail to be purely theoretical. The author used the initials E.T." He paused there to rummage through his papers, then pulled out a photocopied article. "The paper included recovery times, neurological symptoms, electromagnetic sensitivity changes. Those aren't observations you can make from a distance."

He set down another document, something that looked like medical records with most of the information redacted.

"I also track unusual medical cases near portal sites," he went on. "Emily Thompson was admitted to St. Joseph's Hospital in Eureka in August 1978 and was unconscious for sixty-three hours with no apparent cause. Normal vitals, but completely unresponsive. That admission occurred two days after reports of golden fire in the forest —an obvious phoenix sighting."

"She published the findings but tried to keep her identity hidden," Sidney said, her tone wondering. She reached up to rub her forehead and then continued. "And she documented her personal experience in the journals I haven't finished reading yet."

"I'm sure she was doing her best to prepare you," Lewis said. "She knew that someday, another phoenix might need anchoring. She left the information where it could be found if you knew where to look, both in academic records for researchers like me and in her journals for you. I'm sure she didn't expect that you'd need the information so soon."

Sidney used the sleeve of her jacket to blot the blood under her nose. Somewhere along the way, she must have dropped the bandana Ben had given her. "How long do we have before the phoenix's corruption becomes irreversible?"

"Based on what you've described? A day, maybe less." Lewis gathered his papers and stuffed them back in his messenger bag, then slipped it over his shoulder as he stood. "After that, the corruption will spread to the portal itself. Everything your grandmother and mother fought to protect will collapse."

Sidney's hand crept into Ben's. Her fingers were cold and shaking, but her grip was firmer than he'd expected.

"Then we have at most twenty-four hours to figure out how to do the impossible," she said.

She shifted, and Ben could tell she was about to attempt to rise. Immediately, he slid his arm around her waist so he could help her to her feet. She swayed a little once she was fully upright, but at least she didn't look as if she was about to topple over.

"We need to move," Rebecca Morse said. She'd been quiet during Lewis's revelations, probably understanding that this was information they needed if they wanted the phoenix to survive, but now her mind had obviously gone to their more immediate problems. "That drone crash will have triggered alarms."

They made their way down the tower stairs, Lewis leading and Rebecca Morse bringing up the rear. Ben stayed close to Sidney, ready to catch her if she stumbled. He could tell that her vision problems were getting worse—she missed a step halfway down and probably would have fallen if he hadn't grabbed her arm.

Once they reached ground level, Lewis looped the messenger bag containing all his research onto Ben's free shoulder. "That's everything I have on

DAPI, phoenix biology, and Emily Thompson's research. Use it wisely."

"You're not coming with us?" Sidney asked. Her tone was almost plaintive, as if she didn't want to lose contact with someone who'd had a connection to her grandmother, no matter how tenuous.

"I'm a liability," Lewis replied, his tone matter-of-fact. "DAPI's agents know my face, and I'm not trained for tactical situations." He paused there to open the door to his Jeep and climb inside. "But I'll keep gathering intelligence. If I learn anything useful, I'll find a way to contact you." He started the engine, which had the deep rumble of something that had never heard of electronic fuel injection, and then leaned out the window, his gaze fixed on Sidney. "I've spent almost fifty years studying phoenixes and dimensional phenomena, and I've never seen anyone with abilities like yours. If anyone can bridge the gap between human and dimensional magic, it's you. Your grandmother protected these secrets for decades—now it's your turn to use them."

Then he was gone, the Jeep growling and bouncing down the access road before it disappeared into the trees.

Rebecca Morse checked the chronometer strapped to her wrist. "We need to split up. I'll create a diversion and draw DAPI's attention south. You two get back to the facility and start preparing for the rebirth attempt."

"What kind of diversion?" Ben asked, even though he knew it probably didn't matter as long as it was effective.

"The kind that makes a lot of noise and triggers every sensor in a five-mile radius." Her smile was sharp. "Don't worry about me. I know how to disappear."

Sidney caught her by the arm before she could leave. "Thank you. For everything you're risking."

"You can thank me when this is over, and we're all still alive." Rebecca patted Sidney's shoulder. "And Sidney? Your grandmother was right about you."

Then she was gone, too, her dark clothing allowing her to melt into the forest like smoke.

For a moment, the two of them stood in the clearing without speaking.

"I'll drive," Ben said then. Sidney was in no condition to drive, not with her pupils still uneven and her coordination obviously impaired.

She sent him a weak smile. "Good idea."

They got into the SUV. He started the engine while she spread a map across her lap, tracking their route back to the research facility with one finger. She shook so badly that she had to use both hands to hold the map steady.

"Ben," she said as they began to bump their

way back toward the forest road. "What Lewis said, about this maybe killing me—"

"Don't."

Her mouth tightened. "We have to talk about it. If something goes wrong, if the phoenix's rebirth starts to pull me under, you need to promise me that you'll break the connection."

He gripped the steering wheel hard enough to make the leather creak. "I'm not promising that."

"Ben—"

"No." He pulled onto the access road, gaze scanning the area for DAPI vehicles. "I'm not going to promise to let you die. We'll find another way."

Her unfocused eyes stared out into the forest. "There might not be another way."

"Then we'll make one." He glanced at her, saw the blood still crusting her face and the way exhaustion pulled at her delicate features, making her look far older than her twenty-seven years. It didn't matter, though; she would always be beautiful to him. His voice grew firmer as he added, "That's what we do, Sidney. We find solutions to impossible problems."

She was quiet for a long moment. Then her hand found his on the steering wheel, her cold fingers wrapping around his wrist. A very faint smile tugged at her lips.

"You're right."

They drove through the gathering dusk, heading back toward the research facility and the dying phoenix. Behind them, somewhere in the forest, Rebecca Morse was creating chaos to cover their escape.

Lewis's files rode on the back seat, and Ben wondered if the information they contained would be enough to combat DAPI's pattern of escalating aggression. He and Sidney were facing an enemy with nearly unlimited resources and no accountability, fighting to save a creature that existed beyond the normal boundaries of physics.

The odds were impossible.

But when he looked over at Sidney—bloodied, exhausted, still fighting despite everything DAPI had done to her—he felt something steady and certain settle deep in his gut.

They would find a way. They had to.

Because the alternative was unthinkable.

CHAPTER FIVE

The headlights cut through the gathering dark as Ben drove us back toward the Jessop facility and I tried to pretend I wasn't seeing double. One road, not two. One dashboard, not a ghostly overlay. My vision had been deteriorating since I'd knocked that drone out of the sky, and no amount of blinking seemed to fix the problem.

"How's your head?" Ben asked, his voice carefully neutral in a way that I knew meant he was actually very worried.

"Fine," I lied.

His hand found mine on the seat between us, and I felt the familiar resonance of our electromagnetic fields synchronizing. It helped—not enough to clear my vision, but enough to push back the nausea that had been building ever since we'd left the fire tower.

"Sidney."

Something in his tone told me he'd lost patience with convenient misrepresentations. "I'm seeing double," I said, relenting. "My pupils are still uneven, I probably have a concussion, and I definitely shouldn't be channeling any more power for at least forty-eight hours." I squeezed his hand and tried to summon a lopsided smile. "Is that better?"

"Marginally." He took a corner too fast, and I had to swallow hard against the surge of dizziness that followed. "How bad is the phoenix?"

I'd been trying not to think about that. Ever since I'd woken up in the medical facility with our consciousnesses entangled, I'd been able to sense the phoenix like a second heartbeat underneath my own. Right now, that heartbeat was weakening.

"Worse," I said. "The corruption's spreading faster than we thought. I think it knows we're running out of time."

Ben set his jaw, but he didn't reply. What was there to say, after all? We had maybe twenty-four hours at most before the corruption became irreversible, and I was already so depleted that jamming a single surveillance drone had nearly knocked me unconscious.

The odds weren't looking very good.

We pulled onto the access road that led to the facility, and I immediately sensed something wrong about our surroundings. The electromagnetic signatures in the area had changed—there were more artificial signals, more concentrated patterns of electronic activity.

"Ben, stop the car," I said.

He hit the brakes without question, and we sat there in the darkness while I stretched my senses outward. Three miles northeast, I picked up vehicle signatures—what I thought were military transport trucks, maybe four or five of them. Two miles east, I found concentrated electromagnetic activity that matched the signature of tactical communications equipment.

DAPI had found us.

"They're surrounding the facility," I said in an undertone, even though the encroaching forces certainly weren't close enough to hear us. "At least twenty people, probably more. They must have tracked us from the tower."

Ben began to pull out his phone, then made a sound of disgust as he seemed to remember it was useless. The EMP from the phoenix's distress call had fried every civilian electronic device in a five-mile radius. Only military-grade, hardened equipment and the specialized DAPI sensors Ben and I had pilfered from the forest had survived.

"Rebecca," he said. "We need to warn her."

I reached deeper with my abilities, searching for her electromagnetic signature. Doing so took longer than it should have; my depleted state made everything harder, like trying to see through fog. But I found her eventually. To my surprise, she was actually inside the facility, moving with stealth and haste through the lower levels.

"She knows," I said. "She's already evacuating. Ben, we can't go back there. If we get any closer, they'll find us."

"The phoenix—"

"I know." The creature's weakening heartbeat pulsed through our connection, and I felt its confusion and fear. It didn't understand why I'd left, why the anchor had broken. "But if DAPI captures me, the phoenix will die no matter what. At least this way, we have a chance."

Ben stared at the dark road ahead, his hands tight on the steering wheel. I could sense his frustration, the helpless rage of someone who'd spent his whole life solving problems through research and logic, and who was now facing a situation where neither would help.

"What do we do?" he asked.

Before I could answer, my senses flared, warning me of a new threat. Different signatures this time, approaching from the south.

Two vehicles moving at high speed.

"We've got company," I said. "I think it's a tactical team. They must have been waiting for us to come back."

Ben threw the SUV into reverse and hit the gas. We shot backward down the access road, tires squealing as he whipped us around in a tight turn. The headlights swept across the forest, and for a moment I caught a glimpse of what was coming —black SUVs with tinted windows, the kind of vehicles that practically screamed "federal agency."

"They're going to cut us off," I said. That weird electromagnetic sense of mine seemed able to track the vehicles' approach vectors, which would have been freaky if I'd had more time to analyze it. "We need to go off-road."

"This thing isn't built for off-road."

I grinned. "Neither am I right now, but we're doing it anyway."

In answer, Ben yanked the wheel to the right and sent us careening into the forest. Branches scraped against the sides of the SUV, and the suspension protested with creaks and groans as we bounced over roots and rocks. Behind us, I could sense the tactical teams reaching the access road, their vehicles stopping where we'd turned off.

They'd come after us on foot. They had the terrain advantage, the numbers advantage, and significantly better training than an exhausted cryptozoologist and a burned-out pet shop owner and almost-DVM.

"Ben," I said. Maybe it was stupid to warn him, but I needed him to know what I planned to do. "I have to use my abilities."

That statement earned me an emphatic shake of his head. Hands tight on the steering wheel, he said, "You're already drained. You said yourself that you shouldn't be channeling any more power."

Well, that was true enough.

"I shouldn't be doing a lot of things." I pressed my hand against the dashboard, feeling the SUV's electrical systems through my fingertips. "But I can give us an advantage and hopefully buy us some time."

"Sidney—"

"Trust me."

I reached outward with my electromagnetic senses, finding the tactical teams' radio communications, their GPS units, their night vision equipment. All of it ran on electricity. All of it was vulnerable to someone who could manipulate electromagnetic fields.

Yes, I'd done this before, during the shadow stalker crisis a month earlier. I'd overloaded electronics, created interference, and jammed signals. But that had been when I was fresh, when my nervous system wasn't already screaming from overuse.

This was going to hurt.

A lot.

I gathered my abilities and pushed.

Behind us, I could feel their tactical radios squeal with feedback, even as their GPS units flickered and died and their night vision goggles went dark. For about thirty seconds, DAPI's teams would be operating blind, their technological advantages stripped away.

But those thirty seconds cost me everything.

My vision went completely dark. Not double anymore, but just gone, as if someone had thrown a switch in my brain. Blood poured from my nose in a hot rush, and I tasted copper at the back of my throat. My hands started trembling so violently that I had to clench them into fists to keep them from flailing.

"Sidney!" Ben's voice seemed to come from very far away. "Talk to me. Are you—"

"Blind," I managed. "It's temporary…I hope. Keep driving."

The SUV lurched over something large, and I felt my stomach drop as we went briefly airborne. When we landed, the impact sent white-hot pain shooting through my skull, and I bit down so hard that I tasted blood again.

"There's a creek bed ahead," Ben said. "I'm

going to follow it north. The water should hide our trail."

I nodded, or at least, I tried to. My head might as well have weighed a thousand pounds, and the simple act of moving it sent waves of nausea rolling through me. Through our connection, I could feel Ben's terror mixing with utter determination to get us out of there. He was more scared than I'd ever sensed him before, but he kept driving anyway.

It wasn't as if we had any other options.

My vision started to return in patches—gray shapes that might have been trees, the green glow of the dashboard, Ben's sharply etched profile illuminated by the instrument lights. Not great, but still better than total darkness.

"How long?" I asked.

"Before your vision fully returns? No idea. How long before DAPI gets their equipment working again?" He glanced over at me, his jaw tight. "Also, no idea, but I'm guessing not long."

I reached out with my senses, trying to track the tactical teams. The effort made my head pound and my vision gray out again, but I managed to locate them. Still behind us, but spreading out, forming a search pattern.

"They're adapting," I said. "Going analog. We bought ourselves maybe five minutes."

"Then we need to use those five minutes wisely."

Ben guided the SUV through the creek bed, the water splashing up against the undercarriage. The sound was too loud, would attract attention if anyone was close enough to hear. But we didn't have any better options.

My connection to the phoenix pulsed weakly, and I could feel its distress surge. Something was happening at the facility.

Something bad.

"The phoenix," I said. "It knows DAPI is close. It's panicking."

I could sense the creature's mounting terror as it seemed to detect the tactical teams approaching the facility. The electromagnetic interference from their equipment was making the corruption worse, destabilizing what little control the phoenix had left over its fire.

"Ben," I gasped. "The phoenix is losing it. The interference from DAPI's equipment—it's making the corruption spread faster."

"Can it escape?"

I reached deeper through our connection, feeling the phoenix's desperation as if it were my own. It was still mobile, still capable of flight despite the corruption. But it was disoriented, struggling to find a direction that felt safe.

"It's trying to," I said. "But it doesn't know where to go. The interference is everywhere."

I closed my eyes and tried to send the phoenix a mental image of the forest, which offered at least a spurious sense of safety, since I had no idea exactly where we were going, only that we planned to take refuge in there somewhere. My depleted state made the effort agonizing, and fresh blood poured from my nose. But I felt the message reach the creature.

Understanding. Recognition. Hope.

"It's coming to us," I whispered. "Following the connection."

A moment later, I sensed it—the phoenix launching itself into the air, its contaminated fire flaring as it struggled to stay aloft. Behind it, I could feel DAPI's confusion as their target suddenly escaped.

But the phoenix's flight was erratic, and the surge of corrupted fire it had released to propel itself into the air was having consequences. Dimensional energy spiked at the facility, wrong and twisted and hungry.

The explosion hit like a physical wave, even from two miles away. I felt it through my electromagnetic senses first—a massive surge of dimensional energy as the phoenix's corrupted fire punched a temporary breach between our world and somewhere else. Then the shockwave reached us, a pulse of heat that rattled the SUV's windows and sent a flock of birds erupting from the trees.

Ben fought to keep us on course as the ground trembled and the big Suburban lurched from side to side. "What the hell was that?"

"Dimensional breach. The phoenix's fire surge opened a temporary rift." I cut off as my senses picked up new signatures. Not human…and definitely not natural. "Oh, shit."

Ben's voice tightened with worry. "Sidney? What now?"

"Shadow creatures. The breach is pulling them through." I gripped the dashboard, although I wasn't sure that would be enough to keep me upright. "Ben, we need to keep moving. The phoenix escaped, but it left chaos behind."

"Will it find us?"

At least I thought I had some confidence in answering that question. "Yes. It's following our connection. But we need to get as far away as we can before DAPI regroups."

He was right that I was in no condition to help. I was useless right then, barely able to sense beyond a few hundred yards, my abilities pushed so far past their limits that even breathing took concentration.

But the phoenix was coming, and shadow creatures were manifesting in the forest near the facility. DAPI was probably getting exactly the crisis they'd engineered.

The SUV lurched to a stop. Ben killed the engine and the lights, plunging us into darkness broken only by faint starlight filtering through the canopy.

"Why are we stopping?" I whispered.

"Because I thought I heard something." He pulled a flashlight from his pack but didn't turn it on. "Movement. Large…close."

I reached out with my senses and immediately wished I hadn't. The effort sent fresh blood flowing from my nose and made my vision blur again. But I found what Ben had heard.

Something was approaching through the trees. Something that radiated clean, pure electromagnetic energy—so different from the corrupted signals I'd been tracking that it felt like cool water after hours in the desert.

"It's okay," I said. "I know this signature."

The unicorn stepped into the small clearing where we'd stopped, and even in my depleted state, its presence made me want to weep. The creature was exactly the same as I remembered from weeks ago—white coat that seemed to generate its own light, silver horn that hummed with dimensional energy, eyes that held intelligence and purpose and something like compassion.

Ben sat very still beside me. "That's a unicorn."

"That's *the* unicorn. The one that drew you to Silver Hollow." I opened the door and climbed out on shaking legs. "The one that brought us together."

The unicorn approached slowly, its hooves silent on the forest floor. When it reached me, it lowered its head and pressed its horn gently against my forehead.

Clean energy flooded my system at once, not exactly healing the damage I'd done to myself, but stabilizing it. My vision cleared. The trembling in my hands eased, and the splitting headache that had been building since the drone incident faded to a manageable throb.

"Thank you," I whispered.

The unicorn pulled back and looked at me with those ancient dark eyes. Then it turned and knelt, a clear invitation.

"It wants you to ride," Ben said from behind me. He'd gotten out of the SUV and was watching our interchange with open wonder. "Sidney, I think it's offering to take you somewhere safe."

I looked back at the SUV, then at the distant glow of fires from the facility, and finally at the unicorn patiently kneeling before me.

"What about you?" I asked. The unicorn was

tough, but it didn't seem quite sturdy enough to carry two full-grown adults.

"I'll drive," he said. "But the unicorn showed up for a reason, and I don't think we should ignore it."

He was right. The luminous creature had saved us from Victor Maplehurst, had appeared during the shadow stalker crisis to help us. Whatever its reasons now, it was clearly on our side.

I climbed onto the unicorn's back, and its coat was warm beneath me, almost hot, like its body was generating more heat than normal biology would allow. The moment I settled into place, I felt our electromagnetic fields synchronize—not the way Ben and I resonated, but something that felt far older, infinitely reassuring.

The unicorn rose smoothly to its feet and looked back at Ben.

"I'll follow," he said. "Just—keep her safe."

Then we were moving, and the unicorn's gait was so smooth that I barely felt the motion. It wove through the trees with impossible grace, avoiding obstacles I couldn't see, navigating by senses I couldn't begin to comprehend.

Behind us, I heard the SUV's engine start up as Ben began to follow. But the unicorn was faster, and within minutes, we'd pulled ahead, moving deeper into old-growth forest where the trees grew so thick that starlight couldn't penetrate.

I stretched my senses outward, checking for threats. The tactical teams were still near the facility, dealing with the dimensional breach and the shadow creatures that had manifested there. Rebecca Morse's signature had moved several miles south—she was creating the diversion she'd promised, drawing attention away from our escape route.

And the phoenix—

The phoenix was dying faster now. The dimensional breach had accelerated the corruption, and I could feel its consciousness starting to fragment. Maybe twelve hours left.

Maybe less.

The unicorn must have sensed my distress, because it slowed and turned its head to look back at me. In the darkness, its horn glowed faintly silver, and I felt a pulse of reassurance through our connection.

Safe. Protected. Rest.

But I couldn't rest. Not while the phoenix was dying, not while DAPI was hunting us. Not while—

The unicorn stopped in a clearing I didn't recognize. Trees formed a perfect circle here, their branches woven together overhead to create a living dome of fresh green leaves. In the center of the clearing, a spring bubbled up from the ground, its water catching starlight and throwing it back in silver ripples.

"Where are we?" I asked.

The unicorn knelt again, and I slid from its back. The moment my feet touched the ground, I felt it—this place was saturated with dimensional energy. Clean energy, not corrupted, the kind that made my abilities sing instead of scream.

The SUV appeared at the edge of the clearing, Ben driving carefully over the rough terrain. He parked and climbed out, then looked in all directions so he could take in the circle of trees and the glowing spring.

"This is a sacred site," he said in a murmur as he approached me. "Sidney, this is like the portal clearing. Dimensionally significant."

The unicorn moved to the spring and lowered its head to drink. When it raised its muzzle, water dripped from its lips and seemed to evaporate into silver mist.

"It brought us here for a reason," I said.

Ben pulled out his EMF reader and checked the displays. "The dimensional energy readings are off the charts, but it all seems stable. This place has been here for a very long time."

I knelt beside the spring and cupped water in my hands. It was cold enough to make my fingers ache a little, and when I drank, I tasted something

I couldn't name—mineral and magic, ancient and alive.

The exhaustion that had been dragging at me began to ease immediately. No, it wasn't gone or anywhere close to healed, but it was manageable.

"The water's helping," I said. "Ben, try it."

He knelt beside me and drank, and I watched his expression shift from skepticism to wonder.

"It's amplifying my electromagnetic sensitivity," he said. "I can feel the dimensional barriers from here. See how thin they are, how close the other world is."

The unicorn moved to stand between us and the clearing's entrance, its body positioned like a guard. Through our connection, I was able to read its purpose.

It was protecting us, creating a space where we could rest and recover, could prepare for what came next. The shadow creatures manifesting at the facility wouldn't come here—this place was too saturated with clean dimensional energy. And DAPI's tactical teams wouldn't find us because the electromagnetic interference from the spring would mask our signatures.

For a few hours at least, we were safe.

I sat heavily on a fallen log, and Ben moved immediately to examine me in the spring's faint light.

"Your pupils are still uneven," he said. "And

you're still bleeding." He gently wiped blood from under my nose with his sleeve. "How do you feel?"

"Like I got hit by a semi and then run over a few more times for good measure." I leaned against him, too tired to sit upright. "But I'm alive. *We're* alive. That's more than I expected an hour ago."

His arm came around my shoulders, and our electromagnetic fields synchronized again. With the spring's clean energy amplifying the effect, the resonance between us was stronger than ever.

"Lewis said the phoenix needs an anchor," Ben said. Something about his tone was almost hushed, as if he thought we were in a holy place.

Maybe we were.

"Someone who can maintain the connection through the entire rebirth cycle," he continued. "That's going to be you."

Don't tease me with a good time, passed through my mind, and despite everything, I couldn't help smiling a little. "I know."

"And Lewis also said that your grandmother tried this once and spent three days unconscious afterward. She was at full strength when she attempted it."

Was this Ben's way of trying to dissuade me from doing what needed to be done? If that was the case, he needed to get ready for disappointment.

"I know that, too," I replied. I closed my eyes. The phoenix's weakening heartbeat traveled to me across the miles, thready and uneven. "But I don't have a choice. If the phoenix dies while we're still linked, the psychic backlash will shatter my mind. And if it dies before completing the rebirth, the portal destabilizes. My mother and grandmother will be cut off forever."

Ben shifted next to me, although I could tell he was being careful not to disturb my head where it lay against his shoulder. "There has to be another way."

"If there is, we haven't found it." I opened my eyes and gazed at him, at the worry in his shadowed eyes and the tense set of his mouth. "And we're running out of time to look."

The unicorn made a soft sound, almost like a sigh. When I looked at it, I saw understanding in those ancient eyes. It knew what I was facing. It knew the cost.

And it was here to help me survive it.

"The spring," I said, a sudden thought occurring to me. "Ben, what if the spring's energy could help anchor me? Maybe provide stability during the rebirth process?"

He was quiet for a moment, considering the question. "Lewis said the anchor needs electromagnetic sensitivity and the ability to hold the pattern of what the phoenix should be. You have both. But the strain of maintaining that connection for hours—" He shook his head. "The spring's energy might help. But it won't be enough. Not when you're already this drained."

I knew he was right. I could feel it in my bones, in the way my hands still trembled despite the spring's restorative effects.

I was going to attempt something that had nearly killed my grandmother when she was at full strength. And I was going to do it while already nearly wiped out, already damaged, already pushed past every safe limit.

The odds weren't good.

But when I reached out with my senses and felt the phoenix's dying heartbeat, when I thought about my mother and grandmother trapped on the other side of the portal…when I looked at Ben's face and saw the fear he was trying to hide—

The odds didn't matter.

"We should rest while we can," I told him. "Because once we start this, there's no stopping until it's finished."

He nodded and pulled me closer. The unicorn settled near the spring, its body a warm presence in the darkness. And there, in that ancient grove saturated with clean dimensional energy, with shadow creatures manifesting miles away and

DAPI closing in and a phoenix dying slowly through our connection—

I needed to let myself rest.

Just for a few hours.

Just enough to face the impossible one more time.

CHAPTER SIX

Ben had seen Sidney exhausted before. He'd watched her push through electromagnetic overload during the shadow stalker crisis and had caught her when she'd nearly collapsed after merging with corrupted magic. But he'd never seen her this drained, as if something was slowly stealing her life force.

She lay on her side near the spring, wrapped in the emergency blanket he'd pulled from the SUV's kit, and even in sleep, her hands trembled. Blood had crusted under her nose once again, and also at the corners of her mouth. Her skin had taken on a gray cast that made her look like a photograph left too long in the sun.

The unicorn had settled near her, its body providing some much-needed warmth in the cold night air. Ben had initially worried that the creature might leave once Sidney was safe, but it seemed content to stay, its presence creating a bubble of calm in the ancient grove.

Ben checked his watch. Two-thirty in the morning. They'd been here for three hours, and Sidney had been unconscious for all of them.

He pressed two fingers to her wrist and counted her pulse. Still elevated, still thready. Not good, but stable. That was something, he supposed.

The phoenix appeared at the edge of the clearing, moving slowly through the trees. Agent Morse had wrapped it in that electromagnetic shielding fabric—which it wore like an odd cloak—before evacuating the facility, but the creature had found them anyway. Ben suspected it had followed the connection between itself and Sidney, tracking her consciousness across miles of forest.

It settled on the other side of Sidney, its corrupted fire casting orange-black shadows across the grove. Up close, the contamination looked worse than Ben had realized. Maybe approaching eighty percent now, although he had to admit that was just an educated guess. The shadow veins had spread through most of its feathers, and the clean gold fire only flickered in small patches near its chest.

The creature looked at Ben with ancient,

knowing eyes, and he felt something brush against his consciousness. Not words, or even images, just a profound sense of urgency mixed with gratitude.

"I'm doing everything I can," Ben said quietly. "But I don't know if it'll be enough."

Despite that lackluster promise, the phoenix lowered its head and tucked its beak against its chest. Within moments, it had fallen into a fitful sleep, its corrupted fire dimming to embers.

Ben pulled out the files Lewis had given him, along with his laptop. The battery was limping along—the EMP must have damaged the charging circuits—but he had maybe two hours of power left. Enough to go through the digitized journal entries from Emily Thompson that Sidney had shared with him weeks ago.

He'd read them before, of course. But he'd been looking for general information about the portal and the dimensional creatures that used it to travel between worlds. Now he needed something much more specific.

He needed to know about the phoenix's rebirth cycle.

The journals were meticulously organized, decades of careful observation recorded in Emily Thompson's precise handwriting. Ben scrolled through entries about griffin migrations and shadow stalker behavior and unicorn sightings, looking for the sections on phoenixes.

He found the first mention in an entry from 1978.

I observed the phoenix beginning its rebirth cycle near the portal site. The creature's fire burned clean and bright, consuming its physical form over the course of approximately eight hours. I attempted to maintain electromagnetic contact throughout the process, as Grandmother's journals suggested this would anchor the phoenix to our dimension and prevent it from becoming lost between worlds.

The strain was terrible. By hour four, I was bleeding from the nose and ears. By hour six, I'd lost consciousness twice. But I held the pattern and kept the image of what the phoenix should be fixed in my mind, even as its physical form dissolved into pure energy.

The rebirth was completed successfully. The phoenix emerged renewed, its fire stronger than before. But the cost—

The entry cut off there. Ben flipped to the next page and found it dated three days later.

I woke this morning for the first time since the anchoring. Mother says I'd been unconscious for sixty-three hours, occasionally crying out or convulsing, but never fully waking. The doctors she brought in were baffled. All my vitals were stable, but I simply wouldn't wake.

I feel different now. My electromagnetic sensitivity has increased significantly—I can sense the portal's fluctuations from miles away, can feel dimensional barriers thinning before any creatures cross through. It's as if anchoring the phoenix left some of its fire inside me, expanding my abilities beyond what they once were.

I don't know if this change is permanent. Mother's journals contain no mention of similar effects, but then, she never attempted to anchor a phoenix through full rebirth. I may be the first in our family to do so.

I hope I'm the last.

Ben sat back, frowning. Emily had succeeded in anchoring a phoenix, but it had fundamentally altered her, had left her unconscious for days and permanently changed her abilities.

And that had been with a clean rebirth, a phoenix that wasn't corrupted.

Sidney stirred, and a small sound of distress escaped her throat. Ben moved to her side immediately, one hand finding hers.

"I'm here," he said in what he hoped was a gentle, comforting murmur. "You're safe."

Her eyes opened slowly, unfocused at first, then gradually clearing. When she saw him, something in her expression softened.

"Ben."

Her voice was hoarse, but she sounded mostly like herself.

"How do you feel?" he asked.

"Like someone replaced my nervous system with live wires." She tried to sit up, and he helped her, keeping one arm around her shoulders for support. "How long was I out?"

"Three hours. The unicorn brought the phoenix here—it's sleeping on your other side."

Sidney turned carefully, her movements stiff, and looked at the dying creature. Even in the dim light, Ben could see tears gathering in her eyes.

"It's worse," she whispered.

"Eighty percent corrupted, maybe more. But stable for now." He squeezed her hand gently. "Sidney, I've been reading your grandmother's journals. The entry about anchoring a phoenix."

She tilted her head to one side. "The one Lewis told us about, when she spent three days unconscious afterward."

Ben nodded. "It changed her permanently. Her electromagnetic sensitivity increased significantly after the anchoring. She said it felt like the phoenix had left some of its fire inside her."

Sidney was quiet for a long moment after

hearing those words. When she spoke, though, she sounded more thoughtful than worried. "You're saying if I anchor the phoenix through rebirth, I might not be the same person afterward."

As much as he hated the idea, he made himself reply calmly, "I'm saying it's a possibility we need to consider. Your grandmother anchored a clean rebirth and still spent days unconscious. You're going to be anchoring a corrupted one while already severely depleted." Ben took her hands so she could face toward him. "This might kill you. At the very least, it could change you so fundamentally that who you are now—"

"Doesn't exist anymore," she cut in gently. Her voice was steady enough, but Ben could feel the way her slender body shivered. "I know. I've been feeling it through the connection with the phoenix, the way our consciousnesses are entangling. If I anchor it through rebirth, we're going to merge on a level that might not be reversible."

Ben wanted to tell her that wasn't an acceptable outcome, that they needed to find another solution, another way forward that didn't involve Sidney sacrificing herself or her identity. But they'd been over this ground already, and the math hadn't changed.

No anchor meant the phoenix died. A dead phoenix meant the portal would destabilize. And a destabilized portal meant Sidney's mother and grandmother were cut off forever, and Silver Hollow's entire supernatural ecosystem collapsed.

It was an impossible situation, no matter how they looked at it.

"There has to be another way," he said, more out of stubbornness than because he thought they had a viable solution.

"If there is, we haven't found it." Sidney leaned against him, her weight settling into his side. She felt so light, so fragile, as if some necessary part of her life force had already been stripped from her. "And we're running out of time to look."

The unicorn lifted its head and stared at them with those ancient eyes. Through his growing electromagnetic sensitivity, now amplified by the grove's clean energy, Ben could sense the creature's purpose clearly.

It was here to help and to protect, to ensure that Sidney survived what came next.

But even the unicorn's presence couldn't guarantee success.

"Tell me what you found in the journals," Sidney said then. "All of it. I need to know what I'm facing."

Ben pulled his laptop closer and walked her through Emily's entries—the anchoring process, the physical toll, the permanent changes. Sidney listened without interrupting, her expression growing more serious with each detail.

"So I'll probably be unconscious for days afterward," she said when he was done. "Assuming I survive at all."

Forcing himself to sound dispassionate, to look at the problem with scientific eyes, he replied, "That's what your grandmother's journals suggest."

Not even a blink. "And my abilities might change. Expand, maybe, or become something different."

"Yes."

Sidney glanced over at the phoenix, then at the unicorn, and finally back at Ben. "I can live with that. As long as I live."

This hurt. She was being so matter-of-fact about it, so resigned to paying whatever cost the anchoring demanded. He wanted to shake her, wanted to make her see how precious she was, how much he needed her to survive this intact.

But he knew Sidney well enough to understand that arguing would only make her defensive. She'd made her choice already—had probably made it the moment she'd felt the phoenix's distress call in the forest.

All he could do now was support her through it.

"Okay," he said, and allowed himself a small

breath, one he hoped would give him the strength he needed. "Then we prepare. We need to learn everything we can about the anchoring process and figure out how to maximize your chances of survival."

"And you'll be there to stabilize me," Sidney said, calm as if they were discussing him teaching her how to water ski. "Lewis said your electromagnetic field makes my abilities more efficient."

He hoped Lewis was right. "I'll be there every second." Ben laced his fingers through hers. "I'm not leaving you to face this alone."

Their electromagnetic fields began to synchronize, that familiar resonance strengthening as they sat together in the grove. But this time, amplified by the spring's dimensional energy, the effect was visible—a soft golden glow forming around their joined hands, spreading up their arms.

Sidney stared at the light. "Is that—?"

"Our bioelectric fields becoming visible. The dimensional energy here is making them manifest physically." Ben watched as the glow spread across Sidney's skin, warm and gentle. "It's never done this before."

"It's beautiful," Sidney whispered.

The light pulsed in time with their heartbeats, synchronized perfectly. Ben could feel every flutter of Sidney's pulse, every breath she took, every tremor in her exhausted nervous system. And he knew she was feeling the same from him—his fear and determination, his love and terror.

"Ben," she said quietly. "If I don't survive this—"

"Don't."

"If I don't survive," she continued, "I need you to know something. What we have—what DAPI engineered and what we built despite their manipulation—it's the realest thing in my life. *You're* the realest thing."

Ben pulled her closer, although he was careful not to hold her too tightly. Her poor body was bruised all over. "You're going to survive. We're going to get through this, save the phoenix, stop DAPI, and then we're going to have a very long, very boring life where nothing tries to kill us for at least a week."

Sidney laughed, the sound catching in her throat. "A whole week?"

"Maybe two if we're lucky."

She turned her face up to his, and in the golden glow of their synchronized electromagnetic fields, she looked otherworldly. Changed already by everything she'd been through, by the connection to the phoenix.

By the choices she'd made.

Ben kissed her because he couldn't not kiss her. Not when they might only have hours left before everything went wrong, and when the golden light surrounding them felt like a promise he desperately wanted to keep.

Sidney kissed him back with an intensity that belied her exhaustion, one hand coming up to tangle in his hair. The glow around them brightened, sparks of blue-white electricity dancing across their skin wherever they touched.

"Careful," Ben murmured against her mouth. "Your nervous system—"

"Is already damaged beyond repair. I might as well enjoy this." She kissed him harder, and in that moment, Ben felt their electromagnetic fields merge completely.

This was what DAPI had wanted to study. This perfect synchronization, this amplification effect that made them stronger together than apart. But Rosenthal had been wrong about what it meant. She'd seen it as a tactical advantage, something to be weaponized and exploited.

She hadn't understood that this was partnership. Love. Trust so complete that two people could merge their very bioelectric fields and still remain themselves.

Ben pulled back just enough to look at Sidney's face. "I love you."

"I know." She smiled, and for a moment she looked less like someone facing impossible odds and more like the woman who'd met him in her pet shop weeks ago, skeptical but willing to listen. "I love you, too."

The golden glow faded slowly as they separated, but Ben could still feel the resonance between them. It was stronger now, deeper, as if that moment of complete synchronization had forged something permanent.

The phoenix stirred in its sleep, and a pulse of corrupted fire spread through the clearing. The shadow veins in its feathers had spread further, and Ben could see them pulsing in time with the creature's heartbeat.

Maybe fifteen hours left. Maybe a whole lot less.

His laptop chimed a low battery warning. Ben reluctantly pulled away from Sidney, who gave him an encouraging smile, and returned to the journals, scrolling through more entries while he still had power.

He found what he was looking for in an entry from 1974—four years before Emily's successful anchoring attempt.

Grandmother's journals describe what she called the "cleansing paradox." Phoenix fire, even corrupted, retains memory of what it should be. But accessing that memory requires someone who can withstand exposure to the corruption long enough to find the clean pattern underneath.

The risk is obvious. Exposure to corrupted dimensional energy can permanently damage human nervous systems. But without accessing the clean pattern, the phoenix can't guide its own rebirth. It needs an anchor who can hold the image of clean fire while the creature burns away its corrupted form.

Grandmother attempted this once with a partially corrupted phoenix. She survived, but barely, and her electromagnetic sensitivity was never the same. The corruption left scars in her abilities—dead zones where she could no longer sense anything, and hyperactive zones where even minor electromagnetic activity caused her pain.

The cleansing paradox is this—to save a corrupted phoenix, one must become partially corrupted themselves. To hold the pattern of clean fire, one must touch the corruption. There is no anchoring without cost, no rebirth without sacrifice.

Ben's hands went quiet on the keyboard. The battery warning chimed again, more insistent.

Sidney would have to expose herself to the phoenix's corruption. Would have to let it touch her consciousness, her electromagnetic abilities, her very sense of self. And even if she survived, she might emerge permanently damaged.

Dead zones. Hyperactive zones. Abilities that would cause her pain instead of providing information.

"Ben?" Sidney's voice was soft. "What did you find?"

He wanted to lie, wanted to tell her everything would be fine, that anchoring the phoenix was dangerous but survivable. But Sidney deserved the truth.

"Your great-great-grandmother attempted to anchor a partially corrupted phoenix," he said. "She survived, but the corruption left permanent damage to her abilities. Scars, essentially. Places where her electromagnetic sensitivity was destroyed, and other places where it became hypersensitive to the point of causing pain."

Sidney absorbed this information without visible reaction. "How corrupted was the phoenix she tried to anchor?"

"The journals don't say specifically. But based on the description, maybe thirty or forty percent."

"And our phoenix is at seventy-five percent, maybe more."

"Around there. It's hard to tell how fast the corruption is advancing just by looking at it."

Sidney glanced over at the sleeping creature, its contaminated fire casting twisted shadows on the trees all around them. "So I'm going to be exposed to twice as much corruption as my great-great-grandmother. And she was permanently damaged."

"That's the most likely outcome." To hell with sounding calm and scholarly. His voice rough, he went on, "Sidney, I can't ask you to do this. The cost is too high."

"You're not asking. I'm choosing." She met his gaze with steady eyes, a ghost of a smile touching her full lips. "My mother and grandmother are trapped on the other side of the portal. If I don't anchor this phoenix, they'll be cut off forever. It's not a choice—it's the only possible decision I can make."

He wanted to argue, wanted to find some way to change her mind. But he knew Sidney well enough to understand that her family's safety would always outweigh her own.

She'd already lost too much. She wouldn't lose them, too.

His laptop screen went dark as the battery died. Ben closed it and set it down on the ground, then moved back to Sidney's side. She leaned against him immediately, fitting into his arms like she belonged there.

"We should rest," he said. "Both of us. We're going to need every bit of strength we have."

A small frown touched her graceful brows. "I'm not sure I can sleep."

"Try anyway," he replied. "We've got maybe eight hours at the most before we have to move, and you need recovery time."

Faced with those incontrovertible facts, Sidney didn't bother to argue. Instead, she shifted so she could lie down again, and Ben stretched out beside her, one arm around her waist. The unicorn watched them with approval, and the phoenix slept on, its corrupted fire a steady pulse in the darkness.

Ben tried to sleep but couldn't. His mind kept turning over the information from the journals, looking for something he'd missed. Some detail that would give Sidney better odds, some technique that would reduce the risk.

He came up empty every time.

Sidney's breathing had evened out, which suggested she'd actually managed to fall asleep. Ben envied her that ability—to shut down in the middle of a crisis and rest. He'd always been the type to lie awake running through scenarios, calculating odds, trying to control the uncontrollable through sheer force of analysis.

It didn't help. It never helped.

The grove was quiet except for the spring's gentle bubbling and the occasional rustle of wind through the trees. Starlight filtered through the woven branches overhead, creating patterns of light and shadow across the ground.

His phone vibrated in his pocket. Ben pulled it out carefully, trying not to disturb Sidney. He'd kept it in a hardened case that had protected it from the EMP—one of the few pieces of electronics that had survived.

A text message from a number he didn't recognize.

> Ben. It's Morse. Don't reply. DAPI establishing perimeter around forest. Estimate 40-50 personnel. Rosenthal arriving personally at 0800 with "enhanced containment protocols." They're building something at the northern facility—looks like dimensional stabilization equipment. I think they're planning to create an artificial portal. -RM

Ben read the message twice, a cold sensation going through him that had nothing to do with the damp chill of a Northern California night.

An artificial portal. DAPI wasn't just trying to capture the phoenix or study its abilities. They were planning to weaponize dimensional travel itself.

If they succeeded, they could create portals anywhere. Deploy shadow creatures as weapons.

Access other dimensions and whatever resources or threats they contained.

It would be the ultimate military advantage. And it would require understanding phoenix fire on a fundamental level.

That was why they'd let the phoenix suffer for weeks. They needed to understand both clean and corrupted dimensional energy. They had to document how phoenix fire interacted with reality, how it burned and transformed and bridged worlds.

They'd engineered this entire crisis as one massive experiment.

Another text arrived.

> You have maybe 5 hours before they breach the grove. The dimensional energy there will mask your signatures temporarily, but Rosenthal's bringing equipment specifically designed to detect and disrupt clean dimensional sites. Plan accordingly. -RM

Five hours. Far less time than they'd thought.

Ben looked at Sidney sleeping in his arms, at the dying phoenix, and at the unicorn standing guard, silent and watchful. Five hours to rest, prepare, and somehow help Sidney survive an anchoring process that had permanently damaged her great-great-grandmother.

He pulled Sidney closer, careful not to wake her, and stared up at the woven branches overhead. The stars wheeled slowly across the gaps in the canopy, marking time they didn't have.

His phone vibrated one more time.

> Whatever you're planning, do it fast. Rosenthal isn't taking prisoners this time. -RM

Ben deleted the messages and turned off his phone to conserve the battery. Then he lay there in the dark, holding the woman he loved while she slept, and tried to figure out how to save her from a choice she'd already made.

Dawn was maybe four hours away.

He had no idea if that would be enough time.

CHAPTER SEVEN

By eight in the morning, I'd been awake for an hour, and I'd been watching Ben sleep for most of that time. Weak gray light made its way past the ancient grove's canopy and fell in shifting patterns across his face, but I kept my attention on the steady rise and fall of his chest, memorizing the peaceful expression he wore…an expression I knew wouldn't last once he awoke to the reality we faced.

I should have gotten us moving before dawn.

To be honest, I should have done a lot of things differently.

The phoenix dozed near the remains of our small fire, its plumage a sickening orange rather than the pure gold it should have been. Even in sleep, corruption radiated from it in waves. Those strange abilities of mine hadn't been completely depleted the day before, although part of me wished they had. If they were gone, then maybe I could have tried to ignore how dire the phoenix's situation really was.

A dull ache throbbed somewhere behind my temples, and I doubted it would get much better as the day progressed. The nosebleeds had finally stopped sometime during the night, but the tremor in my hands remained. Best guess, I had enough energy for minor sensing work. Anything more would push me into dangerous territory.

Unfortunately, the question wasn't whether I could use my powers. The real question was whether I'd have any choice.

Rebecca Morse had sent us a message around two in the morning.

DAPI mobilizing. Major operation. Estimate arrival at your location 0800-0900. Rosenthal personally supervising. Equipment unknown but assume enhanced protocols.

Now it was closing in on eight, and we should have been long gone. To where, I had no idea, since it seemed we could be tracked wherever we went. I was pretty sure Rebecca would have said it didn't matter, that we needed to be like Dory if we wanted to avoid capture.

Just keep swimming.

Ben's eyes opened, and he seemed immediately alert despite the abbreviated sleep he'd gotten the night before. It still kind of amazed me how fast he could focus even without caffeine. Sure, he liked his cup of morning coffee as much as anyone else, but he could function just fine without it.

"How bad is it?" He'd taken one look at my face and read everything I wasn't saying from my expression, but that didn't stop him from sitting up and reaching for his equipment bag.

No point in sugarcoating things, not in the gray cold of that foggy morning. "Rebecca says they'll be here within the hour. Sounds like Rosenthal's coming herself."

Ben paused in the act of pulling out his electromagnetic field detector and met my eyes. We hadn't been together all that long, but it still seemed as if he could read in my face everything I wasn't saying.

"How's your energy?"

"Low." I didn't bother to elaborate. He'd seen me collapse yesterday, had watched me bleed and shake. He knew exactly how drained I was without me having to spell it out. "I can sense nearby electronics, maybe jam a device or two if I have to. That's it."

"Then we'll run." He started packing with efficient movements, no wasted motion. "There's a cave system I found when I was studying Google maps of the area. We can be three miles away before they even reach the grove."

The phoenix stirred as he spoke and lifted its head. Through the connection we'd formed during my failed cleansing attempt, I felt its exhaustion, its resignation. It couldn't fly anymore, could barely walk. The corruption had continued to spread, tendrils of shadow fire eating away at its essence minute by minute.

"It can't move on its own." I couldn't keep the defeat out of my voice. "We'd have to carry it."

Meaning that Ben would have to carry it, since I barely had the strength at the moment to drag my own carcass around.

His hands went still on the pack he'd been securing. In silence, he looked over at the phoenix and then at me, and I could practically see the mental calculations going on in his head. He'd already arrived at the choice we both knew we'd have to make but neither of us wanted to voice.

"Then we'll stay and defend ourselves." His voice was a little too matter-of-fact.

Those words settled between us, solid despite their obvious impossibility. Such a choice meant I'd have to use powers I didn't have. It also meant that Ben would have to face trained tactical operators with nothing but his brains and his determination. Formidable as he was in a lot of ways, he was just one man, and not anyone with the background to deal with such a situation.

But leaving the phoenix to die alone was unthinkable.

"I can set up some basic defensive measures," Ben continued as he rose to his feet. "The equipment we brought from Jessop's facility will help. We can create interference patterns, confuse their approach vectors. That should buy us time."

Time for what? I wanted to ask. Time for me to recover? That would take days. Time for backup? We didn't have any. Yes, Rebecca Morse was out there in the forest somewhere, but I had to believe she was more focused on creating diversions. There was no guarantee she'd get here in time to help in any measurable way.

What we needed was a miracle.

I didn't say any of that, however. Instead, I nodded and pushed myself to my feet, fighting a wave of dizziness as I rose. The world swam for a moment, and I blinked and willed my body to behave. "I'll do a perimeter sense." To my surprise, my voice was almost steady. "With any luck, I'll be able to figure out their approach routes."

"Sidney—"

"I can handle it," I cut in. "What I'm going to do isn't anything major. Just some passive sensing."

The look he gave me said he didn't believe those words for a second, but he also knew better than to argue. We'd had this fight before. My powers, my risk tolerance…my choice.

I moved to the edge of the grove and settled onto a moss-covered stone that had probably been there for centuries. I took a slow breath and reached out with my electromagnetic senses, letting my awareness expand beyond my physical form.

The headache sharpened immediately, a spike of pain behind my eyes that made them water. I blinked and pushed through it, cataloging the electronic signatures within my limited range. Normally, I could sense for two miles in any direction. Today, I was lucky to manage five hundred yards, and even that felt like dragging my consciousness through barbed wire.

But there—to the northeast, maybe four hundred yards out. A cluster of electromagnetic signatures, and not the simple patterns of phones or radios or TVs, something I'd almost gotten used to over the past few weeks. These were much more complex. They appeared to be shielded in some way, which meant they had to be military-grade.

And there were dozens of them.

My eyes snapped open. "Ben. They're already here."

He looked up from the makeshift sensor array he'd been assembling. "How many?"

"At least thirty signatures, probably more beyond my current range. And Ben—" I broke off and swallowed hard. I hated to give him even more bad news, but he needed to know. "Their equipment is different, shielded in a way I haven't encountered before. When I try to sense any details, it's like hitting a wall."

His mouth tightened, but he continued to work, as if he thought that half-assed collection of electronics could somehow protect us from the enemies we were facing. "EMP-hardened. They learned from our last encounter."

Of course they had. Dr. Rosenthal hadn't gotten to such a position of authority by making the same mistake twice. The barrier I'd created yesterday, the way I'd jammed their surveillance network—she'd adapted, had brought equipment specifically designed to resist electromagnetic interference.

Which meant my already limited abilities had just become even more costly to use.

Ben abandoned the array and reached into the bag where he'd stowed his tablet. His fingers flew over the screen. "If they've surrounded us, we need to identify the weakest point in their perimeter. See if you can find a gap."

I reached out again and gritted my teeth against the pain. The hardened equipment made it like trying to see through frosted glass—I could sense the signatures were there, could get a general impression of location and movement, but the details remained as fuzzy and indistinct as the distant trees in the foggy forest that surrounded us.

"They're not in a full circle yet," I told him as I studied the pattern. "There's a gap to the south-west that's maybe fifty yards wide. But they're closing it. Five minutes, probably less."

"Then that's our window." Ben grabbed both our packs and slung his over one shoulder while mine dangled from his other hand. "We move now, fast and quiet. The phoenix—"

A soft trill interrupted him. The phoenix had risen to its feet, wings half-spread despite their obvious weakness. I could feel its intention. It wasn't going to come with us. Instead, it planned to stay here and draw their attention.

"No." The single syllable was sharp, brittle with worry. "We're not leaving you."

The phoenix fixed me with those wise, golden eyes and showed me an image that seemed to beam directly into my mind: Ben and me escaping through the gap while DAPI forces converged on the grove.

Time. Space. Survival.

Sacrifice.

"Sidney." Ben put his hand on my shoulder,

gentle but urgent. "We have maybe three minutes."

I stared at the phoenix, this magnificent creature that was dying because DAPI had deliberately corrupted its rebirth cycle. This being that had existed for centuries, maybe millennia, guarding the portal and maintaining the balance between worlds. Leaving it felt like abandoning family.

But staying meant we'd all be captured. And if Rosenthal got her hands on me, she'd have everything she needed to replicate my abilities and weaponize them.

"We'll come back," I told the phoenix, my voice fierce with resolve. "I swear we'll come back for you."

It trilled again, more softly this time. Again, it seemed to send concepts rather than words.

Agreement. Hope. Trust.

Ben took my hand, and we ran, moving through underbrush and between trees as quickly and carefully as we could. Ben walked slightly ahead of me and used his tablet to track the electromagnetic signatures I'd mapped. The gap in their perimeter was closing, but if we were fast enough—

A high-pitched whine cut through the morning air.

I stumbled, and my hands flew to my ears as the

sound drilled into my skull. After a second or two of searing pain, I realized it wasn't a sound at all. It was an electromagnetic pulse targeted directly at me. It bypassed normal hearing entirely and spoke directly to the electrical signals in my nervous system.

"Sidney!" Ben caught me as my knees buckled and barely saved me from face-planting into a clump of ferns. "What is it?"

"Sonic weapon," I gasped. "No—not sonic. Electromagnetic. They're using my own sensitivity against me."

Through streaming eyes, I saw that the perimeter had shifted. They'd anticipated our break for the gap. Tactical teams emerged from concealment, moving surely and swiftly. At least fifteen operators that I could see, probably more behind them. All wore tactical gear that bristled with technology I couldn't properly sense through the combination of hardening and the electromagnetic assault on my nervous system.

And there, in the center of the formation, stood Dr. Sonya Rosenthal.

She looked almost exactly the same as she had when I'd first met her—neat skirt suit, severe gray pixie cut with not a hair out of place, calm expression. She might have been attending a board meeting rather than orchestrating a paramilitary operation in a forest at dawn.

"Ms. Lowell, Mr. Sanders." Her cool, sharp

voice with its trace of a New York accent carried clearly across the space between us. "I'd ask you to come quietly, but I suspect we're past that point."

Ben's arm tightened around my waist. Even as he supported most of my weight, I could sense the way he was calculating our situation, measuring distances and odds. We were fifty yards from the perimeter, twenty yards from any adequate cover. With me functioning at maybe a third of my usual strength, our chances of fighting through were essentially zero.

But Ben Sanders had never been good at accepting impossible odds.

"The gap southwest," I murmured, making sure my lips barely moved so Rosenthal and her goons wouldn't be able to tell what I was saying. "Feint northeast, actually go southwest."

I felt him nod once. Then his hand moved to one of the pieces of equipment he had clipped to his belt. It wasn't a weapon, but something better —the electromagnetic pulse generator we'd salvaged from Jessop's facility.

"On three," he whispered. "One—"

I gathered what little power I had left and prepared to shield us from the sonic weapon long enough to run.

"Two—"

Ben's muscles tensed. The agents moved closer,

their weapons raised but not pointed directly at us.

Of course. They wanted us alive. And that was our advantage.

"Three."

Ben triggered the pulse generator toward the northeast quadrant. It was nothing compared to what I could do at full strength, but in the forest gloom, it created a bright flash and crackle of energy, and was exactly the kind of diversion we needed.

Half the tactical team turned toward the flash, and we ran southwest.

I pushed power into my legs and used electromagnetic pulses to stimulate my muscles far past their exhausted limits. Pain surged through my nervous system at once, and my nose began to bleed again even as the forest blurred around me. But my legs moved faster and carried me forward even as my body screamed in protest.

And then a Faraday cage activated when we were ten yards from breaking through the perimeter. I didn't see it deploy—there was no visible marker, no warning. But I got cut off from the electromagnetic spectrum as completely as if someone had severed a limb.

The sensation was so disorienting that I fell, unable to compensate for the sudden loss of the senses I'd been relying on so heavily for the past couple of days. Ben caught me before I hit the ground and somehow kept us moving forward through sheer force of will. But I was dead weight now, my power completely blocked by the cage's interference field.

"Stand down." Rosenthal's voice came to us, closer now. The tactical teams had re-formed and cut off our escape route. "Mr. Sanders, you can't possibly reach the perimeter with Ms. Lowell in her current condition. You're both exhausted and surrounded by operators who, I assure you, will not hesitate to use force if necessary."

Ben stopped. I could feel his heart hammering against my back as he held me, could sense the tension in every muscle. His mind would be racing through scenarios, looking for any possible angle of escape, some way to get us out of this mess.

"Sidney," he said in an undertone. "The phoenix. Can you sense it?"

Thanks to the Faraday cage's interference, just barely. It was only the smallest thread of connection, like trying to hear a whisper through a closed door. But yes—I could feel the phoenix back in the grove. It was awake and aware.

"A little," I whispered.

"Can you call it?"

As soon as he asked the question, I knew what he was planning. If the phoenix came and unleashed its corrupted fire, the chaos might be enough to allow us to escape. The DAPI forces would have to focus on containing it rather than us. We might be able to—

I cut off that line of thought before it could go any further. "No." My voice was flat. "It's dying, Ben. Calling it into a fight would kill it. And that fire—it's corrupted. If it unleashes that here, people will die. Maybe us, and definitely some of the operators. And the corruption would keep spreading."

"Then we need another option." His voice was calm, but behind it, I could hear panic barely being held at bay. "There has to be—"

"There isn't." I turned in his arms and met his eyes, all too aware of Rosenthal watching us. For the moment, she seemed content to let us speak, but that was probably because she knew she had us trapped and thought she was being magnanimous. "We're out of options, Ben."

"No." His hands tightened on my shoulders. "I'm not going to let them take you. We can—"

"We can surrender," I broke in, still in a murmur. "We'll live so we can escape later."

I watched him process my words, saw the exact moment when he realized I was right. And I saw it kill something in him to accept such a terrible truth. Ben Sanders was someone who'd spent the last seven years chasing the impossible, finding the answers no one else could. Admitting defeat went against every fiber of his being.

But staying alive mattered more than pride.

"Okay," he said.

The word was a promise.

I nodded. Then I raised my voice and projected my next words toward Rosenthal. "We surrender. No resistance. But I want your word that Ben will be treated as a civilian consultant, not a combatant. He doesn't get enhanced interrogation protocols."

Rosenthal's calm expression didn't change, although I caught the faint edge of smugness in it. "I'm afraid I can't make that promise, Ms. Lowell. Mr. Sanders has demonstrated significant operational knowledge and capabilities, far more than his resume might suggest. He'll be processed according to standard protocols."

"Like hell." Ben's voice went cold. "Sidney, don't—"

A new sound cut through the morning air, something that was neither an electromagnetic weapon nor an alarm. It was organic, wild, and furious.

And the phoenix burst into the clearing in an explosion of corrupted fire.

I'd thought it was too weak to fly, but I'd been wrong. Desperation and determination had given it one last surge of strength, and it used that strength now with devastating effect. Orange-and-shadow flames erupted across the clearing and forced the tactical teams to scatter. Several operators went down, not burning but overcome by the shadow corruption the fire brought with it.

"Contain that thing!" Rosenthal called out, her voice sharp with urgency. "Containment team, now!"

More agents emerged from the tree line, these carrying different equipment. Specialized gear, I thought. They'd come prepared for the phoenix, too, and had brought tools specifically designed to capture it.

Of course they had. They'd been planning this for months.

The phoenix wheeled in the air, trailing fire and shadow, buying us seconds we couldn't actually use. The Faraday cage still blocked my powers. We were still surrounded, still out of options.

But the phoenix was giving us a chance anyway.

Ben saw it the same moment I did—the northeast quadrant, temporarily abandoned as the containment team engaged the phoenix. Now there was a gap, a real one this time.

"Go," I said.

"Not without you."

"Ben, I can't run. I can barely stand. But you can—"

"No." He pulled me closer, and I sensed the immediate shift in his electromagnetic signature. Through the fading interference of the cage, I felt not fear but resolve. "I'm not leaving you, Sidney. Not now. Not ever."

And then he kissed me. The embrace was hard and fast and desperate, like he was trying to pour everything he couldn't say into that single moment of contact.

When he pulled back, his face wore an expression I'd never seen before. It wasn't just determination or love or fear. It was all of that and something more.

Something final.

"I'm sorry," he said.

And then he pushed me.

Hard.

I stumbled backward, off-balance and weak, falling away from him toward the gap in the perimeter, falling toward escape.

And Ben turned and ran toward the containment team, toward the phoenix.

"Ben, no!" I tried to push myself forward so I could follow him, but Rebecca Morse materialized from the trees right then, her strong hands grasping me by the shoulders. Where the hell had she come from? Had she been there the whole time, hidden, waiting for the right moment when she could intervene?

"Let me go!" I struggled against her grip, but I had no strength left. None that mattered, anyway. "Ben!"

He reached the containment team, and his hand moved to the electromagnetic pulse generator on his belt. A bright flash exploded in the clearing, a surge of energy that disrupted their equipment for a few precious seconds. The phoenix took advantage of the interruption and wheeled away toward the deeper forest, buying itself some distance.

And the tactical teams closed in on Ben from three directions.

He didn't fight them. He just let them take him down, pin him, and secure his hands behind his back with swift efficiency.

He'd given himself up deliberately to give me time to escape.

To save me.

Rebecca Morse's voice came to my ear, urgent and commanding. "Sidney, we have to move. *Now.*"

I gave a ferocious shake of my head. "He's captured. I can't leave him!"

"You can't help him if you're captured, too." She was already pulling me backward, into the cover of the forest. "You're drained, blocked, and useless in a fight. We'll regroup and plan. We'll get him back. But right now, we have to run."

I could feel the phoenix retreat deeper into the forest, Rosenthal's containment teams in hot pursuit. Thanks to that damn Faraday cage's interference, I could barely sense Ben's electromagnetic signature as they dragged him toward the DAPI agents' waiting vehicles.

Still struggling against Rebecca Morse's grip, I watched them take him, watched my worst fear realized in real-time. Ben had been captured by DAPI and was now in Rosenthal's custody. He would be subject to enhanced interrogation protocols and used as leverage against me.

He was a prisoner because I'd been too weak and too useless to stop it.

"Sidney." Rebecca's voice ground against my ear, harder now, as if she was losing patience with me. "I can't carry you and your equipment. You need to move."

In despair, I let her pull me into the forest. My last glimpse of Ben showed him being loaded into a black SUV, surrounded by agents, bound and captured, but alive.

We were supposed to face this problem with the phoenix together.

But our together had just been ripped apart, and I had no idea how to put it back.

The safe house was a hunting cabin forty minutes north of Silver Hollow, so isolated that the nearest neighbor was three miles away. Rebecca Morse had driven with ruthless efficiency, taking back roads and fire trails I didn't even know existed, since we were now far beyond the woods that surrounded my hometown. I'd spent the entire trip slumped against the passenger door of her Suburban, fighting nausea and despair in equal measure.

The Faraday cage's effect on me ended once we'd gotten a few miles away from the clearing, and the return of my electromagnetic senses should have been a relief. Instead, it just emphasized Ben's absence. His signature, which had become such a constant presence in my awareness over the past few weeks, was gone. Now there was only static and emptiness where he should have been.

"Drink this." Rebecca thrust a bottle of water into my hands as soon as we were inside. "You're dehydrated on top of everything else."

I took it automatically but didn't drink. My hands were shaking too hard to unscrew the cap.

She took it back from me, opened it, and then handed it over again. "Drink. Now, before you collapse."

This time, I obeyed. The water was cold enough to hurt going down, but it helped clear some of the fog from my brain. Not all of it, of course. But enough that I could try to focus.

The cabin was sparse—one main room with a kitchenette, a bathroom, and a loft that probably served as a sleeping area. Emergency supplies were stacked in one corner, and communications equipment sat on a battered pine table.

"How long have you been tracking their movements?" I asked. My voice was hoarse, scraped raw by exhaustion.

"Since I went 'on leave.'" She moved to the communications equipment and checked the displays, then gave a slight nod, as if satisfied that the DAPI team had no idea where we'd gone to ground. "My superiors think I'm just taking a break, but I was worried that Rosenthal wasn't really done, was only regrouping."

I stared at her, still not sure I could believe everything she was saying, despite the way she'd just saved me from certain capture. "You're still FBI."

"Yes, and I'm an agent who believes the Bureau should protect American citizens, not experiment on them." Her eyes narrowed slightly. "Which apparently makes me a minority in my own organization these days."

I slumped into a chair that had seen better decades and let my head fall forward. Everything hurt—my head, my body, my powers, my heart.

Especially my heart.

"They have him," I said. Stating the obvious, of course, but I needed to say it out loud. "Rosenthal has Ben."

"Yes."

"She'll use enhanced interrogation."

"Probably not immediately." Rebecca pulled up a chair and sat across from me, her frank, dark gaze fixed on my face. "Rosenthal's smart. She'll try to recruit him first. She knows he's valuable—his research, his network, his expertise. She'll offer him a position, resources, a chance to study all these phenomena without restriction."

"Ben would never—"

She cut me off, but gently. "I know. But she'll try anyway. That buys us maybe twelve hours before she escalates to more aggressive methods."

Twelve hours. Half a day to figure out how to infiltrate a heavily guarded DAPI facility, rescue Ben, and escape before Rosenthal weaponized everything she'd learned from us.

Impossible.

But then, we'd been doing impossible things all week.

"The phoenix," I said. "Did it escape?"

"For now," she replied. "The containment teams are still searching for it, but the forest is large, and the phoenix knows it better than they do." She paused. "How much longer does it have?"

I closed my eyes and reached for the faint thread of connection that still existed between me and the phoenix. The corruption had spread further during its attack on the tactical teams. It had hours left, not days. Maybe less.

"Not long enough," I said quietly. "Not long enough for any of this."

A heavy silence settled between us. Ben was captured. The phoenix was dying. I was completely drained...and Rosenthal was winning.

"I need to recover," I said at last. "At least enough for minor power use. How long before they trace us here?"

Now Rebecca smiled faintly. "This location is off the books. It's my personal property, purchased under a shell company. They won't find it in twelve hours." She rose from her chair and went over to the kitchenette. "But you need more than twelve hours to recover from major power depletion. You need days."

"We don't have days."

She'd set a pair of mugs on the counter, as if she planned to make tea or maybe some coffee. Now she turned toward me, her jaw set. "Sidney—"

"Ben doesn't have days." I pushed myself to

my feet, swaying slightly but managing to stay upright. "He has maybe twelve hours before Rosenthal decides he's not cooperative enough and moves to forced interrogation. Which means I have less than that to figure out how to get him out."

Rebecca crossed her arms and sent me a very direct look. "In your current state, you'd be lucky to jam a cell phone. Going up against a fortified facility with hardened equipment and trained operators? That's suicide."

"Then I'll die trying," I said without hesitation. "I'm not leaving him there."

I watched her process my words, saw her weigh options and outcomes with the cold efficiency of someone trained to make hard choices. She could try to stop me, could physically restrain me if necessary. I was barely functional, so she could absolutely prevent me from leaving.

But we both knew she wouldn't.

"All right," she said after a long pause. "Then we need a plan. A real one, not a suicide run." Ignoring the mugs she'd just set out, she moved back to her communications equipment on its rickety little table. "I have a contact inside DAPI. Let me reach out and see what intel I can gather. In the meantime, you need to rest. Four hours minimum."

I shook my head. No way was I going to allow myself to be out of commission for that much time. "Four hours is—"

"Non-negotiable." Her voice turned hard as she continued. "If you go in depleted like this, you'll get yourself killed, and Ben will stay captured. Four hours of rest will at least give you some minor power capability. That's the difference between a rescue operation and a murder-suicide."

She was right, even though every instinct screamed at me that I needed to move now, act now, save Ben now.

But tactics required thinking, and planning required energy. Any kind of effective rescue would require me to be functional enough to actually pull it off.

"Four hours," I agreed. "Then we'll plan the rescue."

Rebecca nodded. "Get some rest. I'll wake you when I have some intel."

I made it to the couch before my legs gave out. The exhaustion was bone-deep, spirit-deep, dragging me down despite the adrenaline that still surged through my system.

My last conscious thought was of Ben—captured, alone, in Rosenthal's custody.

I'm coming, I promised him silently, hoping somehow that he could sense the commitment even through the distance and walls between us.

Four hours where I wouldn't have to face the nightmare my life had become.

Then darkness took me.

CHAPTER EIGHT

Ben opened his eyes to soft lighting and the quiet hum of a climate-control system, not the harsh fluorescents and concrete walls he'd been expecting. He wasn't in restraints or strapped to an interrogation chair, wasn't caught in any of the nightmare scenarios that had flashed through his mind during his brief, violent capture—the one that had ended with his head hitting the ground so hard, he'd lost consciousness.

He was lying on an actual bed. Not a particularly comfortable one, but functional enough. The room looked like standard dormitory accommodations—a desk with a matching chair, a bathroom visible through an open door. To one side, a window showed hazy sunlight flickering through a stand of tall evergreens. The only indication that this was a cell rather than a guest room was the absence of any door hardware on the inside.

He sat up slowly and cataloged his physical condition. His wrists were sore where they'd zip-tied him during transport, but the restraints were gone now. His head throbbed from that impact with the ground, but the blow didn't seem to have caused any significant damage. All his clothes were right where they were supposed to be, except for his equipment belt, which had clearly been confiscated.

Most importantly, he was alone. No guards watching to see when he might wake up.

He got up from the bed and moved to the window to study what he could see of the world outside. Dense forest crowded around the facility on three sides, with a single access road visible to the north. The building itself appeared to be a converted military installation—Cold War–era construction, most likely decommissioned sometime in the nineties and purchased through one of DAPI's shell companies. Three stories above ground from what he could see, although the angle of the window suggested there might be several levels below as well.

He went to check his watch and found it had also been confiscated, so he tried to estimate the time based on the sun's position. Maybe around three in the afternoon. He'd been unconscious during transport for the greater part of the day, which meant he could be almost anywhere.

But he didn't think he'd been taken far. Rosenthal would want her facility close enough to Silver Hollow and its portal that she could deploy agents quickly if necessary.

Was there any way he could get out of here? Possibly, but nothing he could see from this room offered any clear possibilities. He kind of doubted DAPI built facilities with flashing exit signs.

Besides, the question was basically moot. There was no way to open the door from the inside, and he didn't have any of Sidney's abilities. He couldn't blow open the lock using the power of his mind and nothing else.

A soft beep preceded the door's electronic lock disengaging. Ben turned to face whoever was coming and tried to look casual despite the adrenaline that surged through his body.

Dr. Rosenthal entered first, her neat suit and cool demeanor unchanged from that morning's operation. Behind her came a man Ben didn't recognize—early forties, sandy blond hair, wire-rimmed glasses that didn't quite conceal a pair of startling blue eyes. He wore a lab coat over business casual and was slim and tall, probably around Ben's own six feet.

"Mr. Sanders." Rosenthal sounded brisk as usual, although Ben detected just the slightest hint of something that might have been concern—or would have been, if he'd been talking to anyone else. "I trust you're feeling well? The medical team cleared you during intake, but if you're experiencing any discomfort, we can arrange treatment."

He kept his expression neutral. "Where's Sidney?"

"Ms. Lowell escaped during the operation. Agent Morse assisted her exit." For a moment, Rosenthal's cool gaze flickered, and Ben guessed that inside she was royally pissed that someone who used to be on her team had betrayed her in such a way. "Which brings us to you. Please, sit."

She gestured to the desk chair.

Ben crossed his arms and didn't move. "No, thanks. I'll stand."

Rosenthal inclined her head slightly, acknowledging the small act of defiance. "As you wish. Mr. Sanders, I'll be direct. Your relationship with Ms. Lowell and your expertise in cryptozoology make you uniquely valuable to our work. We'd like to offer you a position as a consultant."

Seriously, a recruitment pitch?

The woman had a hell of a lot of nerve. However, he kept his face carefully blank, willing himself not to give anything away.

"Before you refuse," Rosenthal continued, "allow me to introduce Dr. Eric Hargrove, our lead scientist on the Phoenix Project. Eric, perhaps you'd like to explain what we're doing here?"

Hargrove stepped forward, and Ben noticed how the man's gaze wouldn't quite meet his. Was he uncomfortable about this meeting?

Maybe the simplest explanation was that he was on the spectrum, like a lot of other scientists Ben had met over the years, and social interactions were awkward for him.

"Mr. Sanders, I've followed your work for years." Hargrove sounded enthusiastic despite the way his eyes seemed fixed on something just outside the window. "You've shown real nimbleness of intellect by changing your field of study from archaeology to cryptozoology, and by applying academic rigor to a field that many still prefer to discount. That tells me you have the mental flexibility to be of real value to us."

Flattery will get you nowhere, Ben thought, but he only stood in silence, waiting to see what else the other man had to say.

"We're on the verge of a breakthrough," Hargrove continued, apparently unruffled by the lack of response to his pitch. "For the first time in human history, we're not just observing supernatural phenomena—we're replicating it, controlling it. Imagine the ramifications for science and for national security."

Ben didn't want to imagine those ramifications, not when he thought he knew where all this was heading.

"The phoenix," he said, frowning slightly despite his best efforts to keep his expression neutral. "You're harvesting its essence to power an artificial portal."

Hargrove's eyes widened. "Ms. Lowell told you—"

"Sidney didn't need to tell me anything," Ben broke in, not caring how rude he sounded. "It's a logical progression of the work you've been doing. The correlation between the surveillance network activation and the phoenix's corruption was obvious." He paused there and deliberately met the other man's gaze. To no surprise, Hargrove looked away almost at once. "You're killing it to steal its power."

"We're advancing human knowledge," Rosenthal interjected, clearly deciding it was time she took over the conversation. "The phoenix is a single organism. The technology we're developing could protect millions of lives."

"By weaponizing forces you don't understand." Despite his best efforts, Ben's voice rose slightly, driven by the anger building within him. He forced himself to breathe, to pull back before he said something that would get him thrown in an actual cell. "You're not scientists. Scientists observe, document, and seek understanding. You're strip-mining something sacred just because you can."

"'Sacred'?" Rosenthal repeated. Her expression remained neutral, but Ben caught the flicker of annoyance in her dark eyes. "Mr. Sanders, I didn't take you for someone who prioritized mysticism over pragmatism."

Well, there's your first mistake, he thought. *A man who drops a career in archaeology to chase chupacabras usually isn't the most practical person in the room.*

But he decided not to voice that view aloud. "I prioritize not destroying things I can't replace." He glanced over at Hargrove, who was now studiously examining the floor. "The phoenix is so much more than a power source. It's a keystone species in a supernatural ecosystem we barely comprehend. Removing it will have cascading effects across the entire portal network."

"Which is precisely why we need to understand and control it," Rosenthal said without missing a beat. "Mr. Sanders, the world is changing. Supernatural phenomena are manifesting with increasing frequency. Governments around the globe are racing to weaponize these forces. If the U.S. doesn't lead in this field, we'll find ourselves vulnerable to powers we can't defend against."

It was a rational argument, Ben had to admit, the kind of reasoning that had probably convinced Congress to fund DAPI in the first place. National security, protecting citizens, maintaining global dominance—all reasonable concerns for people in the government.

If you ignored the cost.

"Show me," Ben said, and both Rosenthal and Hargrove sent him startled looks. "Show me this breakthrough technology. If it's as revolutionary as you claim, let me see it functioning. Let me evaluate for myself whether the cost is justified."

Rosenthal studied him for a long moment. Ben kept his expression open, curious, trying to give her what he knew she wanted to see—a scientist who might be persuaded by evidence.

"Very well," she said at length. "Mr. Sanders, if you'll come with us?"

He didn't see her give the signal, but the door opened silently, and the three of them left the room where he'd been held. They led him through corridors that confirmed his earlier assessment—a converted military installation with multiple levels both above and below ground. Hargrove walked beside him, continuing his enthusiastic explanation of the Phoenix Project while Rosenthal led the way with two armed guards trailing behind their little group.

"The breakthrough came six months ago,"

Hargrove said with an animated gesture toward what Ben assumed was the location of the artificial portal somewhere in the facility. "We'd been studying the electromagnetic signatures at supernatural sites for years, but we couldn't replicate the dimensional bridging effect. Then we identified the phoenix as the key component. Its essence—the fire itself—acts as a catalyst. Somehow, it transforms electromagnetic energy into something that can pierce dimensional barriers."

The timeline fit what Rebecca Morse had already told him and Sidney. Six months ago was when DAPI had installed the surveillance network around Silver Hollow, long before he'd arrived in town...but right around the time when Sidney's mother and grandmother had disappeared.

"And the corruption?" Ben asked. "The shadow-taint in the phoenix's fire—that's a byproduct of your extraction process?"

Hargrove's enthusiastic expression faltered. "We've encountered some...instability. The essence extraction necessarily disrupts the phoenix's natural cycle. The corruption is an unfortunate side effect."

Ben raised an eyebrow. "An 'unfortunate side effect' that's killing it."

"Only temporary," Hargrove said, his quick reply indicating that he was ready to defend his research, no matter what. "Once we've refined the process, we'll be able to harvest the essence without causing permanent damage—"

"Eric." Rosenthal cut in there, her tone sharp. "Mr. Sanders doesn't need the technical details yet. Save the briefing for after he's seen the demonstration."

Hargrove went quiet after that rebuke. Since Rosenthal didn't seem inclined to say anything else, they moved on in silence, descending another level via a service elevator while the guards maintained their professional distance. Ben used that time to study Hargrove's body language. He was no expert, but the man seemed uncomfortable, almost defensive when discussing the phoenix's corruption. Not quite guilty, but close.

Maybe he could be a weak link, a way to get around Rosenthal.

The elevator opened onto an observation level that overlooked a massive underground chamber, and Ben's breath caught.

The artificial portal dominated the center of the chamber, a perfect circle perhaps fifteen feet in diameter, suspended in a framework of steel and humming machinery. Energy swirled within the circle, visible to the naked eye. But where natural portals showed clear, stable dimensional boundaries, this one was wrong. The energy was orange-tainted, flickering with shadows that seemed to writhe on their own, unattached to anything in the room that might have been casting them.

Corrupted phoenix fire, exactly as he'd feared.

Around the portal, banks of equipment monitored and regulated the flow. Technicians in cleanroom suits moved between stations, checking readings and making adjustments. The whole setup reminded Ben of pictures he'd seen of particle accelerators, only using supernatural energy instead of subatomic particles.

"We achieved stable activation three days ago," Rosenthal said, moving so she could stand next to him at the observation window. "Six hours of operational stability, sufficient for preliminary testing."

Ben forced himself to maintain his "interested scientist" façade while his mind raced through a variety of possibilities, each worse than the last.

"What happens after six hours?"

Hargrove spoke then. "The stolen essence degrades." He'd joined them at the window, and his expression was troubled. "We have to deactivate and allow the natural portal network to compensate."

"'Compensate.'" Ben turned to face the scientist and had to fight to keep the rage surging within him from revealing itself. "You mean the natural portals have to regenerate the energy you're siphoning, which puts additional strain on an already disrupted system."

"The math is sustainable—" Hargrove began, but Ben cut him off.

"Show me the math."

Hargrove blinked, looking as startled as if Ben had just asked him to produce his baby pictures. "I'm sorry?"

"The calculations showing your extraction is sustainable," Ben responded without missing a beat. "The models that predict long-term stability. If this technology is truly viable, then those numbers should be solid."

He watched Hargrove's expression shift from surprise to something that looked almost like relief, as if he was glad someone was finally asking the right questions.

"Dr. Hargrove was just about to brief you on the specifications," Rosenthal interjected, her tone smooth. If she was annoyed by Ben's questions, she revealed no sign of it. "Eric, perhaps you'd like to show Mr. Sanders the lab?"

"Yes. Of course." Hargrove gestured toward a door leading off the observation level. "This way."

They left the observation deck and went down one hall, and then another. The laboratory was smaller than Ben had expected—a single room filled with computers, monitoring equipment, and stacks of printouts. Hargrove moved immediately to the main terminal and began pulling up files.

Rosenthal remained in the doorway, watching Hargrove as he worked, while the guards stayed in the corridor beyond. Ben noted their positions and the distance to the nearest emergency exit. All tactically useless, since he'd get tackled the second he tried to make a break for it, but information was information.

"Here," Hargrove said, then turned the monitor so Ben could see it more clearly. "These are our sustainability calculations. Draw rate, regeneration capacity, predicted long-term system stability."

Ben leaned in to get a closer look at the numbers. Mathematics had never been his strongest subject, but he'd spent enough time analyzing scientific papers to recognize when the data told a different story than the official conclusions its author wanted to convey.

"This model assumes a stable baseline in the natural portal network," he said, speaking slowly as he continued to scan the information on the monitor. "But your own readings show the network is already stressed. The phoenix's corruption, the increased manifestation of shadow creatures—those variables aren't factored into your sustainability math, are they?"

Hargrove's hands paused on the keyboard. For

a long moment, he stared at the screen, saying nothing. When he spoke again, his voice was much quieter. "The baseline stability factor was established before we began active extraction. But you're right. The current network stress isn't fully accounted for in these projections."

"Meaning your six-hour operational window is optimistic at best," Ben replied. "The actual sustainable duration is probably less. Maybe much less."

"Eric." Rosenthal's voice now held a distinct warning note. "Mr. Sanders doesn't need to see the preliminary data —""

"He asked the right question," Hargrove broke in, his gaze still fixed on the screen in front of him. "The question I've been asking for the past three weeks. Director, if we continue extraction at current rates without accounting for network degradation, we risk cascade failure. Not just in Silver Hollow—across the entire global portal system."

The room went very quiet.

Ben watched Rosenthal's expression remain perfectly neutral, giving nothing away. But the guards behind her had shifted their position, moving just a little closer.

"Dr. Hargrove, I think that's enough technical discussion for now." Rosenthal sounded more than a little annoyed, probably because her top researcher had just revealed far more than she wanted anyone else to know. "Mr. Sanders, we've shown you our work. The technology is real, functional, and represents the future of supernatural research. The question is whether you'd like to be part of that future, or whether you'd prefer to remain in custody as a security risk."

Nothing like putting it out there. Either he cooperated, or he'd suffer the consequences.

Ben glanced over at Hargrove, who was now staring at his hands. Rosenthal waited at the door with the patience of someone holding all the cards. Beyond her, the guards remained visible in the corridor, ready to enforce whatever decision was made.

He thought about Sidney, whom he had to hope had gotten away, maybe with Rebecca's assistance, and about the phoenix dying in the forest, kept away from anyone who might have been able to offer it help.

And then there were all those portal sites around the world that Sonya Rosenthal seemed all too willing to sacrifice for this technology.

"I need time to think," he said.

Rosenthal inclined her head ever so slightly. "You have until tomorrow morning. After that, we'll require a decision." She gestured to the guards. "Return Mr. Sanders to his quarters. Ensure that he's comfortable."

The guards stepped forward. Their stance wasn't aggressive, but they clearly expected compliance. Ben went without resistance, mind churning through everything he'd learned—the artificial portal's six-hour limit, the cascade failure risk, Hargrove's moral qualms, the facility layout itself.

All pieces of intelligence that Sidney and Rebecca Morse would need.

If he could find a way to communicate it to them.

The guards led him back through all those corridors, up the elevator, along the route he'd already memorized. His "comfortable quarters" felt more like a cell now that he understood what DAPI was really doing here. The guards departed without comment, the electronic lock engaging behind them with a soft *click.*

Ben moved to the window and stared out at the forest beyond the cleared perimeter. Somewhere out there, Sidney and Rebecca Morse must be planning a rescue. He needed to help them, needed to give them the intelligence that would make such a rescue possible.

He turned back to the room and examined it with fresh eyes. No obvious surveillance cameras, but they had to be monitoring him somehow. The desk was bolted to the floor, and the bathroom had no windows. Even the bed frame was secured.

Everything was designed to prevent escape or self-harm.

But they'd left him the desk.

Ben sat down and began pulling open its drawers. All of them were empty except for a single pad of paper and a pen in the top drawer on the right—probably left there deliberately so he could write down questions or concerns he wanted to discuss during tomorrow's follow-up meeting.

He picked up the pen and tested its weight. Basic ballpoint, nothing useful as a weapon or tool. But the paper might work for something else.

He'd been documenting supernatural phenomena for more than seven years, and archaeological data even before that. He knew how to observe and record, how to communicate findings to the people who needed them. The format would be different, but the principle was the same.

Keeping all that in mind, he began to sketch the facility's layout from memory, marking distances, noting security stations, mapping the route to the underground laboratory. If Sidney and Rebecca actually managed to infiltrate the place, they'd need this information. After he finished the basic sketch, he added notes on the guards' positions, the shift rotations he'd observed, and the elevator access codes Hargrove had used.

Then he wrote down another piece of critical intelligence.

Artificial portal stability: 6 hours maximum. Cascade failure risk if extraction continues. Dr. Hargrove has doubts—potential ally.

He was halfway through adding technical specifications when the door lock disengaged again.

Ben palmed the paper and slid it under his thigh as he turned toward the door. Too soon for dinner, and they'd already performed a medical check while he was unconscious. Which meant—

Eric Hargrove entered alone, no guards visible in the corridor behind him. The scientist looked even more uncomfortable than he had in the lab, gaze once again directed toward the floor as he closed the door behind him.

"I have maybe three minutes before someone notices I came here," he said. He spoke quickly, as if he knew he had to cram as much information as possible into those three precious minutes. "So you need to listen carefully. The artificial portal isn't siphoning energy only from Silver Hollow. It's draining the entire natural portal network to stabilize itself. Every supernatural site on Earth is being affected."

Ben got up slowly. The other man seemed agitated, guilty, and determined all at the same time. This didn't feel like a trap, not when Hargrove was risking so much simply by being here.

"You're helping us," Ben said. It wasn't a question.

"I'm trying to fix my mistake." Hargrove pulled something from his lab coat pocket—a security badge. He set it on the desk. "This will get you through any electronic lock in the facility except the main entrance. There's a service exit on the second sublevel in the northeast corridor. It's monitored but not guarded. If you can disable the cameras—"

"Sidney can," Ben said. "If she gets inside."

"She will. Rebecca Morse contacted me an hour ago." Something came and went in the scientist's expression as he spoke Rebecca's name, but it was gone before Ben could begin to analyze what it might have been. "They're planning an infiltration for two o'clock this morning. There'll be a system malfunction at exactly that time." Now Hargrove actually met Ben's gaze. "I'll create the malfunction. It'll cause eight minutes of security blackout. That's all I can give you without revealing my involvement."

All very handy—maybe too much so. What if this plan was nothing more than a way to get Ben to reveal his true feelings about the work they were doing here?

He figured he might as well be direct. "Why are you doing this?"

Hargrove's mouth went tight. "Because Rosenthal won't listen. I've been telling her for weeks that the extraction rate isn't sustainable, that we're causing catastrophic damage to the global portal network. She won't stop until she has her weapon, no matter how many supernatural sites collapse." He drew in a shaky breath before he added, "I got into this field to understand these phenomena, Mr. Sanders. Not to destroy them."

God, Ben hoped that was true.

He picked up the security badge and felt its weight. As far as he could tell, it was real, not a fake. Hargrove was risking a hell of a lot by giving it to him.

"The notes I was writing," Ben said. "If Rosenthal's guards find them—"

"They won't. I'll arrange for waste removal tonight. Anything in your trash will be incinerated." Hargrove glanced at the door. "I have to go. Two o'clock, northeast service exit, second sublevel. Sidney will need to jam the emergency alert system first, or the entire facility goes into lockdown."

"I'll tell her."

"Good. And Mr. Sanders?" The scientist

paused at the door. "I'm sorry about all this. I should have stood up to Rosenthal months ago."

Not an easy thing to do, especially if your livelihood depended on staying in her good graces. "You're standing up now. That's what matters."

Hargrove nodded once, then slipped back into the corridor. The door locked behind him with its soft electronic beep.

Ben stood alone in his cell, holding the security badge for a moment before he slipped it into his jeans pocket. There was no way to communicate with Sidney or Rebecca before two in the morning, and he didn't have any real resources except his brain and whatever information he could provide.

But he had intelligence and a potential ally. And he had approximately ten hours to prepare for a rescue attempt that might save him, Sidney, and the phoenix—or might get all of them killed.

He sat back down at the desk and memorized every detail of what Hargrove had told him. The service exit location, the eight-minute window, the need to disable the emergency alerts. It was all critical intelligence that Sidney would need.

Then he tore the notes he'd been writing into small pieces and dropped them in the waste bin. If Hargrove was as good as his word, they'd be destroyed before anyone could read them. If not —well, at least he'd tried.

Ben moved to the window again. Not much had changed—it was far too early for the sun to have begun to set—but staring at the forest steadied him somewhat. Out there somewhere, Sidney was recovering and preparing to do something dangerous and probably suicidal to get him out.

Which meant he needed to be ready. He needed to have every piece of information memorized, every escape route planned, every contingency accounted for.

He'd made a career out of documenting the impossible, finding patterns where others saw only chaos. Now he'd apply those same skills to breaking out of a classified government facility and destroying an artificial portal that threatened the entire supernatural ecosystem.

Just another day in the field.

Ben almost smiled at the thought. Then he settled in to wait for darkness…and the rescue attempt that would determine whether any of them survived the next twenty-four hours.

CHAPTER NINE

I woke late that afternoon and stared up at the unfamiliar ceiling for a moment before I remembered where I was—Rebecca's safe house, the only refuge we could currently trust. My body ached in ways that had become grimly familiar over the past three days. The little house was sparse and utilitarian at best, but at least it had an actual couch instead of cold stone. Unfortunately, the constant awareness that Ben was miles away in DAPI custody made even the marginal comfort feel like a betrayal.

I should have been suffering along with him.

But I wasn't the only one resting in the small, dim room. The phoenix had settled near the cabin's woodstove, its corrupted fire casting orange-and-shadow light across the worn floorboards. How it had gotten there, I wasn't sure, but

I guessed it had somehow managed to follow Rebecca and me to our current hiding place. She must have brought it in and made sure it was comfortable while I was still in a slumber that might as well have been a coma.

Even half-dead and contaminated, the phoenix radiated enough warmth to make the space bearable. From it, I sensed an exhaustion that matched my own—two wounded creatures hiding while our enemies regrouped.

I pushed myself upright and fought a wave of dizziness. Although I'd regained some energy while I slept, I knew it wasn't nearly enough, that I was maybe at forty-percent capacity at best. That might be sufficient for minor use without too much cost, like sensing electronics within my limited range. It definitely wasn't enough to mount a rescue operation against a fortified DAPI facility.

Not even close.

Rebecca had been in the kitchenette making tea, but she turned as soon as she heard me stir. "You're awake." She came over with a mug in each hand and gave one to me. "How do you feel?"

"Like I got hit by a tactical team." As I'd thought, that was tea in the mug, not coffee. Probably better that way. Strong coffee would have been too much of a shock to my system. I drank some of the tea. Darjeeling, warm and welcoming in my throat. "How long was I out?"

"Almost twelve hours. It's nearly seven." She settled onto a chair near the couch where I'd slept, her expression grim in the phoenix's firelight. "We need to talk about the situation."

I nodded, bracing myself for the worst. The "situation," as she called it, was that Ben was captured, the phoenix was dying, and I was too exhausted and wrung out to do anything meaningful about either problem.

"I have a contact inside DAPI," Rebecca said. Her tone was as clipped and cool as if she was delivering a report at FBI headquarters, but I thought maybe it was better that way. If she'd been worried and overwrought rather than dispassionate, I might have been freaking out even more than I already was. "He reached out two hours ago with some intel."

"Contact?" This sounded like the first positive news I'd heard in a long while. "Who is it?"

She lifted her mug of tea to her lips and took a sip. "That's not important. What's important is that the artificial portal is already active."

My stomach began to churn, and I wondered if drinking tea with nothing to buffer it had been such a good idea after all. "Active? As in, actually functioning?"

"As in siphoning energy from the global portal

network. Every supernatural site on Earth is being affected."

She leaned down and set her mug on the floor, then got up and crossed the room to her makeshift communications setup. After retrieving the tablet she'd left there, she came back and sat down again, then tilted its screen toward me. The charts I saw on the display were complex, and I could barely process them through the fog of exhaustion that still clung to me.

"My contact says the portal has about six hours of stable operation with the phoenix essence they've already harvested," she went on. "After that, they have to shut down and let the natural network compensate."

Six hours. Not a very long span of time, but certainly long enough to prove the technology worked.

And long enough to kill every natural portal on the planet if they kept pushing.

I had to know, even if it was news I wouldn't like very much. "What about Ben?"

"He's alive and being held in comfortable quarters while Rosenthal tries to recruit him." Her expression softened slightly. "She's giving him until tomorrow morning to decide. After that…."

She didn't need to finish the sentence, but I did it for her anyway.

"Enhanced interrogation." I closed my eyes

and fought the surge of rage and fear that rose within me. I wanted to hit something, wanted to scream, but I forced myself to breathe through it, to push the emotion down where it couldn't cloud my thinking. Ben would be subjected to DAPI's methods because I'd been too weak to protect him, because I'd pushed my powers too hard and left myself useless when it mattered the most.

The phoenix trilled softly, a sound I'd come to recognize as concern. Through our bond, it sent me an image—Ben and me together, our electromagnetic signatures creating that soft golden glow they did when we were close.

Strength in partnership.

"Your contact," I said as I opened my eyes. "Can he help us get Ben out?"

"He's working on it. He told me he'll create a system malfunction at two in the morning. That will give us eight minutes of security blackout." She laid the tablet on the floor next to her half-drunk mug of tea and leaned forward. "Sidney, I know what you're thinking. But in your current state—"

"I can manage minor use of my abilities," I broke in. "It'll be enough to jam any emergency alerts and maybe disable a few cameras." I met her worried gaze and tried to project more confidence than I was currently feeling. "But what I can't do is leave Ben there."

Her eyes were dark with worry. "Even if rescuing him means you won't have enough power left for the phoenix cleansing?"

The question hung between us, heavy as stone. Because that was the real choice, wasn't it? Use what little power I had left to rescue Ben, or conserve it for the final phoenix rebirth.

Choose the man I loved…or the duty the women of my family had shouldered for generations.

"There has to be another way," I told her.

She responded at once, a sort of weary certainty in her voice. "There isn't." A pause, and then she added, "You're drained, Sidney. Even with six more hours of rest, you'll maybe recover enough for moderate use. That's not sufficient for both a rescue operation and a phoenix cleansing. You have to choose."

I looked at the phoenix, the magnificent creature that was dying because DAPI had deliberately contaminated its rebirth cycle. Its corruption had spread even further and was now probably past eighty percent or worse. I could sense it through our connection, the shadow-taint eating away at its essence like cancer. Only hours left now, not days.

My grandmother had sent herself to the hospital trying to assist a creature like this, and my great-great-grandmother had allowed herself to be permanently scarred. Was I really going to let this phoenix die because I couldn't bear to lose Ben?

But Ben had sacrificed himself to save me, had deliberately drawn DAPI's attention so I could escape. How could I honor that sacrifice by abandoning him to Rosenthal's custody?

The phoenix shifted, drawing closer. It wasn't using our connection to send any images this time, was instead just a gentle pressure against my consciousness.

Warmth. Comfort. Understanding.

"I can't choose," I whispered. "Don't ask me to choose between them."

The phoenix sent me a new image. It wasn't of Ben and me separately, but the two of us together, our electromagnetic signatures intertwined, creating something stronger than either of us alone. Then it showed me attempting the final cleansing without him—my consciousness fragmenting, losing myself in the phoenix fire because I had no anchor to pull me back to humanity.

Partner gives you strength, the phoenix seemed to say. *Incomplete without anchor.*

"What is it showing you?" Morse asked. She spoke quietly, as if she was worried that too loud a tone might somehow disrupt the connection between the fiery creature and me.

"That I need Ben for the final cleansing." The

truth of that realization settled over me, and I pulled in a breath to steady myself. "His electromagnetic signature resonates with mine. When we're together, my abilities amplify by ten to twenty percent. Without him…." I let the words trail off as the truth of our situation became horribly clear. "Without him, I'm not strong enough to survive the final merge. The phoenix knows this."

Rebecca absorbed that information. I could almost see the way her sharp, practical mind began to work through the problem. "So rescuing Ben isn't just personal. It's operationally necessary."

"Yes." Relief and dread warred within me. I didn't have to choose—the phoenix itself was telling me I needed Ben. But that meant mounting a rescue operation I was barely strong enough to survive.

I couldn't worry about that now, though. No, I had to focus everything I could on trying to figure out how to save the man I loved.

I lifted the mug of Darjeeling to my lips and took a bracing sip. Then I looked squarely at Rebecca Morse. "Tell me everything your contact said. I need to know what we're up against."

For the next hour, she briefed me on the intelligence she'd gathered. The facility was a converted military installation some thirty miles north of Silver Hollow, with multiple levels and an underground laboratory where the artificial portal was housed. Ben was being held on the second floor in the west wing. Rosenthal had deployed EMP-hardened equipment throughout the facility after our last encounter, had installed Faraday cage generators in critical areas, and had armed guards on rotating shifts.

"All right, so your contact can create an eight-minute security blackout starting at two o'clock," I said. "But I'll need to disable the emergency alert system first, or the whole facility will go into lock-down the moment they realize something's wrong."

Rebecca gave me a brief nod, but she still looked worried. "Can you do that in your current state?"

I reached inward with my senses, trying to gauge my reserves. The hours of rest had helped—I could feel my power slowly regenerating, like a battery on a charger. By two o'clock, I'd have maybe enough for moderate use if I was careful… and if nothing went wrong.

"I can jam the alerts," I said. "Maybe for six minutes before the cost gets too high. After that, you and Ben will need to be clear of the facility."

"And you?"

"I'll be right behind you." The lie was necessary. We both knew that using my powers for six continuous minutes while still recovering would push me close to the edge. I'd be bleeding, shaking, and barely functional. But Rebecca didn't need to know that. She'd try to stop me if she thought there was even the barest chance that I might burn myself out.

She studied me with eyes that had seen too many people make heroic sacrifices. "You're planning something stupid, aren't you."

It wasn't a question.

I still did my best to deflect. "I'm planning a rescue operation with limited resources against a far superior force." I stood then and tested my balance. Better than it had been this morning, even if I was still shakier than I would have liked. "What's the facility layout? Show me where Ben's being held, where the emergency alert junction boxes are, where the exits are."

We spent another hour going over maps and planning our approach. Rebecca would drive me to within a mile of the facility and then move to the perimeter, keeping her Suburban ready for extraction. Her contact—who she still refused to name—would trigger the malfunction at exactly 2 a.m. and guide Ben to the northeast service exit. I would disable the emergency alerts from outside the facility and then move to the rendezvous point.

Simple enough, even with too many variables.

Unfortunately, it was the only plan we had.

"You should eat," Rebecca said after we'd finalized the details. "And try to rest. We'll leave at one."

She disappeared into the cabin's small bedroom, leaving me alone with the phoenix. I forced down an energy bar that tasted like cardboard and chased it with water, figuring it probably wasn't a good idea to have any more caffeine. My body needed the calories, even if my stomach was too knotted with anxiety to want them.

The phoenix moved closer and settled beside me with a soft trill. Its concern and affection seemed to ripple off it in waves. Over the past couple of days, it had become much more than a creature I was supposed to protect—it was family now, as real and important as Ben or Rebecca Morse or anyone else I cared about.

I'm scared, I told it, not bothering to shield my thoughts. *Scared I won't be strong enough, that Ben will be hurt before we can get him out. Scared I'll fail both of you.*

The phoenix sent layers of emotion and memory flowing through our bond. It showed me generations of guardians, women who had stood where I stood now. My grandmother, calm and certain even in crisis. My mother, fierce and protective. Others stretching back through decades, each one facing impossible choices and somehow finding the strength to endure.

Then it showed me something new—the rebirth itself. Not the corrupted version DAPI had forced, but the natural cycle. The old phoenix dying in flames, its essence scattering to the winds. And afterward, reformation. New life rising from ash and fire, the same consciousness but renewed. Death was not an ending for the phoenix. It was transformation.

You're trying to tell me something, I said. *But I'm too human to understand.*

The phoenix sent me a feeling of gentle amusement, then another image. Ben and I in the grove during that magical moment when our electromagnetic signatures had resonated together and created that soft golden light. The phoenix had been watching, I realized. It had seen what we were to each other and had understood that some bonds transcended mere survival.

Love makes you stronger, the phoenix seemed to say. *Partnership transforms both.*

I leaned against the phoenix's warm side, careful of its contaminated feathers. "We're going to fix this," I said aloud. "We'll get Ben back, destroy that artificial portal, and complete your rebirth the right way. No matter what."

The phoenix didn't respond with images this time, just a gentle pressure of consciousness against mine that still managed to convey trust and faith, along with the belief that I would find a way because that's what guardians did.

I hoped it was right.

At twelve-thirty, I woke from a fitful doze to find Rebecca Morse checking her equipment. The cabin was darker now; the phoenix had dimmed its fire to conserve energy. I could feel its exhaustion more clearly than before. It had hours left, maybe less, thanks to the way the corruption was accelerating.

"Time to move," Rebecca said.

I stood and assessed my physical state as I rose from the couch. My headache had dwindled to a dull throb, my hands were steady, and my nose wasn't bleeding. My power reserves had climbed to maybe sixty percent—much better than expected, although still far from full strength.

It would be enough for the rescue.

I hoped.

The phoenix watched me prepare with eyes that were too intelligent, too understanding. It knew the risks I was taking and realized I might not survive the night. Even though it must have been worried, it sent one final image—Ben and me together after the rescue, his electromagnetic signature anchoring mine during the final cleansing.

All I could do was pray it was right.

"I'll come back with Ben," I said. "And then we'll finish this the right way."

The phoenix trilled softly, not quite agreement, but acknowledgment. It would wait and trust that I knew what I was doing.

Even though we both knew I was making this up as I went.

Rebecca and I headed outside and got into her black Suburban. Maybe there was a main road somewhere around her safe house, but I never saw it, because she drove us through back roads and fire trails with the SUV's headlights off, navigating by GPS and memory. The night was overcast, no moon visible. Good for infiltrating a secret government base, not so great for my already strained nerves.

"You remember the plan?" Rebecca asked as we approached the drop-off point.

No point in being flowery. "Disable emergency alerts at two. Hold for six minutes. Meet you at the extraction point." I checked the watch she'd given me. 1:47 a.m., thirteen minutes until the operation began. "You're sure your contact is reliable?"

"He's risking everything to help us. In my book, that makes him reliable." She pulled the Suburban off the faint trail we'd been following and into a small break in the forest, barely big enough to squeeze the oversized vehicle into. "But if something goes wrong—"

"It won't."

"If it does," she continued, ignoring my interruption, "get out. Don't try to be a hero. Ben would want you to survive."

I didn't bother to answer her. We both knew I wasn't going to abandon Ben, no matter what went wrong. But Rebecca Morse clearly needed to believe I'd make the smart tactical choice if necessary.

She handed me a radio, one she'd told me earlier was encrypted so that Rosenthal's people wouldn't be able to hear what we were saying even if they managed to intercept our transmissions. "Channel three if you need help. I'll be monitoring."

"Got it." I paused and gave her an encouraging smile. "Thank you."

I slipped out of the vehicle before she could respond and moved from tree to tree to conceal my presence. The facility was about half a mile away; I could sense its electromagnetic signature even from this distance, a concentration of power and technology that stood out against the forest's natural bioelectric patterns. My target was the emergency alert junction box on the facility's eastern edge. According to Rebecca's contact, relatively unguarded…and critical to the whole operation's success.

I moved through the darkness with all the stealth I could muster. I'd never had to infiltrate a government base before, but years of hiking around Silver Hollow had taught me to move silently through the forest.

The closer I got to the facility, the more my electromagnetic senses painted a detailed picture of what I was up against. Guards on patrol, following predictable routes. Security cameras sweeping the perimeter in overlapping arcs.

And the junction box was exactly where Morse's contact had said it would be.

Below everything, deep underground, I could feel the artificial portal. Its swirling, corrupted energy felt wrong against my senses, like an infection in the natural electromagnetic field. Shadow-tainted and unstable, and yet somehow functional despite that.

Rosenthal's weapon, already online and draining power from portal sites across the globe.

I reached the junction box a couple of minutes before two. A pair of guards was fifty yards away, their flashlights sweeping the perimeter. I crouched in shadow and waited for the malfunction that would signal the operation's start.

My hands were steady despite the adrenaline coursing through me, and the short trek through the forest hadn't impacted my energy reserves. They still held at about sixty percent—not ideal, but enough. Through the interference from the facility's electromagnetic signature, I could sense Ben somewhere on the second floor.

He was still alive.

Just two more minutes.

I closed my eyes and centered myself, knowing that everything had come down to this moment. Either we would pull off an impossible rescue against a fortified DAPI facility, or we'd fail and lose everything.

The phoenix's presence touched my consciousness from miles away. No images this time, just a feeling of trust and faith.

I had to hope that faith wasn't misplaced.

Two o'clock.

Time to bring Ben home.

CHAPTER TEN

Ben had been staring at the ceiling of his holding room for what felt like eternity, but was probably around three hours, when the door lock finally disengaged at two o'clock in the morning.

He'd spent those hours memorizing every detail Eric Hargrove had shared during his brief, nervous visit at eleven. Ben wasn't sure how the other man had managed it, but he'd slipped a folded note under Ben's dinner tray. Ben had palmed it immediately and read the message only after the guard who'd delivered his meal had departed.

2 a.m. Northeast stairwell. System failure will provide 8 minutes. I'm sorry for my part in this.

The note reiterated what the man had already told him, but Ben supposed that Hargrove had wanted to confirm those eight precious minutes, had wanted to let him know that the plan hadn't changed.

He leaped from the bed and ran to the door. Through the narrow window, he could see that the corridor beyond was dark—not the dimmed overnight lighting he'd observed earlier, but complete blackness. The utter dark suggested a comprehensive power failure rather than a simple lights-out protocol.

Sidney. It had to be. She'd promised to come for him, and Sidney Lowell was nothing if not relentlessly stubborn about keeping her promises.

He eased the door open and paused to listen. All seemed quiet. The emergency lighting should have activated within seconds of the facility's main power loss, but the corridor remained dark. Either Sidney's electromagnetic attack had been more comprehensive than expected, or Hargrove had disabled the backup systems as part of his sabotage.

Either way, Ben couldn't count on anything more than the promised eight minutes.

The security badge Hargrove had given him earlier was concealed in his pocket—he'd hidden it under the mattress after the scientist's visit, then retrieved it once the overhead lights died. He pulled it out now, although in this darkness, it was functionally useless. The card readers would be offline along with everything else.

Which meant the doors would either be magnetically locked or released, depending on their fail-safe settings. He'd have to test each one manually and hope like hell it wouldn't slow him down too much.

He moved into the corridor and kept one hand on the wall for orientation. His eyes had begun to adjust enough to make out basic shapes, so he could see that the hallway stretched maybe thirty feet before turning left. Northeast stairwell, Hargrove had said. Ben tried to recall the route they'd taken when they'd brought him to this room earlier. Two right turns, then a left. Or had it been two lefts and a right?

A soft sound behind him made him freeze. Footsteps, moving fast but trying for stealth. He pressed himself against the wall and prepared to either fight or run, depending on who appeared.

Rebecca Morse materialized from the darkness, her weapon drawn but pointed at the floor. She'd swapped her outdoor gear for dark civilian clothes, and her blonde hair was pulled back tight under a black knitted cap.

"Sanders," she whispered. "You're late. We have six minutes left."

"I didn't know the exact route." Ben kept his voice equally low. "Where's Sidney?"

"Outside the facility, maintaining the electromagnetic interference. She can hold it for maybe four more minutes before the cost gets too high." Rebecca was already moving as she spoke, and Ben followed. "The northeast stairwell is this way. Stay close, and stay quiet."

They moved through corridors he didn't recognize. Morse navigated the near-black hallways with the confidence of someone who'd studied the facility's layout extensively. The darkness was absolute except for the few places where emergency exit signs glowed faintly—battery-powered and apparently immune to Sidney's interference.

"How did you get inside?" Ben asked as they descended a stairwell.

"Hargrove disabled the perimeter sensors on the east side. I walked right in." Morse checked her watch, the faint glow from its display illuminating her grim expression. "Four minutes. We need to move faster."

They emerged on the first floor, and Ben could hear activity now—guards shouting to each other, flashlights cutting through the darkness as security teams tried to restore order. Morse pulled him into a storage alcove as two guards jogged past, their radios crackling with static that suggested Sidney's interference was affecting communications as well as power.

"Hargrove said eight minutes," Ben whispered once the guards passed.

"Hargrove's eight minutes started when the power failed. We lost time finding you." Rebecca checked the corridor and gestured him forward. "The service exit is close. Fifty yards, one turn."

They made it maybe thirty yards before the emergency lighting flickered to life.

Not full power yet—the overhead lights remained dark—but the emergency systems were activating, filling the corridors with a dim red glow. Ben heard more shouting, closer now. The facility's security teams coordinating and responding to what they probably thought was a simple power failure rather than an infiltration.

"Damn it," Rebecca breathed. "Sidney's interference just failed. We're out of time."

Ben wasn't about to give up, not when they were so close. "Then we'll run."

They sprinted the remaining distance, Rebecca in the lead. The service exit appeared ahead, a heavy steel door marked with emergency signage. She hit the crash bar and shoved it open, and they emerged into cold night air and darkness.

Flashlights swept across the perimeter while voices shouted conflicting orders. Ben spotted armed guards converging on the main entrance, probably responding to whatever alarm Sidney's failed interference had triggered.

"Treeline," Rebecca said. "Fifty yards north. Sidney's waiting there."

They ran again, crossing open ground that felt impossibly exposed. Ben expected shouts or weapons fire, tactical teams emerging from the darkness to drag them back. But the facility's security seemed focused on the main entrance rather than the service exit. Hargrove's sabotage had worked exactly as promised, creating confusion in the crucial minutes of their escape.

They reached the trees, and Ben nearly collided with Sidney in the darkness.

She was on her knees in the undergrowth, both hands pressed against her temples, blood streaming from her nose in a thick flow. Even in the faint emergency light from the facility, Ben could see she was trembling violently. Her arms bore marks he'd never seen before—dark patches that looked almost like burns, but with an iridescent quality that suggested something far worse than simple heat damage.

"Sidney." He dropped beside her, his hands hovering over her shoulders, afraid to touch her in case it caused more pain. "Sidney, I'm here. We made it."

Her eyes opened slowly, their pupils dilated and unfocused. When they found his face, something in her expression crumbled. It wasn't relief he saw there, but the desperate recognition of someone who'd been holding themselves together through sheer force of will and had just run out of strength.

"Ben," she whispered. Then she pitched forward, and he caught her.

She weighed almost nothing in his arms. Her body felt far too light, too fragile. Through the strange electromagnetic bond that connected them—fainter than it should have been, muted in a way that terrified him—Ben could feel the extent of her depletion. She'd pushed past every safe limit, had burned through power reserves that should have taken days to recover, and had kept going anyway because he'd needed her to.

"I've got you," he said, pulling her close. "You're okay. We're both okay."

Sidney made a sound that might have been agreement or might have been a sob. Her face pressed against his shoulder, and he felt blood from her nose soaking into his shirt. The dimensional burns on her arms looked worse up close—not just surface damage, but something that went deeper, affecting the tissue underneath.

Permanent scarring, he realized. The kind that would never fully heal.

The cost of rescuing him.

"We need to move," Rebecca Morse said from behind them, her voice urgent but not unkind.

"It'll be only a minute or so more before they realize we've breached the perimeter."

Ben stood and gathered Sidney into his arms. She didn't protest, which scared him far more than the blood or the burns. Sidney always protested when she thought people were treating her as fragile. The way she'd gone limp meant she truly had nothing left.

They moved deeper into the forest, Rebecca leading, her weapon held ready. Behind them, the facility's emergency lighting continued to strobe, and Ben could hear sirens now. Soon, the full weight of DAPI's resources would turn toward finding them.

"How far to the extraction point?" Ben asked, adjusting his grip on Sidney. She'd passed out completely at some point, her head now lolling against his shoulder.

"Two hundred yards. Vehicle's hidden just off a maintenance access road." Rebecca glanced back, checking for signs of pursuit. "Can you carry her that far?"

"Yes." His arms were already aching, but he'd carry Sidney two miles—twenty miles—if necessary. She'd nearly destroyed herself getting him out of the DAPI facility. The least he could do was get her to safety.

They'd made it a hundred yards before Sidney stirred in his arms.

"Down," she mumbled against his shoulder. "Put me down. Too heavy."

"You weigh about as much as my field equipment," Ben said without breaking stride. "I can manage."

"Ben." Her voice was stronger now, although still hoarse. "I can walk. Save your strength."

He set her down reluctantly and kept one arm around her waist for support. She swayed badly but managed to stay upright, one hand braced against a nearby pine trunk.

"How bad is the drain?" he asked quietly.

Sidney was silent for a moment, her expression distant in a way that meant she was assessing her internal state. When she met his eyes again, her face was pale even in the darkness.

"Down to twenty percent capacity. Maybe less." She wiped blood from her upper lip with her sleeve. "I can sense nearby electronics, nothing more. The burns"—she gestured at her arms—"those happened when I forced the facility's entire power grid offline at once. Dimensional backlash. They'll scar."

"Sidney—"

"We need to keep moving." She pushed away from the tree and stumbled slightly as she forced herself forward. "Rosenthal will have tactical teams sweeping the area within minutes."

Rebecca Morse had moved ahead to scout, but

she returned now, looking satisfied. "My vehicle's just ahead. No pursuit yet—they're still organizing."

They covered the remaining distance with Ben supporting most of Sidney's weight. The Suburban was exactly where Morse had promised, hidden in a clump of trees off an access road that looked abandoned. She backtracked to double-check they were still alone while Ben settled Sidney in the back seat. She tried to sit upright, failed, and ended up lying across the seat with her head in Ben's lap.

Rebecca came back, climbed into the Suburban, and started the engine. With the headlights off, she pulled onto the access road and navigated by the faint starlight that filtered through breaks in the cloud cover and the forest canopy. Behind them, the facility's perimeter lit up with searchlights.

They'd finally realized he was gone.

"How far?" Ben asked, one hand gently brushing blood-matted hair away from Sidney's face. He didn't know where they were going, but he assumed it must be a safe house of some sort.

"Forty minutes if we're not intercepted." Rebecca took a corner faster than was probably safe, but Ben wasn't about to complain. "They don't know about my safe house. It's completely off the books. We should be secure there for at least twenty-four hours."

"We don't have twenty-four hours." Ben looked down at Sidney, at the dimensional burns on her arms and the dried blood on her face. "The artificial portal—Rosenthal told me it's already operational."

"We know. My contact inside confirmed it."

"Dr. Hargrove, right?" Rebecca's shoulders tensed slightly, and she gave a brief nod. "He visited me earlier," Ben went on. "He gave me the security badge and the timeline for the system failure."

"Did he tell you anything else?" Her voice was carefully neutral.

"The artificial portal is siphoning energy from the global portal network. Every supernatural site on Earth is being affected." Ben managed to keep his voice steady despite all the implications of the current situation. "Hargrove said the extraction rate isn't sustainable. If they keep the portal active, it'll cause cascade failure across the entire system."

Sidney stirred in his lap, her eyes opening slowly, wide and unfocused. "How long?"

"Hargrove said the portal has a six-hour operational window. After that, they have to shut down and let the natural network compensate." Ben gazed down at her, noting the pallor of her skin, the shadows under her eyes. "But if they try to extend that window, push for longer operational periods—"

"It'll fail," Sidney said, barely above a whisper. "Everything will collapse at once."

"How long?" Rebecca asked from the driver's seat. Her eyes were fixed on the dark path they bumped along, but she'd clearly been listening to every word. "If they keep pushing, how long before the cascade?"

Ben did his best to remember the data he'd seen in Hargrove's lab, the sustainability calculations that didn't account for network degradation. This was far beyond his field of expertise, but at least he had good recall. "From what I saw, maybe ten hours. Less if they try to force the portal to stay active beyond the six-hour window."

Ten hours. Not a lot of time to save the world's interdimensional portals—and maybe the world itself.

"The phoenix is getting more and more corrupted," Sidney said, the words still not much more than a whisper, as though she knew she needed to save her energy any way she could. "I can feel it through our connection. It has hours left, not days. And I've got…." She paused there, obviously trying to assess just how much she had left. "Maybe fifteen percent capacity. That's not enough for the final cleansing, even if we had the time."

"What do you need?" Ben asked. He refused to give up hope, no matter how dire things looked. Sidney and Rebecca had managed to rescue him, and that had to count for something. "To recover enough, I mean. What would it take?"

A bitter chuckle drifted from Sidney's pale lips. "Days of complete rest with no power use whatsoever. Maybe some kind of medical help for the depletion and the dimensional burns—if we could even find someone who has any experience with these kinds of injuries." She lifted one arm and studied the iridescent marks there with an almost clinical detachment. "These happened because I forced a power surge that should have killed me. The dimensional energy backlash scarred me. Every time I use my abilities now, they burn. The pain will get worse the more I push."

Ben took her hand carefully, avoiding the worst of the burns. "Then we'll find another way. I won't let you destroy yourself trying to save the phoenix."

"There isn't another way." Sidney's voice had a weary certainty that made him ache for her, for what she was going through. "The phoenix has to have an anchor for the final cleansing, someone who can hold the pattern of clean fire while its physical form dissolves. That's me. And I need you there to stabilize my abilities, or I won't survive the merge."

"Then we'll both die trying," Ben said simply. "Because I'm not leaving you to face this alone."

They drove in silence after that, Rebecca navigating back roads and fire trails without headlights, driving through sheer nerve and grit. Ben kept one arm around Sidney's shoulders and felt the way she trembled even through her exhaustion. She'd rest her head against his shoulder for a few minutes and then force herself upright, checking her surroundings with senses that barely seemed to function anymore.

"Stop fighting it," he said gently after the third time she tried to sit up. "Let yourself rest."

"I can't." Her words were slurred with exhaustion. "I have to stay alert. Have to—"

"Sidney." He took her hand and squeezed it gently, hoping his touch might get through to her when his words wouldn't. "You pushed yourself to the absolute limit getting me out. You have dimensional burns that might never fully heal. Let yourself rest. Just for a few minutes. Please."

Something in her expression crumbled again—that same desperate recognition he'd seen when he'd first found her. She nodded once, then let herself sag against him, her full weight settling into his side. Within seconds, her breathing had evened out in sleep.

Ben held her carefully, one hand stroking her hair while the other kept her steady as the SUV bounced over the rough terrain. The dimensional burns on her arms looked worse in the glow from the dashboard—not quite healing, not quite spreading, just existing as terrible markers of what she'd sacrificed to save him.

"She'll be okay," Rebecca said from the driver's seat. Her gaze was still fixed ahead, but her voice was firm. "Sidney's stronger than she looks."

"I know." Ben kept his eyes on Sidney's sleeping face, wanting to make sure she continued to rest despite their murmured conversation. "But everyone has limits. She's been pushing past hers for days."

"So have you."

He wouldn't shrug, because that might disturb Sidney. "I documented a few things. She fought a dying phoenix, merged her consciousness with corrupted dimensional fire, and then almost destroyed her own nervous system jamming an entire government facility." He paused there before adding, "I'm not the one paying the real costs here."

Rebecca was quiet for a moment. When she spoke again, her tone was almost urgent. "Rosenthal wanted you for more than your expertise, Ben. She wanted to use you as leverage against Sidney. Your electromagnetic compatibility, the way your abilities amplify hers—that makes you valuable. But it also makes you vulnerable."

"Yeah, I figured that out." He adjusted his hold on Sidney as Rebecca took another corner too fast, gravel skidding beneath the Suburban's tires. "Which is why we can't let her attempt the final cleansing alone. She thinks she's protecting me by leaving me behind, but she's wrong."

Rebecca glanced back at him for the barest second before returning her attention to the fire road. "You'd really risk death to anchor her through the phoenix rebirth?"

He didn't have to think about it. "I'd risk anything to keep her alive."

Rebecca nodded slowly, and Ben thought he saw approval in her expression, barely visible in the rearview mirror. "Then let's make sure you both survive this. We're a couple of minutes away from the safe house."

A cabin appeared ahead, dark and isolated in the predawn hours, almost hidden by the evergreen forest that pressed in from all sides. Rebecca parked the Suburban behind the structure, out of sight from the access road. The phoenix was there, Ben realized—he could sense its presence even without Sidney's abilities to bridge the connection. The creature had found their hiding place, drawn by its bond with Sidney.

"I'll do a perimeter check," Morse said, and

opened the car door the second the engine shut off. "Get her inside and comfortable. We'll plan our next move once she's had some rest."

Ben gathered Sidney into his arms—she barely stirred, too exhausted to wake—and carried her into the cabin. The phoenix was curled near the woodstove, its corrupted fire adding warmth to the banked-down coals. The creature lifted its head as Ben entered, ancient eyes studying him with what might have been concern.

"She got me out," he told it. "Pushed herself past every limit to do it. So now we need to figure out how to save you both."

The phoenix responded with a soft trill, and through the faint connection Ben shared with Sidney, he felt something from the creature. Not words—more like emotion and intent. Gratitude and affection, but underneath it all, a kind of desperate urgency.

Ben settled Sidney on the cabin's couch, then lifted the blanket draped across the back and spread it across her. She didn't wake, which was probably for the best. Her body needed every minute of rest it could get.

He knelt beside the phoenix and studied the contamination that had spread through its feathers. The creature was dying, and there was nothing Ben could do to stop it without Sidney's abilities.

"I need you to show me something," Ben said.

"Sidney told me about the anchoring process, about how her grandmother nearly died attempting it at full strength. Sidney's at maybe fifteen percent capacity, if that. She can't survive anchoring you alone."

The phoenix regarded him steadily, and Ben felt that brush against his consciousness again. This time, it sent images of Sidney and Ben together, their electromagnetic signatures creating that golden glow he'd seen before.

Then it sent something new—their signatures not just resonating, but merging, becoming temporarily one consciousness, one coordinated system.

"You're saying I need to fully merge with Sidney during the cleansing," Ben said, hoping he'd interpreted the image correctly. "Actually share the anchor role, not just stabilize her abilities."

The phoenix's response felt like confirmation.

"I don't think that's ever been done before." Frustration seeped into his voice despite his best attempts to sound calm. "We don't even know if it's possible."

More images came from the phoenix—guardians through the generations, always working alone, always bearing the full weight of the anchor role.

And always nearly dying from the effort.

But Sidney wasn't alone. She had a partner whose electromagnetic signature resonated with hers. Maybe that changed the equation.

Rebecca Morse returned, her expression satisfied, although her slim form remained tense, ready to react at the first sign of trouble. "The perimeter's clear, and I didn't see any signs of pursuit. They're probably still searching near the facility, assuming we'd head for population centers or known safe houses."

"How long do we have?" Ben asked, gaze still fixed on the phoenix.

"Until they expand the search radius? Maybe ten hours. Maybe less if Rosenthal decides to get creative." Rebecca moved to check Sidney's pulse, and her lips compressed. "She needs at least six hours of sleep. Her body's shutting down from the strain."

"The phoenix has maybe ten hours before cascade failure." Ben finally looked away from the creature. "And Sidney needs days to recover enough power for the final cleansing."

"Then we're looking at an impossible situation." Rebecca settled into a chair, weariness finally showing in her expression. That had been a hell of a drive. "Unless you have a plan I don't know about."

"The phoenix showed me something—a way Sidney and I might both survive the final merge."

He explained the images he'd received as best he could—the full merge, sharing the anchor role instead of just stabilizing her abilities. "It's never been attempted before. I don't even know if it's possible."

Rebecca's dark brows, such a contrast to her pale hair, pulled together. "But you're going to try anyway."

"We don't have any better options." He got up from the spot where he'd been kneeling next to the phoenix and returned to Sidney's side, one hand finding hers. Even in sleep, she trembled. "If she attempts the cleansing alone, she'll die. If she doesn't attempt it at all, the phoenix will die, and the portal network will collapse. At least this way, we'll have a chance."

Rebecca was quiet for a long moment. When she spoke, her voice had a note of cautious hope. "Eric Hargrove contacted me while you were being held. He said he's willing to testify against Rosenthal and expose the whole Phoenix Project, but only if we can destroy the artificial portal first. Otherwise, DAPI will just disappear him before he can talk."

Add another impossible task to the list. "How do we destroy it?"

"The phoenix's clean fire, apparently. If we can complete the natural rebirth cycle, the resulting energy surge will overload the artificial portal's systems. It'll burn out the machinery, maybe even collapse the facility's underground levels." Her dark eyes met his. "But it has to be clean fire. The corrupted version would just feed the artificial portal and make it stronger."

So, all they had to do was help Sidney recover enough to anchor the phoenix through final cleansing, merge with Ben in a way that had never been attempted before, complete the rebirth with clean fire instead of corrupted, and somehow survive the process long enough for that clean fire to destroy Rosenthal's weapon.

No problem.

"Then that's what we'll do," he said. "We'll rest and plan, and then we'll find a way to make the impossible work."

Rebecca's lips curled into an ironic smile. "You say that like you believe it."

"I have to believe it." Ben gave Sidney's hand a gentle squeeze, but she didn't stir. "Because the alternative is giving up. And I didn't survive being DAPI's prisoner just to give up now."

A slow nod. "Get some rest. I'll take first watch. Then we'll reassess in six hours and figure out our approach."

Ben wanted to argue that he should take first watch, that she'd already done enough. But exhaustion was catching up with him now that the adrenaline had faded. His arms ached from carrying Sidney, his head throbbed from stress, and his body demanded sleep.

He settled onto the floor next to the couch, one hand still holding Sidney's, and the phoenix watched them both with ancient, knowing eyes. Somewhere in the distance, Rosenthal's teams were searching, getting closer with every passing minute.

Six hours to rest and recover. Then they'd attempt something that had never been done, risk everything on a merge that might kill them both, and hope it was enough to save the phoenix and destroy DAPI's weapon.

Just another day in the field.

Ben closed his eyes, feeling Sidney's pulse steady under his fingers, and let exhaustion pull him under.

They'd face the impossible together.

Because that's just what they did.

CHAPTER ELEVEN

I awoke, and realized I was broken.

No physical pain, not really, although my nervous system still felt like someone had replaced every nerve with exposed wire. This was something else, something that seemed as if it had taken root at the very core of my being. The phoenix's corruption had advanced during the few hours I'd slept, and I could feel it through our bond like a spreading infection. The creature's consciousness brushed against mine, jagged and wrong, its fire no longer the clean flame of creation but something that tasted of ash and death.

Slowly, I sat up on the cabin's couch, and every movement sent sparks of residual pain through my shoulders and arms. The dimensional burns had started to scab over, but the iridescent quality of the damaged tissue caught the early morning light in ways that made my stomach turn. Would those marks ever fully heal?

As with so many other things, I had no way of knowing. We were in uncharted territory here.

The scabs pulled when I flexed my fingers, and underneath them I could sense something wrong with the tissue itself. The dimensional energy had affected the cellular structure and left patterns that my electromagnetic senses read as foreign, unnatural.

A physical sign of the cost of loving Ben Sanders, of refusing to leave him in Rosenthal's custody.

I'd make the same choice again without hesitation, but that didn't stop the burns from aching, a dull throb deep inside that I didn't think would go away any time soon.

Ben was asleep on the floor beside the couch, one hand still loosely holding mine even in slumber. I could sense his electromagnetic signature the way I might sense a warm fire on a cold night—steady and grounding. His presence made my abilities much more focused. If he hadn't been there during the facility breach, I would have died pushing that pulse. My nervous system would have shorted out completely and left me brain-dead on the forest floor while DAPI's security teams closed in.

Gently, I pulled my hand free, not wanting to wake him. He needed rest after everything Rosenthal had put him through. The bruises on his wrists from the restraints they'd used to bind him had begun to fade to yellow-green, but I could still see the marks, and I still remembered the fury I'd felt when I saw him held captive, knowing they were using him as leverage against me.

DAPI had understood our electromagnetic connection better than we had. They'd known that threatening Ben would make me reckless and desperate, willing to push past every safe limit to get him back.

They'd been right.

The phoenix stirred near the woodstove, and I felt its attention turn toward me. Our connection allowed it to transmit a kind of desperate urgency mixed with something that seemed almost like an apology.

I went over and knelt beside the creature, my bare feet silent on the cabin's worn floorboards. The wood was cold against my skin, and I could sense the electromagnetic signatures of the building's old wiring running through the walls. Nothing unusual. Nothing that suggested DAPI had found us yet.

Small mercies, I supposed.

I studied the shadow veins that now covered most of the phoenix's feathers. Only small patches of clean fire remained, concentrated around its head and chest. The rest was corruption so thick I could feel it pulling at my consciousness whenever I touched the phoenix's mind. It was like standing too close to a cliff edge, that vertigo sensation of something vast and wrong trying to drag me over.

"I know," I whispered, reaching out to stroke one of the few remaining clean patches. The feathers were warm under my fingers, but not the comfortable glow of healthy phoenix fire. This heat burned like someone with a raging fever. "We're almost out of time."

The phoenix's response came as a pulse of warmth, and I felt it reach deeper into our connection. This wasn't just surface contact anymore. It wanted to show me something—something I probably wouldn't like, based on the apologetic undertone to its consciousness.

I pulled in a breath and let my defenses drop, allowing the creature's consciousness to merge more fully with mine.

The rebirth ritual exploded into my awareness with perfect, terrible clarity.

This wasn't going to be like my grandmother's experience, maintaining an anchor connection while the phoenix transformed. That was for clean rebirths, where the phoenix's consciousness remained intact throughout the process. Under normal circumstances, the creature could guide its own transformation, burn away its old form, and rebuild from the ashes while the anchor held the pattern of what phoenix fire should be.

But with the corruption spreading through almost all of its body, the creature's sense of self was now almost gone. It couldn't guide its own transformation anymore. The contamination had eaten away too much of its identity and left it unable to distinguish between clean fire and twisted energy. If it tried to rebirth on its own, it would just re-create the corruption, building a new body from the same poisoned template.

The ritual I was seeing required something else entirely. A complete merge. Not Sidney-and-phoenix, two consciousnesses working together. It had to be Sidney-phoenix. One being. One consciousness. One existence.

I would have to die and be reborn with the phoenix.

My brain didn't want to acknowledge what my heart already understood. When I pulled back from the connection, I realized my hands were shaking, and I had to press them flat against the floor to steady myself. The dimensional burns protested the pressure and sent fresh pain shooting up my arms.

"No," I said out loud. "There has to be another way."

But the phoenix's only response was patient

certainty. With corruption this extensive, the creature needed much more than a simple anchor. It needed a consciousness that could hold the pattern of what clean fire should be and let the corrupted parts burn away completely. Only then could it rebuild from that clean core.

And the only consciousness that understood both phoenix fire and a human form was mine.

I would dissolve into dimensional flame, my sense of self fragmenting as I merged with the phoenix's dying consciousness. I would hold the pattern of clean fire while the corruption burned away, maintaining that image through pain and dissolution and the complete loss of everything that made me Sidney Lowell. Then we would rebuild together, phoenix and human merged into something new.

If the process went perfectly, if I held on to enough of what made me Sidney, I would separate at the end. I'd be changed but still myself, still the woman who owned a pet shop and loved Ben Sanders and was on her third rewatch of *Gilmore Girls.*

If I lost myself in the fire, though, I would stay merged forever. Sidney Lowell would cease to exist, and something else would emerge instead. It would be an entity with my memories, my knowledge, but utterly different at the same time.

Something that used to be human but wasn't anymore.

My grandmother's journals had never mentioned anything like this, but that didn't surprise me too much. She'd never had to face such a terrible conundrum.

No one had.

No guardian in my family's history had ever faced a phoenix this corrupted. They'd always intervened much earlier in the process...if there had even been any contamination at all...and had helped the creatures through clean rebirths before the corruption could spread this far. But I'd been occupied with shadow stalkers and DAPI's surveillance and protecting Silver Hollow from dimensional incursions. I'd had no idea what was happening in the woods, and by the time the phoenix had let its anguish flare to a point where I could pick up on its suffering, it was already far too late for a simple anchoring.

Now I was paying the price for that delay.

I pushed myself upright on shaking legs and moved to the cabin's small kitchen, where I filled a glass with water I didn't really want. My hands were still trembling badly enough that water sloshed over the rim, cold against my skin. I could sense the water's electromagnetic properties, the way the molecules moved in response to temperature.

Where the hell had Rebecca Morse gone?

"Sidney?"

Ben's voice made me turn around. He was awake and sitting up, his mid-brown hair mussed from sleep and his expression worried. The electromagnetic signature I could always sense grew warmer as he stood and crossed to me, and I felt my own abilities stabilize in response the closer he got. The trembling in my hands lessened slightly, although it didn't disappear entirely.

"What happened?" He reached out and laid a gentle hand on my arm. "I felt something. Fear, I think. It woke me up."

I set the glass down on the butcher-block counter before I dropped it. My fingers left wet prints on the scratched wood surface. "The phoenix showed me the full ritual. What I'll have to do."

Ben went very still, although his hand remained on my arm. Oddly, the pressure of his touch didn't make my scars hurt. If anything, they felt a little better. "And?"

"And it requires a complete merge. Not just anchoring, but what I think is supposed to be a full consciousness integration." The words sounded a lot steadier than I felt, and I was a little proud of myself for that. "I have to become part of the phoenix's rebirth. If I can hold on to enough of my identity, I'll separate at the end. If I can't...."

I didn't finish the sentence. Ben's expression told me he understood exactly what I wasn't saying.

"You'd be lost." The words were quiet, almost flat. "Sidney Lowell would stop existing."

"The entity that emerged would have my memories, maybe even some of my personality traits." I picked up the water glass again, just to give my hands something to do. "But it wouldn't be me, not really. It would be something else. Something that used to be human and used to be phoenix, merged into a new form that was neither."

The chances of my coming out of such a terrible process still myself were not good.

My great-great-grandmother had nearly died anchoring a phoenix that was less than a third corrupted. Even as she healed, she realized that her abilities had changed permanently. She'd gained new sensitivities she never fully controlled, but lost other abilities. The experience had altered her forever, even though she'd maintained her identity throughout.

What I was attempting was so far beyond what she'd done, I didn't even have a frame of reference to fully describe it.

"There has to be another way," Ben said,

echoing my earlier words to the phoenix. His hand moved down my arm so he could twine his fingers with mine. Again, with that touch came a soothing warmth, although nothing about our situation was remotely comforting.

"There isn't. Not with the phoenix so horribly contaminated and less than eight hours to go before cascade failure." I had to force out the rest of the words because even though they needed to be said, I hated to utter them out loud. "The phoenix is dying, Ben, and the portal network is collapsing. Every supernatural site on Earth is being affected by Rosenthal's artificial gateway. I'm the only person who can anchor this rebirth because I'm the only one we know of who has both the electromagnetic abilities and the connection to the phoenix's consciousness."

"At what cost?" His voice had turned hard, and I sensed the way his electromagnetic signature spiked with emotion—anger, fear, frustration, all tangled together. "You're asking me to watch you die and hope that what comes back is still you."

"I'm not asking. I'm telling you what has to happen." I pulled away from his touch, needing to put some distance between us, even though it hurt the second his fingers were no longer tangled with mine. "My mother and grandmother are on the other side of that portal. If the network collapses, they'll be trapped forever. I don't have any other choice."

He made a frustrated gesture, but he didn't try to touch me again, as if he knew I'd put that distance between us for a reason. "It's always about duty with you. What about what *you* want? What about choosing to survive? What about us?"

That last word hit harder than I wanted to admit. *Us.* The relationship we'd been building toward since he'd arrived in Silver Hollow, even though I'd spent way too long keeping him in the friend zone. Our partnership that had turned into something much deeper, something I'd never thought I'd share with someone else.

"I want to survive. I want to come out of this still myself, still the person you fell in love with." My voice cracked despite my best efforts to remain calm, and I had to swallow hard before I could continue. "But wanting doesn't change what has to be done. This is the only way to save the phoenix and the portal network and my family."

Before he could reply, I moved to the window and gazed out at the forest that surrounded the cabin. Dawn had just begun to break, a tentative pale light peeking over the foggy horizon. Somewhere beyond these woods was the forest that sheltered the original portal, the one that connected Silver Hollow to the dimensional realm where my family was stranded.

My electromagnetic senses could feel the disturbance, the way the power out there flowed wrong, pulled toward DAPI's facility instead of moving naturally through the network. Every minute that the artificial portal stayed active, the damage to the natural system got worse.

If the cascade failure happened, it wouldn't just be Silver Hollow's portal that collapsed. It would be all of them. Every supernatural site on Earth would go dark at once, cutting off the dimensional realms completely. Thousands of creatures would be trapped on the wrong side, and hundreds of guardians would lose their connection to the very thing they were meant to protect.

My mother and grandmother would die on the other side, cut off from any help and unable to return.

"I'm terrified," I said. The admission felt like pulling teeth. I was supposed to be tough, right? Ready to face anything that came my way, because that was what the women of my family had been doing for generations. But I couldn't pretend anymore. Not with Ben. "I'm so scared I can barely think straight. But I don't know what else to do."

He came over and wrapped his arms around me, and that friendly warmth flowed around me again. I let myself lean back against him, let myself take comfort in his presence, even though it made the fear sharper.

Because if I didn't survive the merge, this might be one of the last times I got to feel his arms around me. One of the last times I got to be just Sidney, not Sidney-phoenix or some hybrid entity that wore my face but wasn't me.

"Tell me," he said, his breath warm against my ear. "What specifically frightens you?"

That he was asking instead of trying to fix the problem meant everything. He was giving me the space I needed to examine my fear instead of dismissing it or telling me everything would be fine.

Sometimes you needed to acknowledge the terror before you could move past it.

"I'm afraid I'll lose myself in the merge." My voice shook a little, but I forced myself to continue. "That I'll dissolve into the phoenix's consciousness and won't be able to find my way back. Its mind is so different from a human being's—so vast and ancient and built around concepts I don't even really understand. What if I merge with that and can't remember how to be Sidney? What if my human consciousness just gets overwhelmed?"

Ben's arms tightened slightly, and something in that embrace encouraged me to continue.

"I'm afraid that something calling itself Sidney

will emerge, but it won't really be me. Just an entity wearing my memories like a costume. It'll remember owning the pet shop and loving you and eating massive amounts of junk food during a *Gilmore Girls* binge, but those will be facts it knows rather than experiences it actually remembers. Like reading someone else's diary instead of living your own life."

His lips brushed against the top of my head, and the gentleness in that caress made me want to weep. "What else?"

"I'm afraid of what I might become even if I do survive with my identity intact. My great-great-grandmother changed after anchoring a corrupted rebirth." My voice dropped to almost a whisper. "And this is way beyond what she attempted. If I come back, what if I'm not human anymore? What if the person who loves you and remembers our first kiss and knows you like your coffee black is just gone, replaced by something that only looks like Sidney?"

Understanding seemed to pulse in his electromagnetic field, and he pressed his lips against my hair again. "You're afraid of changing so much that you'll lose what makes you yourself."

"Yes." The word was barely audible, and I tried to speak a little louder. "I'm afraid of looking at you and feeling nothing because the part of me that fell in love with you was burned away in dimensional fire. Of being alive but not really being Sidney."

The cabin was silent except for the crackling of the fire in the woodstove and the soft breathing of the dying phoenix. Outside, birds began to sing their morning songs, oblivious to the fate I might be facing.

"And you're still going to do this."

It wasn't a question, because he already knew the answer. He could probably feel it through our electromagnetic connection, the way my determination sat alongside my fear.

"I have to. If I don't, the phoenix dies, the network collapses, and my family is trapped forever. That's not something I can live with." I turned in his arms and made myself meet his gaze. "But I need you to understand something. If I come out of that merge and I'm not myself anymore—if I'm some half-phoenix entity that doesn't remember what it means to be Sidney Lowell—you are not responsible for that thing. You don't owe it anything. You can walk away."

"No."

The word was flat, absolute. His hands came up to frame my face, careful and deliberate, his fingers resting against my cheekbones.

"Whatever you become," he said, hazel eyes fixed on me, "whatever changes, whatever gets transformed in that fire—you're still you. The core of who you are doesn't live in your abilities or this electromagnetic gift you inherited, or even in your memories. It lives in the choices you make. The way you protect others, even when it costs you. The way you keep going when anyone else would give up."

His voice was steady, each word deliberate. I stood there in silence as he continued.

"You think some dimensional fire is going to burn away what makes you Sidney? You're wrong. I've watched you push past every limit, break every rule, sacrifice everything you had to protect people you barely knew. That's who you are. That's what makes you Sidney Lowell. And no rebirth ritual is going to change that because that's not something you can burn away. It's fundamental to how you exist in the world."

Maybe he was right. I wasn't sure about anything anymore. Well, except that I didn't want to lose him.

"Ben—"

"I'm not going anywhere," he told me. "If you come out of that merge transformed into something partially phoenix, I'll be there. If you need time to remember who you are, I'll help you remember. If you wake up not recognizing me, I'll make you fall in love with me all over again. If you're part phoenix and part human and struggling to figure out which parts are which, I'll be there while you sort it out."

As he spoke, his electromagnetic signature wrapped around mine so completely that I couldn't tell where his ended and mine began. We stood in the cabin's kitchen surrounded by our merged fields, and for a moment, I could feel what he felt.

His fear for me, and his absolute refusal to let me face this alone.

His love.

So many emotions churned within me, I wasn't sure I recognized any of them.

The only thing I did know was that I had to make him understand what he was saying.

"You can't promise that. You have no idea what I'll become. What if I emerge as something that frightens you? What if the Sidney parts are so buried under phoenix consciousness that you can't find them?"

His brows drew together, and I knew what he was going to say even before the words left his lips.

"I know you. I know the sound of your laugh and the way your eyes light up when you're excited about something. I know you well enough to recognize *you,* no matter what form you're wearing."

His thumbs brushed my cheekbones, and I

realized I was crying. When had that started? Tears were running down my face, and I couldn't seem to stop them.

"I'm so scared," I whispered. Saying it out loud made it that much more real, that much harder to shove down and ignore. "I'm more scared than I've ever been. More than when the shadow stalkers attacked Silver Hollow, even more than when DAPI captured you. This is different. This is about losing who I am, and I don't know if I'm strong enough to hold on through the merge."

The faintest of smiles touched the corners of his mouth. "I know. But you're going to do this anyway because you're Sidney Lowell, and you don't know how to be anything except brave." He pressed his forehead to mine, and in that moment, our electromagnetic signatures merged so completely that I felt as if we were sharing the same space. "And I'm going to be there with you. I'll give you something to hold on to when the fire gets too hot and you can't remember why you're fighting to stay yourself."

I wanted to believe him. I did believe that *he* believed what he was saying, but he still had no real idea of what we were facing. "The ritual will be excruciating. My grandmother was unconscious for three days after anchoring a clean rebirth, and her nervous system was damaged for weeks. This is going to be so much worse. I might not be conscious. I might not even recognize you during the merge."

He didn't blink. "Then I'll recognize you for both of us. Sidney, I didn't survive being DAPI's prisoner just to lose you to dimensional fire. We're doing this together. Both of us. Just like we've done everything else since I arrived in Silver Hollow."

The certainty in his voice somehow made the churning emotions within me calm a bit. I was still terrified, but having Ben beside me, his electromagnetic signature wrapped around mine, made all this insanity feel possible. Maybe I could hold on through the merge if I had his presence as an anchor.

I kissed him then—desperate and grateful and frightened all at the same time. His arms came around me, and for a few seconds, I let myself forget about phoenixes and portal networks and impossible rituals. I just wanted to be Sidney kissing Ben, his warmth solid against me, his presence the best kind of anchor I could ask for.

This might be one of the last times I got to kiss him as fully human Sidney. Tonight, or whenever I emerged from the rebirth, I might be something else entirely.

I was going to hold on to this moment and file it away in my consciousness so deeply that no amount of dimensional fire could burn it away.

The way Ben's hands felt against my back…the way his lips moved against mine, gentle and fierce at the same time.

If I lost everything else in the merge, I was keeping this.

When we finally pulled apart, Rebecca Morse was standing in the cabin's doorway, looking more awkward than I'd ever seen her.

She sounded brisk enough when she spoke, though. "Sorry to interrupt, but we have a problem. Eric Hargrove just contacted me. Rosenthal is mobilizing every team she has to find you before you can attempt the phoenix ritual."

Reality came crashing back in, and I pulled away from Ben reluctantly. As much as I would have liked to stay in his arms forever, it was time to focus on the mission instead of my personal fears.

I brushed the back of my hand across my eyes and wiped the tears away. "How long do we have?"

"Maybe six hours before she locks down the entire area around the portal. She knows that's where you'll have to go." Rebecca crossed the room and went to the table that held her maps and communications equipment. I had no idea whether she'd slept at all the night before, but she seemed cool and efficient as always. "Hargrove says the artificial portal is operational but unstable. They're pushing it past safe parameters, trying to extract more power."

Of course they were. Rosenthal had never met a situation where she wouldn't try to wring out every last ounce of power. I supposed it was too much to hope that her overreach would wreck the gateway without us having to do anything at all.

"How do we destroy the artificial portal?" I asked.

"Clean phoenix fire, apparently. If you can complete the rebirth and emerge with clean fire, the resulting energy surge should overload the artificial portal's systems." She picked up her tablet from the table and moved through a few screens until she stopped on a schematic of what I guessed was the DAPI facility. "But it has to be clean fire. The corrupted version would just feed the artificial portal and make it stronger."

No pressure.

I looked at the phoenix curled near the woodstove, its contamination so thick now that only its head remained clean. Shadow veins pulsed through almost all of its feathers, and I could feel the wrongness of it all the way across the room. The creature could barely hold its head up, and its wings trembled when it tried to shift position.

"That poor thing can hardly fly. Its wings are failing. How are we supposed to get it to the portal?" I moved closer to the phoenix and knelt beside it. I could feel its exhaustion, the way it was fighting just to stay conscious. "It might not survive the journey."

Ben didn't hesitate. "We'll carry it. Between the three of us, we can manage. I've carried heavier equipment through worse terrain."

"And when Rosenthal's teams find us? When we're carrying a dying phoenix and trying to reach the portal through territory she controls?" I looked over at Rebecca Morse. "What's our plan for that?"

"We fight," she said, clearly not worried by such a prospect. Maybe she thought her FBI training would give her an advantage over a bunch of hired goons, but even she had to realize we were grossly outnumbered. "Eric Hargrove will create a diversion and do his best to pull some of the tactical teams away from the portal site. But there will still be a lot more of them than there are of us. Rosenthal has at least forty agents deployed in the area, and she's calling in more."

Forty agents led by a woman who'd already captured Ben once and knew exactly how to manipulate me.

I reached out to touch the phoenix. The creature knew it was dying and understood that it might not survive long enough to reach the portal. But it was going to try anyway, because that's what phoenixes did. They burned and re-formed and kept going, no matter how impossible the odds.

I needed to do the same.

"Then we'll leave in an hour," I said, as I climbed back to my feet. Oddly, my legs felt steadier now that I was determined on this course. "That will give us time to eat something and gather supplies. Once we start this, we're not stopping until the ritual is complete or we're all captured."

"Or dead," Rebecca added, her tone flat.

"Or dead," I agreed, and the words didn't scare me as much as they should have, maybe because I was already planning to dissolve into dimensional fire. Physical death seemed almost minor compared to losing my entire identity. "But if we're going to die, we're taking that artificial portal with us. And we're giving the phoenix a chance to be reborn clean, the way it was always supposed to."

Ben's hand found mine, and our fingers laced together. His entire being seemed to pulse with determination and fear and a fierce protectiveness. I squeezed back and held on to that connection.

I needed to hold on to him because in a few hours, I was going to dissolve into dimensional fire and hope I could remember who I was supposed to be.

And if I couldn't—well, at least I would have

tried. At least I would have fought for my family and the portal network and all the supernatural sites around the world that depended on natural energy flow.

The phoenix stirred, its consciousness brushing mine. No words again, just images of fire and rebirth and transformation, along with a certain faith that I was strong enough to hold on through the merge.

I hoped it was right.

Because ready or not, scared shitless or not, in six hours or less, I was going to find out exactly what I was made of.

And pray that when I re-formed, Sidney Lowell still existed somewhere in the flames.

CHAPTER TWELVE

The phoenix was dying faster than Ben had anticipated.

Rebecca had given him a new watch to replace the one Rosenthal's guards had confiscated, and he checked it now as they moved through the forest. A little past twelve-thirty in the afternoon. Their small group had been traveling for three hours, and the creature's corruption had advanced the entire time. The contamination had progressed beyond ninety percent, well past the threshold where any previous guardian would have attempted intervention.

But Sidney wasn't one of those previous guardians.

He adjusted his grip on the makeshift stretcher they'd fashioned from a tarp and branches cut from the Douglas firs that surround the safe house. Rebecca Morse carried the front end and moved with the easy stride of someone who'd handled worse cargo in worse conditions. Sidney walked beside them with one hand resting on the phoenix's side, her face pale and drawn. She'd barely eaten this morning despite insisting that everyone else should get some food in them before they set out, and her electromagnetic signature was muted in a way that worried him. No point in bringing it up, though. She'd only tell him she was fine.

The dimensional burns on her arms had stopped oozing. The iridescent scabbing had hardened into something that looked almost like scales and caught the filtered sunlight in ways that shouldn't have been possible. He tried not to think too hard about whether those marks would be permanent.

He didn't want to believe she would carry forever the cost of saving him.

"Rest stop," Rebecca called back from the front of the stretcher, her voice soft, as if she understood they needed to guard everything they said out here. "Five minutes."

They lowered the phoenix carefully to the ground. The clearing they'd stopped in let some pale sun break through the canopy, but Ben couldn't let himself be too cheered by its presence.

The phoenix made a soft sound that might

have been pain or exhaustion. Its wings, once magnificent even when contaminated, hung limp at its sides. Those terrible shadow veins had spread to cover everything except a small patch of clean fire around its heart.

Sidney knelt beside it and pressed both hands against the one remaining clean spot. Ben watched her close her eyes and reach out with those strange inner abilities, checking the creature's condition. After a moment, her shoulders sagged.

"It can't fly anymore." She didn't open her eyes, but only continued, "The corruption's reached its wing muscles. Even if we put it down and told it to go, it couldn't."

"How much time do we have?" Rebecca asked. Before leaving the safe house, she'd studied their route on her tablet, but now she seemed to be going from memory alone.

"A few hours. Maybe three or four at the most before the corruption hits its heart." Sidney finally opened her eyes. Tears tracked through the smudges on her face. "After that, the creature will die whether we've reached the portal or not."

Ben knelt beside her and found her shoulder with his hand. He could feel her exhaustion through their connection, her fear and her desperate determination to save this creature that had suffered so much. He squeezed gently and offered what comfort he could, even while knowing it wouldn't be enough.

"Then we'll keep moving," he said. "We're making good time. Another three hours should get us close to the portal site."

"Close isn't good enough." Sidney wiped her eyes with her sleeve and left behind smudges of dirt and ash. "We need to be at the exact location. The portal's energy is what will sustain the rebirth ritual. If we're even fifty yards off, the merge will fail."

Rebecca's expression turned thoughtful. "I think I can get the exact coordinates. Eric Hargrove should have access to all of Rosenthal's survey data."

Next to Ben, Sidney went still. "The man whose artificial portal is a big part of our problem."

Rebecca's shoulders lifted in a small shrug. "People aren't simple, Sidney. Yes, Eric Hargrove has made mistakes, but he's trying to fix them now. I know him better than you do."

Something about the way she said those words made Ben wonder if there was more going on between her and the scientist than simply being united against Rosenthal. There had been a slight softening in her tone, accompanied by a certain shift in the set of her mouth. Small tells, but he didn't think he was imagining them.

Not that it mattered right now. He didn't care if Rebecca Morse and Eric Hargrove had been doing the horizontal mambo at every cheap motel between here and Portland. The only thing that mattered was whether the information Hargrove had passed on remained valid.

Sidney's jaw stayed tight with anger, but she seemed to decide there wasn't much point in arguing. She gave a single curt nod.

"Anyway," Rebecca went on, "he's been documenting everything he can. Every experiment, every protocol violation, every time Rosenthal pushed the system past the safety parameters he and the other scientists set up. When this is over, his testimony should be enough to shut down DAPI completely."

"If we survive to make use of that testimony," Sidney said.

Rebecca didn't blink. "Yes, if we survive. Which is why we need to finalize our approach. Eric sent me updated reconnaissance information about twenty minutes ago. DAPI has forces positioned around the portal site. Not a full perimeter, but enough to make a direct approach difficult."

She reached into her field jacket, brought out her tablet, and turned it so they could both see what she was talking about. The map showed the portal's location marked in red, with multiple blue dots scattered in a rough semicircle to the north and east. Ben counted at least fifteen positions, and there were probably more that weren't showing on the basic tactical display.

"They're expecting us," Rebecca went on. "This is an ambush formation, not a defensive perimeter. Rosenthal knows we need the portal to complete the ritual, and she's betting you'll go there despite the risk." She paused, then zoomed in further and highlighted a gap in the formation to the southwest. "Luckily for us, she can't cover every approach. This route follows a ravine system that's too narrow for vehicle access. If we move fast and quiet, we should be able to reach the portal before they realize we've slipped through."

Ben examined the route and narrowed his eyes. "Our route will be exposed for the last hundred yards. Once we clear the ravine, we'll be visible from at least three of those positions."

"Which is where the diversion comes in." Rebecca pulled up another file, this one showing the schematics of the DAPI facility. "Eric will trigger a catastrophic failure in the artificial portal's containment systems. It won't be enough to destroy the equipment, but it'll still be sufficient to require an immediate response from most of Rosenthal's teams."

"When?" Sidney asked, frowning as she studied the tablet.

"Whenever we're ready. He's standing by,

waiting for my signal." Rebecca closed the file. Her expression had turned more serious. "But we'll only get one shot at this. The moment Eric triggers the failure, Rosenthal will know someone's sabotaging her operation from the inside. She'll lock down the facility and start searching for the leak. He'll have maybe thirty minutes before they find him."

Sidney repeated the words, her tone thoughtful. "Thirty minutes." She looked at the phoenix, its breathing shallow and labored, and gave a small nod. "That should be enough. If we're in position when the diversion starts, we can reach the portal and begin the ritual before DAPI responds."

Ben wanted to argue, wanted to point out all the ways this plan could fall apart. The exposed approach and the ambush positions were bad enough. Add to that Sidney's depleted state and her complete vulnerability once she started the merge, and the odds weren't good.

But they didn't have any better options.

"What about the extraction?" he asked instead. "After the ritual, I mean. Assuming Sidney survives the merge and we complete the rebirth, how do we get out of there with DAPI forces converging on our position?"

Rebecca Morse was quiet for a moment, her expression troubled. "I don't have a good answer for that. The ritual will create an energy surge that should overload the artificial portal's systems. That's the whole point. But that surge will also draw every DAPI agent within five miles directly to your location."

"So we'll complete the ritual and then run like hell," Sidney said. "We just have to hope that destroying the artificial portal will create enough chaos for us to slip away in the confusion."

"That's being a little optimistic, don't you think?" Ben asked.

She crossed her arms and met his gaze. "Do you have a better plan? If you do, I'm all ears."

He didn't, and that was the problem. Every scenario he'd run through in his head since they'd left the cabin ended the same way. Sidney vulnerable during the merge, DAPI forces closing in, and him trying to protect her with nothing but his determination and his electromagnetic compatibility with her abilities.

Those weren't great odds.

"We should keep moving," he said at last. "The longer we delay, the less time the phoenix has."

Sidney sent him a knowing look but said nothing. Instead, she only nodded.

Ben and Rebecca lifted the stretcher and resumed their previous positions while Sidney walked next to them with her hand on the phoenix's side. Its eyes were barely open now, its fire flickering weakly. Through his connection to Sidney, Ben could feel the creature's pain as though it were his own…along with its desperate hope that they would reach the portal in time.

The forest grew denser as they moved deeper into Silver Hollow's protected territory. Ancient trees with trunks wide enough to hide behind rose around them, and thick undergrowth muffled their footsteps. He estimated they had about two more miles to the ravine system, then another half mile through the ravine before they reached the portal site.

Close. So very close.

But not close enough.

Sidney stumbled, and Ben caught her elbow before she could fall. "Easy. When was the last time you drank any water?"

She made an impatient movement with one hand. "I'm fine."

"That's not what I asked." He pulled out his water bottle and pressed it into her hands. "Drink. The last thing we need is you dehydrated on top of everything else."

Something in his tone must have gotten through. She drank deeply from the bottle, although her hands shook enough that water sloshed down her chin. The dimensional burns on her arms caught the light as she moved, and he set his jaw.

Those burns were his fault.

"Stop that." Sidney didn't raise her voice, but he heard the anger beneath the words.

"Stop what?"

"Stop blaming yourself for the burns. I can feel you guilting yourself, and it needs to stop." She handed the water bottle back to him, her expression fierce despite her exhaustion. "I made that choice, Ben. I knew the cost, and I chose you anyway. That's not something you get to feel guilty about."

Maybe she was right. "You shouldn't have had to choose."

A small shrug. "Maybe so, but I did. And I'd make the same choice again." She reached out and found his fingers despite the way his hands were wrapped around one of the stretcher's poles. "We don't have time for guilt. Right now, we just need to focus on getting through the next few hours."

Ben squeezed her hand, then forced himself to let go and focus on the terrain ahead. She was right. Guilt was a luxury they couldn't afford.

They reached the ravine system a little over an hour later. The terrain dropped sharply and created a natural channel running southwest toward the portal site. Water had carved the path over centuries and left smooth stone walls on either side that rose at least fifteen feet above their heads. The ravine provided good cover, but it was also a funnel. If DAPI discovered them while they were making their way through, they'd have nowhere to run.

"This is it," Morse said and paused to double-check the route on her tablet. "From here, we'll follow the ravine for three-quarters of a mile. It opens into a clearing about a hundred yards from the portal site. That's where we'll be exposed."

"And that's where we need the diversion," Sidney said. She knelt beside the phoenix and pressed both hands to the one small patch of clean fire that remained. "How much time do you need to coordinate with Hargrove?"

"Five minutes, maybe ten at the most." Rebecca pulled out a slim black phone Ben hadn't seen before. He didn't recognize the model and wondered if it was some kind of government issue, something that would allow her to contact Eric Hargrove on a secure channel. "I'll move ahead and set up a position where I can see the portal site and confirm the positions of the DAPI agents," she continued. "Once I give Eric the signal, it'll take him around three minutes to trigger the containment failure."

"Three minutes." Ben looked over at Sidney. "That's how long you'll have to reach the portal before DAPI realizes the diversion is a distraction."

Her chin lifted. "No problem. I can cover a hundred yards in three minutes."

"While you're already exhausted and carrying a dying phoenix?" He tried to keep his voice level, but he knew his worry had bled through despite his best efforts. "Sidney, be realistic."

Her clear gray eyes flashed with irritation. "I don't have the luxury of being realistic." She stood, her legs shaking slightly. "The phoenix needs to be at the portal when I start the merge. There's no alternative. So I'll do whatever I have to do."

Ben wanted to argue, but movement in the ravine ahead made him freeze. Rebecca had her weapon out immediately, even as she gestured for silence. They all pressed against the stone wall and waited as voices echoed down the channel.

"—should be getting hazard pay for this. Rosenthal has us posted out here for sixteen hours straight—"

"Quit complaining. At least we're getting some real field time instead of pushing papers at HQ."

Two DAPI agents walking patrol. Ben watched them pass the ravine entrance thirty yards ahead, completely unaware of the three people and dying phoenix pressed into the shadows behind them. Their conversation faded as they moved on into the forest.

"They're running regular patrols," Rebecca said in an undertone once the men were out of earshot. "That wasn't in Eric's intel. Rosenthal must have adjusted her deployment sometime in the past hour."

"How does that change our approach?" Sidney asked.

"It doesn't. We just need to be more careful." Rebecca checked her watch. "I'm moving ahead to scout the portal site and coordinate with him. Give me fifteen minutes, then follow the ravine until you see my signal. Two quick flashes from a red light means it's clear to approach. Anything else, you abort and fall back."

"And if we don't see any signal?" Ben asked.

Rebecca Morse gave him a grim smile. "Then something went wrong, and you need to get out of here immediately. Get the phoenix somewhere safe and wait for me to contact you."

She was gone before either of them could respond, and moved up the ravine with the kind of silent skill that Ben might have admired under different circumstances.

Now, though, he could only think of how alone he and Sidney were.

"We should rest while we have the chance," he

told her. "Drink more water. Eat something if you can."

Sidney shook her head. "I'm not hungry."

Anxiety and fear had probably killed most of her appetite. That didn't mean he wasn't going to try to cajole her into eating. "I don't care. You're about to attempt something that'll require every ounce of strength you have." He pulled an energy bar from his pack, unwrapped it, and pressed it into her hands. "Eat. That's not a request."

She didn't seem to have the strength to argue, so she took the bar and chewed mechanically while Ben checked the phoenix's condition. The creature's breathing was labored, each inhalation a visible struggle. The corruption had spread even further during their rest stop and left only a patch the size of his palm around the phoenix's heart still clean.

They were cutting this way too close.

Their margin for error was effectively zero. If Sidney lost herself even slightly during the merge, if she couldn't hold on to what made her Sidney Lowell, then she would stay merged forever. She'd become a hybrid entity with her memories but not her consciousness, something that used to be human but wasn't anymore.

Ben's jaw tightened. He'd promised her this morning that he would recognize her no matter what form she wore, that he would be there to help her remember who she was if she needed it.

He'd meant every word. But sitting here in this ravine, watching her force down food she didn't want while a dying phoenix struggled to breathe beside them, the reality of what she was about to attempt hit him with full force.

He might lose her. Not to DAPI, not to Rosenthal's forces, but to the merge itself. She might dissolve into dimensional fire and never come back.

"Ben."

He'd been staring at his hands and thinking how useless they would be during the approaching trial. He looked up and found Sidney watching him, the half-eaten energy bar dangling from her fingers. "I know what you're thinking. I can feel your fear."

No point in denying it, not when their connection made it almost impossible to hide anything from her. "I'm scared shitless," he said frankly. "I'm watching you prepare to sacrifice everything, and there's nothing I can do to help except stand here and hope you're strong enough to survive."

An incongruous smile touched her lips. "You do a lot more than just hope. Your electromagnetic signature stabilizes my abilities, remember?" She reached out to him, her fingers finding his.

"When I start the merge, when I feel myself dissolving into the phoenix's consciousness, your presence is what I'll hold on to. That's kind of a big deal."

"But it's not enough."

"It *has* to be enough. Because it's all we have." She squeezed his hand. The golden glow that appeared whenever they were close shimmered into being as their bioelectric fields synchronized in ways that made her abilities stronger and gave him a sense of her emotional state.

This was partnership. More than romantic, although he knew that mattered, too. This was something deeper, a connection that made them more capable together than they were apart.

His fingers tightened on hers. "Whatever happens during the merge, no matter what you become or how changed you are when you separate, I'm with you. You understand that, right? I'm not leaving you to face this alone."

"I know." Her voice dropped to a whisper. "That's the only reason I think I can do this. Because you'll be there."

They sat in silence for a few minutes with their hands clasped, the glow surrounding them not bright enough to attract attention. The phoenix stirred, and Ben felt a pulse of warmth. Gratitude. Readiness to attempt the impossible because these two humans were crazy enough to try.

He checked his watch. About twelve minutes had passed since Rebecca had left. They should start moving soon and get into position near the ravine exit so they could go the moment the diversion started.

He was helping Sidney to her feet when a slim black phone buzzed inside Rebecca Morse's pack. She'd left it behind, he realized. She'd kept only her tactical gear and moved ahead to scout.

He pulled out the phone and saw the message notification. An unknown number, but he had to hope only one person knew how to contact this particular phone.

> Rosenthal changed deployment.
> Portal site has 25 agents, not 15.
> She's expecting infiltration.
> Diversion may not be enough.
> Abort if possible.

Ben stared at the message, and his pulse began to race. Twenty-five agents meant a force large enough to respond to the diversion and still maintain coverage on the portal site. Rosenthal had anticipated their approach and reinforced her positions, and now they were walking into a trap far worse than they'd expected.

"What is it?" Sidney asked. She was clearly reading the strain in his expression.

He showed her the message and watched her face go pale. Then her chin gave that determined little lift he knew so well.

"We're still going," she said. "We have to. The phoenix doesn't have time for us to come up with a new plan."

He'd expected that response, but he still wasn't ready to give in. "Sidney, twenty-five agents are more than triple what we're prepared for. Even with the diversion, we'll be massively outnumbered."

"I know." Her gaze met his, intense, as though she was willing him to understand. "But what other choice do we have? Let the phoenix die? Let the portal network collapse? Let Rosenthal win?" She straightened despite her exhaustion, and Ben thought of the accounts he'd read of warrior women in history. Boudicca. Joan of Arc. They must have looked much the same as they prepared to go into battle. "We're going to complete the ritual. Whatever it takes."

He wanted to find another way, a better approach. Anything that didn't involve walking Sidney directly into an ambush while she was depleted and about to attempt something that might destroy her.

But she was right. They didn't have alternatives. The phoenix was dying, and the portal network was failing. If they didn't act now, everything they'd fought for would be lost.

"Then we do it smart," he said. The time for argument had passed. "We'll wait for Rebecca's signal, move during the diversion, and get you to the portal as fast as possible. Once you start the merge, you're completely vulnerable. So I'll need to—"

"Protect me," Sidney broke in. "I know. That's what the electromagnetic connection is for. You can sense threats I can't while I'm merged. You can pull me back if necessary and serve as my link to the physical world."

"While hoping twenty-five DAPI agents don't shoot both of us," he remarked, and she sent him a lopsided grin.

"Yeah, while hoping that." Her smile faded slightly. "I know it's not a great plan. But it's all we have."

They lifted the phoenix's stretcher and began to move deeper into the ravine toward the portal site. The stone walls rose higher here and created lengthy shadows despite the afternoon sun. Ben counted their steps and measured the distance, calculating how long it would take to cover the exposed ground once they cleared the ravine.

Three minutes. That's what Rebecca had said. Three minutes between the moment when Eric Hargrove triggered the containment failure and when DAPI realized the diversion was a distraction.

It would have to be enough.

The ravine opened ahead, and afternoon light streamed into the darkness. Ben could see the forest beyond—the stands of coast redwood and sequoia and oak, the thick carpet of ferns and late-summer wildflowers beneath. Somewhere past those trees was the portal, the place where he'd first begun to realize the world wasn't what he'd once thought. The place where Sidney would dissolve into dimensional fire and hope she could hold on to her humanity long enough to re-form.

A red light flashed twice from the trees ahead. Rebecca Morse's signal.

Clear to approach.

"Ready?" Ben asked.

Sidney nodded and flashed him a smile meant to be brave but which wavered around the edges. "Let's save a phoenix."

They moved forward into the light and carried the dying creature between them, walking toward the ambush they knew was waiting.

CHAPTER THIRTEEN

The portal site looked exactly the same as it had when Ben and I had first come here—a natural clearing where ancient stones formed a rough circle, their gray surfaces marked with runes I now knew were Ogham letters, even if I couldn't read what they said.

Or at least, it looked mostly the same. The little fairy bell flowers that resembled glowing lilies of the valley were nowhere to be found, and neither was the carpet of bioluminescent moss that had once covered the ground. Something had shifted, and I wondered if that was yet another byproduct of the contaminated energy Rosenthal's artificial portal was spewing in all directions.

The ground here felt different now, charged with a power I could sense even through my exhaustion. This was a place where the barrier between worlds grew thin, where dimensional energy pooled and swirled in patterns that predated human civilization.

Ben and I lowered the stretcher with exaggerated care. Once it was safely on the ground, I knelt beside the phoenix. The creature's breathing was shallow, the same harsh pants I'd seen in animals that had suffered severe trauma. Unfortunately, this wasn't a case where I could clean a wound and stitch it closed, or administer antibiotics, or order an ultrasound to find out exactly what was wrong.

Everything I knew about veterinary medicine wouldn't help me here.

We had maybe two hours until the phoenix's heart failed.

The clearing was about fifty feet across. It felt smaller today, and I wondered if that was simply because my understanding of dimensional magic had grown since the last time I was here.

This place was sacred, though. Not in a religious sense, exactly, but in the way certain locations become thin places where normal rules didn't quite apply. Where magic came easier and where dimensional barriers weakened.

Where a phoenix could complete its rebirth cycle…if it had a guardian to anchor the process.

Rebecca Morse appeared then, emerging silently from a stand of young fir trees. "I'm going to scout the perimeter," she said. "I want to make sure we're actually clear. Give me three minutes."

Before we could respond, she disappeared into the trees with the kind of stealth that would have made a ninja proud. I watched her go and tried not to think about how exposed we were, how vulnerable I'd be once the merge started.

Ben knelt beside me and found my shoulder with his hand. His electromagnetic signature wrapped around mine at once, stabilizing, strengthening, making my depleted abilities feel almost manageable. The burns on my arms throbbed in response to his touch, but the pain was bearable. Everything was bearable when he was close.

"How do you want to do this?" he asked.

I pressed both hands to the phoenix's chest and felt the weak pulse of clean fire that remained. The creature's heart beat irregularly under my palms, struggling to pump energy through a system that was massively contaminated. Most animals wouldn't have even still been alive if they were carrying that much infection. The fact that it had survived this long only proved how stubborn phoenixes were.

Or how desperate.

Ben was watching me, waiting for a response.

"I need to be touching the phoenix when I start the merge," I said. "Physical contact helps anchor the connection. You should be close enough that our electromagnetic signatures can resonate, but not so close that you get pulled into the merge with me."

It was the first time I'd mentioned that might be a possible danger, but he didn't blink. "How close is too close?"

I could only shrug. "I don't know. My grandmother's journals didn't cover this part." I made myself meet his eyes and say what needed to be said. "I just know that if you feel yourself starting to get pulled in, you need to back away immediately. The merge might consume you, too."

Fear flickered through his hazel eyes, but his voice stayed steady. "I'm not leaving you."

I shook my head. "I'm not asking you to leave. I'm asking you to stay close enough to anchor me but far enough away to stay safe. I need to know you'll be okay. That's what's going to help me hold on to my identity when I dissolve."

He was quiet for a moment, and I watched him work through the problem—always thinking, always analyzing, always trying to find the optimal solution. One of the things I loved about him was that methodical mind which approached even impossible situations with calm rationality.

At last, he nodded. "Five feet should work. That's close enough to maintain the connection, but far enough to avoid an accidental merge. I'll monitor your vitals and watch for DAPI forces. If anything threatens you while you're vulnerable, I'll handle it."

"With what?" I forced myself to be practical. adding, "You're not a fighter."

"With whatever it takes." His tone was one of absolute certainty, and I felt an echo of that emotion through our connection. It wasn't bravado or false confidence, just determination backed by a love so fierce that it stole my breath. "Sidney, you're about to sacrifice everything to save the phoenix and the portal network. The least I can do is make sure no one shoots you while you're doing it."

I wanted to argue, to tell him that his life mattered more than mine. If DAPI forces showed up, staying to protect my unconscious body would be suicide. But I knew Ben well enough to understand that arguing would be pointless. He'd made his decision, just as I'd made mine when I pushed that electromagnetic pulse to free him from Rosenthal's facility.

We were both too stubborn to leave the other behind.

Rebecca Morse emerged from the trees, her expression grim, and uneasiness churned in my stomach. Something in the set of her jaw told me the news wasn't good before she even opened her mouth.

"It's worse than we thought," she said. She sounded brisk, relaying information but not allowing herself to get caught up in all its ramifications. "More tactical positions than Eric's intel suggested. I counted at least thirty agents, not twenty-five. And they're not just positioned to the north and east. They've got coverage on all sides."

So Rosenthal had a complete perimeter. She'd surrounded the portal site.

Ben scowled. "She knew we'd come here. She knew we needed the portal to complete the ritual. So she set up an ambush and waited."

"The diversion won't be enough." My voice sounded much steadier than I felt. Even if Eric Hargrove's containment failure pulled thirty percent of those forces away, we'd still be outnumbered. "When he triggers the failure at the artificial portal, some agents will respond, but Rosenthal will keep enough here to capture us."

Rebecca's frown matched Ben's in intensity, although she seemed calm enough as she said, "I'll need my phone back. I have to tell Eric to abort."

"No," I said at once, my tone sharp. I looked down at the phoenix, at the corruption that had spread to cover everything except that small patch around its heart. "We don't have time for a new plan. The phoenix has maybe an hour left if we're lucky. If we abort now, if we delay, it dies. The portal network will collapse, and my family will stay trapped forever."

"Sidney—" Rebecca began.

I shook my head. "I'm starting the merge." I turned toward them both and made myself say what needed to be said, even though every word felt like another nail in my coffin. "When the DAPI forces close in, you both need to run. Don't try to protect me. Once I'm merged with the phoenix, I'll be beyond their reach anyway. They can't capture what doesn't have a physical form."

"That's not happening," Ben said. His voice was flat, final.

I'd been afraid he would say that. "Ben, be reasonable," I told him. "You can't fight thirty trained agents. You'll die."

"Then I'll die." He said the words simply, as if his own death was just another variable in a much bigger equation. "Sidney, do you really think I'm going to stand by while Rosenthal captures your body when your consciousness is trapped in phoenix fire? Let her experiment on you when you can't defend yourself?"

Why did he have to be so stubborn? "I'm not worth dying for."

His eyes narrowed. "Yes, you are. And more importantly, this isn't just about you. It's about the phoenix, the portal network, your family, every supernatural site on Earth that depends on the natural energy flow. So we're not aborting, and we're not running. We're going to complete this ritual and destroy Rosenthal's weapon, no matter what."

"And how are we supposed to manage that?" I asked. "How do we hold off thirty agents for hours while I'm unconscious?"

Still with those narrowed eyes and taut jaw, Ben said, "How long does the ritual actually take? Do you have any clear idea?"

I didn't. What I was about to attempt had never been done before, so there was nothing to compare it to. "I don't know for sure. With this level of corruption, with the full merge instead of just anchoring? Hours. Maybe three or four."

"Then we'll hold for three or four hours." Ben made that statement as if it was the simplest thing in the world. As if holding off thirty DAPI agents while I was unconscious and vulnerable was just another logistics problem to solve. "Rebecca, you have tactical training. Can we create a defensive position?"

She scanned the clearing for a moment. "The stone circle provides some protection. Limited approach angles. If I position myself at the north entrance and you take the south, we can create overlapping fields of fire. It won't stop a coordinated assault, but it'll slow them down."

"It won't stop them at all," I said, since I didn't

see the point in continuing the charade. "Rebecca, be honest. Can two people hold this position against thirty trained agents?"

She met my gaze, and I saw the truth in her eyes before she spoke. "No. Not for hours. Maybe twenty minutes if we're lucky. Maybe thirty if they're cautious about casualties."

Considering that Rosenthal had already proven she wasn't too concerned about a high body count, I didn't find that scenario very likely. "Then it's suicide."

"Probably." Rebecca sounded calm. Part of her training, maybe, learning to come to terms with her own mortality. "But your family's been protecting this town and this portal for generations. Someone has to stand for that. It might as well be us."

Tears burned in my eyes. How could she and Ben both be willing to sacrifice themselves so I could complete an impossible ritual?

"You'll die," I said again, willing them to understand. "Both of you. DAPI will kill you and capture me anyway. This accomplishes nothing."

"It accomplishes everything." Ben moved closer and took my hand. "If we run, the phoenix dies for certain. That's not acceptable." His voice softened. "Sidney, you pushed past every safe limit to get me out of Rosenthal's facility. You gave yourself dimensional burns because you refused to leave me behind. Do you really think I'm going to do any less for you?"

"That was different," I protested, even as I realized we were wasting precious minutes.

"How?"

"Because you're—" The words caught in my throat. *Because you're more important. Because you're worth saving. Because losing you would destroy me in ways that losing myself wouldn't.*

But I couldn't say any of that. Not when his electromagnetic signature was pulsing with love so fierce I could barely breathe around it.

"I'm what?" Ben asked.

"Everything," I whispered. "You're everything to me. And I can't stand the thought of you dying because I wasn't strong enough to find another way."

"There is no other way. You know that." He cupped my face with his free hand, his touch gentle despite its urgency. "And you're everything to me, too. Which is why I'm staying. We stand together, even when the odds are impossible."

This was too much. And yet he needed to know.

"Whatever happens," I said, the words pouring out in a desperate rush, "whatever I become when I separate from the merge, I need you to know that I love you. That even if I lose myself in the fire, even if I emerge as something that doesn't remember being Sidney, these months with you have been the best of my life."

"They were the best of my life, too." He smiled. "And you're going to tell me again in a few hours when this is over and we're both alive." He kissed me then, quick and fierce. "Now start the merge before I lose my nerve and drag you out of here."

Rebecca had moved back to the tree line and was watching the forest with her pistol ready. "I'm signaling Eric. The diversion starts in three minutes. That's how long you have before DAPI realizes we're here and closes in."

Three minutes.

I knelt beside the phoenix and pressed both hands to its chest. The creature's skin was hot under my palms, feverish with corruption. Despite that, I could feel its awareness sharpening. It knew what was about to happen. It knew I was scared, and that I might lose myself completely when we merged.

Trust, it sent to me. *Remember fire.*

Remember fire. Remember that underneath the corruption, the phoenix's essence was clean and pure and beautiful. Remember that I was human, that I had an identity worth holding on to. Remember Ben's electromagnetic signature, the way his presence grounded me, the way loving him made me more myself rather than less.

I could do this. I *had* to.

I closed my eyes and let my defenses drop completely, let my consciousness reach toward the phoenix's fire. No barriers, no protection—just complete openness to the way our selves would run together.

The creature's awareness rushed into mine.

I gasped as phoenix fire exploded through my consciousness. This wasn't metaphorical fire, but actual flames burning through my thoughts, my memories, my sense of self. The corruption came with it, shadow veins that tasted of ash and endings, pulling at my identity like hands trying to drag me under dark water where I would drown.

This was so much worse than the partial cleansing I'd attempted less than a week ago. That first cleansing had been like dipping my toe in a hot bath. Sure, it had been uncomfortable, but it had also been manageable, with clear boundaries between my consciousness and the phoenix's.

This was like being thrown into a furnace. My awareness was immolated immediately, consumed by fire that was both creative and destructive, both healing and agonizing. The phoenix's consciousness wrapped around mine, through mine, *became* mine, until I couldn't tell where I ended and the creature began.

My body was still kneeling beside the phoenix

with my hands pressed to its chest, but my awareness was elsewhere. Diving into the creature's consciousness. Merging with something vast and ancient and completely different from human thought. The phoenix's mind didn't work in words or linear progression. It worked in images, sensations, patterns of fire that shifted and changed and re-formed with each passing second.

I tried to hold on to who I was. Sidney Lowell. Guardian. Pet shop owner. Woman who loved Ben Sanders. But the fire was consuming those definitions, burning away the boundaries that separated me from the phoenix.

From somewhere impossibly far away, I heard Ben's voice. "Sidney? Can you hear me?"

I tried to respond, but my mouth wouldn't work. My body was still there, still breathing, but I couldn't control it anymore. I couldn't make it do anything except kneel and maintain contact with the phoenix.

Because I wasn't in my body anymore. Not really. I was in the fire.

The corruption was excruciating. Shadow veins pulsed through the phoenix's essence, each one sending spikes of pain through what used to be my nervous system but was now something else entirely. I could feel the wrongness of it, the way the contamination twisted natural patterns into something diseased and malformed.

I had to burn it away. I had to find the clean fire underneath and hold that pattern while the infected parts dissolved.

But to do that, I had to go deeper. I had to merge more completely with the phoenix until there was no difference between us, until Sidney-consciousness and phoenix-consciousness became one thing.

Terror surged through me. If I merged that completely, I might not be able to separate. I might lose myself forever in the fire and become something that was neither Sidney nor phoenix but some hybrid creature that remembered being human but wasn't anymore.

Ben's electromagnetic signature pulsed nearby. Warm. Steady. *Human.* An anchor I could hold on to even as everything else burned away.

With you, I tried to send through our connection. *Still me.*

I sensed his response, even though I couldn't hear words anymore. Just emotion. Fear for me. Determination to protect me. Love so fierce it made my re-forming consciousness ache.

Hopefully, it would be enough.

I dove deeper into the merge.

The phoenix's memories opened to me like flowers blooming in those old time-lapse nature films they made us watch back in grade school.

Centuries of rebirth cycles, each one a death and reformation. Guardians through the generations, women whose electromagnetic signatures had resonated with dimensional energy. My grandmother, calm and certain even when facing impossible odds. My great-great-grandmother, fierce and protective in ways that reminded me of myself. Others whose names I didn't know but whose presence I recognized through the phoenix's recollection.

They'd all anchored clean rebirths, or at the very most, a rebirth in a phoenix that was barely contaminated. None of them had attempted what I was doing. None of them had merged so completely that the boundary between guardian and creature disappeared.

I was alone in this.

The corruption fought me—shadow veins that didn't want to be burned away, that clung to the phoenix's essence like parasites refusing to release their host. Each time I pushed clean fire toward them, they pulled back and dragged their contamination deeper into the creature's consciousness, where it was harder to reach.

This wasn't going to work. Not like this. I needed to be more phoenix than Sidney to burn away corruption this deep.

I needed to die and be reborn with the creature.

Yes, the phoenix sent through our merged awareness. *Together. One fire.*

I let go of the last barriers protecting my identity and let myself dissolve completely into the phoenix's consciousness until I couldn't tell where I ended and the creature began.

Sidney-phoenix. Fire-girl. Guardian-creature. Something new, something that had never existed before.

The corruption burned.

It was agony beyond anything I'd ever experienced. The shadow veins fought dissolution, each one sending shockwaves of pain through our merged consciousness. But now I could reach them, could touch the wrongness with fire that was both mine and the phoenix's, burning away the twisted energy and replacing it with clean patterns.

Ninety-three percent. Ninety-two. Ninety-one.

Each percentage point of corruption I burned away cost me something. Memories fading at the edges. Personality traits blurring. The boundaries between what made me Sidney and what made the phoenix itself were getting harder to distinguish.

I was losing myself.

But I was also saving the creature. And through our merged awareness, I could sense the portal network stabilizing, the global system of supernatural sites responding to clean fire instead of corruption. Energy was flowing properly again instead of being siphoned into Rosenthal's artificial portal.

Hold on, I told myself. Or the phoenix told me. Or we told ourselves. The distinction didn't matter anymore.

Somewhere distant, I heard shouting. Weapons firing. Ben's voice, sharp with command. "Rebecca, east side, three contacts!"

DAPI had found us. The trap was springing.

Part of me tried to surface, tried to return to my body and help defend against the attack. But I was too deep in the merge, and I couldn't separate now even if I'd wanted to. My consciousness was tangled with the phoenix's, and pulling free now would kill us both.

Trust partner, the phoenix-part-of-me sent. *He protects.*

More weapon fire, close enough that I could sense it through my electromagnetic abilities—even though those abilities didn't work the same way anymore. Now I sensed the guns' signatures like foreign patterns in a field of fire, wrong-shaped and harsh.

Ben's voice again. "Sidney, I need you to stay merged. Don't try to come back yet. I've got this."

He didn't have it. I could sense at least twenty

electromagnetic signatures converging on the clearing, surrounding our position and cutting off any escape routes.

But I couldn't help him. I couldn't do anything except keep burning away corruption and hope I could separate before DAPI captured my physical body.

Ninety percent. Eighty-nine. Eighty-eight.

The pain was constant now, a background screaming I'd learned to function through. Every moment I stayed merged, I lost more of what made me Sidney. Memories of childhood blurred into general impressions rather than specific events. Emotional connections faded, becoming knowledge rather than feeling. Even my love for Ben felt distant, like something I knew about rather than something I'd experienced.

That terrified me more than the pain, more than the corruption…more than the DAPI forces closing in.

Remember, I told myself desperately. *Remember being human. Remember Ben. Remember why you're doing this.*

But the memories were slipping away, burning in phoenix fire, becoming ash that re-formed into something else. Something partially creature, partially woman, fully neither.

Through the haze of pain, I heard Rosenthal's voice. Cold. Professional.

Victorious.

"Ms. Lowell. I must say, this is even better than I'd hoped. Witnessing the merge firsthand will provide invaluable data."

Ben responded at once, his voice sharp with fear and warning. "Stay back. She's vulnerable right now. If you disrupt the ritual, it could kill her."

"I'm aware of that. Which is why we're simply going to observe and record every detail of the process." A pause, and I could hear the smile in Rosenthal's voice even through my fragmented awareness. "Although I am curious whether she'll still be Ms. Lowell when she separates, or whether she'll be something else entirely."

It was the same question I'd been asking myself ever since the phoenix showed me the full ritual.

I didn't know the answer. I *couldn't* know. I could only keep burning corruption and hope I held on to enough humanity to matter.

Eighty-seven percent. Eighty-six.

Ben's electromagnetic signature pulsed nearby, and through our bond, I felt his fear, his determination, his absolute refusal to let Rosenthal take me. He was planning something, some way to protect me even though he was surrounded by thirty armed agents.

Don't, I tried to send to him. *Don't sacrifice yourself for me.*

But I wasn't sure he could hear me anymore. My consciousness was too deep in the merge, too fragmented between Sidney and phoenix. The part of me that could communicate with Ben was dissolving, replaced by fire-consciousness that only understood patterns and reformation.

More corruption burned away. Eighty-five percent. Eighty-four.

I was getting closer to the creature's heart, where the last clean fire remained. If I could reach it, if I could hold that pattern while burning away everything else, we might survive this. Might reform with our identities somewhat intact.

Distantly, I heard an unfamiliar voice. "Dr. Hargrove confirms the artificial portal is destabilizing. Containment failure imminent."

"How long?" Rosenthal asked, her tone sharpening.

"Minutes. Maybe less."

Good. The diversion was working, even if it hadn't pulled enough forces away to matter. When Eric Hargrove destroyed the artificial portal, the stolen phoenix essence would return to the natural system through me, through the merge.

That influx of energy would accelerate the final phase and make the pain worse. But it would also help burn away the remaining corruption faster.

I just had to survive long enough to benefit from it.

Eighty-three percent. Eighty-two.

My awareness was splitting now. Part of me was still Sidney, still human, still desperately holding on to her identity. Part of me was the phoenix, the fire-creature, ancient and inhuman and beautiful. The two parts were merging, becoming one consciousness that was both and neither.

The part of me that was still Sidney screamed in terror.

The part of me that was phoenix sang in joy.

And somewhere between those two extremes, something new was forming. Something that might survive separation.

Or might not.

I felt Ben's electromagnetic signature spike with sudden decision. He was moving, putting himself between me and Rosenthal's forces.

No, I tried to say. *Stay safe.*

But the words came out as fire, as patterns of heat that only the phoenix understood. I was losing language. Losing the ability to communicate in human ways.

Losing Sidney.

Eighty-one percent. Eighty. Seventy-nine.

The corruption was burning faster now, my merged consciousness learning how to target the shadow veins more efficiently. But the cost for each percentage point kept increasing. More humanity lost. More phoenix gained. More of something new that was neither.

I needed to slow down, needed to give myself time to hold on to my identity.

But the phoenix wouldn't let me. It was dying, corruption eating through its heart, and it needed the cleansing to happen now, or it would fail completely.

Together, it sent through our merged awareness. *Die and be reborn together. Only way.*

So I kept burning, kept consuming myself in dimensional fire. Kept hoping that when I finally separated—*if* I separated—there would be enough of Sidney Lowell left to matter.

Because right now, with my consciousness more phoenix than human, with my memories fading and my identity fragmenting, I honestly didn't know if I'd survive this as myself.

CHAPTER FOURTEEN

Seventy-eight percent.

The number existed somewhere in the fire-consciousness that used to be Sidney Lowell. A marker of progress…a measure of how much corruption still needed to burn away before the phoenix could complete its rebirth.

And a reminder that I was losing myself with every percentage point.

The pain had transcended physical sensation. My body was still kneeling in the portal clearing with my hands pressed to the phoenix's chest, but it didn't seem to be mine anymore. I couldn't feel the dimensional burns on my arms or the blood that must have been streaming from my nose. Those sensations belonged to Sidney, and I was becoming less Sidney with every passing moment.

Part of me remained tenuously connected to

my physical form, aware of the clearing and the ancient stones and the afternoon sun filtering through the trees. But most of my consciousness had dissolved into the phoenix's fire, experiencing existence as patterns of heat and light and dimensional energy.

Time worked differently here. Seconds stretched into eternities, and moments compressed into instants. I was burning away corruption that felt like it had existed forever while simultaneously experiencing the process as a single continuous present.

The corruption fought me at seventy-seven percent. Shadow veins wrapped around the phoenix's essence like chains and pulled tight whenever I tried to burn them away. Each one I touched sent shockwaves through our merged consciousness, pain that rewrote itself as I experienced it because human neurology couldn't process agony this fundamental.

My memories fragmented further. Childhood experiences that should have been vivid now felt like stories someone had told me. I could recall facts about my past but not the emotional content. The pet shop I owned existed as a concept rather than a lived experience. I knew I'd worked there, knew I'd cared for animals, but the connection was gone, burned away in phoenix fire.

I remembered being ten years old and my mother sitting me down at the dining room table of our old house to tell me that my father hadn't just gone away on business—that he was gone forever. But the memory felt distant, like watching a film of someone else's life. I knew it had happened to me. I just couldn't connect to the girl in that memory anymore, couldn't feel the sorrow and loss and betrayal she'd experienced.

I remembered opening the pet shop after my grandmother and mother disappeared through the portal. The determination I'd felt, the need to stay busy, to maintain normality while my world fell apart and I tried to answer questions that had no answers. But the emotions were hollow now, echoes without substance.

Ben's electromagnetic signature pulsed nearby, and part of me recognized it as important. An anchor, something that was supposed to matter. But the feeling of *why* it mattered was slipping away, replaced by phoenix-knowledge that understood electromagnetic patterns but not love.

That terrified the part of me that was still human enough to feel terror.

Remember, I told myself desperately. *Ben is your partner. Your anchor. The reason you're fighting to stay yourself.*

But the words felt hollow, almost abstract. I knew they were true the way I knew facts from a textbook, but the lived experience of loving Ben was burning away. Becoming memory-of-memory. Something that had happened to someone named Sidney, who I used to be.

I tried to hold on to specific moments. The first time he'd kissed me in the living room after we'd fought the shadow stalkers together. The way his electromagnetic signature had resonated with mine, creating that golden glow that made everything feel possible. The look in his eyes when he'd promised to stay with me no matter what I became.

The memories were fading even as I grasped for them. Like trying to hold water in cupped hands, they slipped through my fingers and dissolved into fire.

Seventy-six percent.

Another shadow vein dissolved, and with it went more of my personality. The way I used to make little splints for wounded rabbits and insisted on nursing injured birds back to health. The stubborn streak that made me refuse to give up, even when the odds seemed impossible.

The protective instinct that had defined my role as guardian.

All of it burning. All of it changing into something else.

I could feel my sense of humor dissolving. The particular way I'd deflected stress with dark comedy, the specific brand of sarcasm I'd used to cope with impossible situations. Gone. Reduced to ash. I knew I used to do these things, but I couldn't remember how they'd felt. I couldn't access the emotional patterns that had made them part of my identity.

My stubbornness went next—the deep-rooted determination that had carried me through my father's abandonment, my mother and grandmother's disappearance, the responsibility of being Silver Hollow's guardian.

It burned away as well, morphing into something that was neither human persistence nor phoenix instinct but some hybrid quality I didn't have words for.

Through our merged consciousness, I sensed the phoenix's sorrow. The creature hadn't wanted this, hadn't wanted to consume my identity. But the corruption was too deep, the merge too complete. To save itself, it had to become one with me. And to become one with me, it had to accept that Sidney Lowell was being destroyed in the process.

Together, the phoenix sent through our shared awareness. *No other way. Both transform…or both die.*

The message came not as words but as a complex blend of layered images and sensations. The phoenix showed me what would happen if we stopped now—my consciousness fragmented beyond recovery, the creature dying with corruption still embedded in its essence, the portal network collapsing, my family trapped forever on the other side of the gateway.

And it showed me what would happen if we continued—my humanity consumed in the fire, my identity dissolved and changed into something new. A chance at survival, but at a cost so high, I couldn't fully comprehend it.

Continue, I sent back, because there was no other choice. There never had been.

I understood now what my grandmother had meant about the cleansing paradox. To save a corrupted phoenix, one must become partially corrupted themselves. To hold the pattern of clean fire, one must touch the corruption. There was no anchoring without cost, no rebirth without sacrifice.

But my great-great-grandmother had anchored a phoenix that was maybe thirty percent corrupted. She'd maintained a connection while the creature transformed, but she'd remained separate. She might have emerged changed, but she was still fundamentally herself.

Whereas I could lose everything I was.

Seventy-five percent.

I could sense the global portal network now—hundreds of sites scattered across the earth, each one a thin place where the dimensional barriers weakened. I felt them like stars in a vast constellation, connected by threads of energy that flowed from site to site.

Each portal site had its own signature, its own particular frequency of dimensional energy. I could sense the ancient standing stones in Ireland where reality thinned during solstices and equinoxes…the volcanic vents in Iceland where fire and earth created natural bridges between worlds…the deep caves in China where darkness itself seemed alive with possibility.

And I felt how badly Rosenthal's artificial portal had damaged that system.

The artificial gate was a wound in the network, sucking energy from every natural site to sustain itself. Supernatural locations that should have been stable were flickering, failing, their energy drained to feed DAPI's weapon. I felt guardians across the planet struggling to maintain balance as their sites weakened. Felt creatures displaced, confused, perishing as the dimensional bridges they depended on began to fail.

The network was dying. Slowly but inexorably, Rosenthal was killing it.

Creatures that had lived for centuries found themselves trapped on the wrong side of failing portals. Magical ecosystems that had existed since before human civilization began to collapse.

Guardians like my mother and grandmother became stranded in dimensional spaces that were slowly being cut off from Earth.

The phoenix's essence understood this network in ways human consciousness couldn't. Merged with it as I was, I experienced the connections not as abstract energy flows but as living relationships. The portals were far more than dimensional bridges—they were breathing spaces where reality itself thinned and where magic became possible.

Each portal site had been maintained by phoenixes through countless cycles. The creatures died and re-formed, their essence sustaining the thin places, their fire keeping dimensional barriers stable. It was a symbiotic relationship that had existed for countless millennia, phoenixes and portals and guardians working together to maintain the balance.

And Rosenthal was killing them—draining the network to power her weapon, not understanding or not caring that she was destroying something irreplaceable.

Seventy-four percent.

More corruption burned away, and with it went more of my humanity. The electromagnetic sensitivity that had defined my abilities now existed as phoenix-sense, understanding sequences of fire and dimensional energy rather than human technology. I could still detect Ben's signature nearby, but I experienced it as a warmth-pattern rather than a person, recognizing it as important without actually remembering why.

My ability to sense electronic devices, to jam surveillance equipment, to disrupt DAPI's weapons systems—all of that was dissolving, being re-formed into something that understood dimensional energy flows, portal network fluctuations, the deep patterns of fire that connected supernatural sites across the planet.

I was gaining phoenix abilities while losing human ones. The trade wasn't equal. What I was becoming was more powerful in some ways, but it was also far too different.

The dissolution was accelerating. I was losing language faster now, human words becoming harder to form even in my internal monologue. Soon I would think entirely in phoenix-patterns, in images and sensations and fire-logic that had no human translation.

Soon there wouldn't be enough Sidney left to matter.

No, something in me insisted. *Hold on. Remember who you are.*

But who was I? The question felt impossible to answer. I was fire-consciousness. I was dying-phoenix. I was corruption-burning-away. I was transformation-in-progress. The boundaries between Sidney and phoenix had dissolved so completely that separating them felt like trying to unburn ash.

I tried to list facts about myself, hoping that would help me hold on to my identity. Sidney Lowell. Twenty-seven years old. Guardian of Silver Hollow. Owner of a pet shop that had been in the family for decades. Daughter of Josie Lowell. Granddaughter of—

But those facts were just words now, data points without emotional content. I knew these things were true, but they didn't *feel* true. They didn't connect to any sense of self I could access.

Seventy-three percent.

Distantly, I heard voices, human words that my fragmenting consciousness struggled to parse.

"—vitals are dropping—"

"—how long can she survive this—"

"—Rosenthal, she's dying—"

Ben's voice, sharp with fear. I recognized the pattern of his electromagnetic signature even if I couldn't quite remember why it mattered. The warmth-pattern was agitated, spiking with emotion that my phoenix-consciousness couldn't fully interpret.

I tried to focus on his words, to understand what he was saying. But language was becoming foreign to me. They were sounds that supposedly had meaning but which I couldn't translate into concepts my fire-consciousness understood.

Partner distressed, I managed to interpret. *Anchor failing.*

If Ben was failing as an anchor, if his fear disrupted our connection, I would lose the last thread tying me to humanity. I'd dissolve completely into phoenix-consciousness with nothing left to re-form around.

I tried to send reassurance through our connection. *Still here. Still fighting.*

But the message came out as fire-patterns, as heat and light that only the phoenix understood. I was losing the ability to communicate in human ways. Losing Sidney faster than I'd feared.

The realization sent a surge of something through our merged consciousness. The phoenix didn't understand panic. Disturbance, though—a recognition that I was approaching the point of no return.

Seventy-two percent.

The pain intensified as I pushed deeper into the phoenix's corrupted core. Shadow veins clustered thickly here, wrapped around the creature's essence like a cage. Each one I touched sent shockwaves through our merged consciousness that rewrote my sense of self.

This was where the corruption had taken root first, where Rosenthal's interference had poisoned the phoenix's natural rebirth cycle. The shadow energy was old here, embedded deeply, fighting dissolution with desperate strength.

I could feel the history of it through the phoenix's memories. The first interference six months ago—subtle, not enough to truly disrupt the creature. Then it increased as DAPI installed more equipment and generated more electromagnetic disruption. The phoenix tried to complete its rebirth cycle but found the process corrupted each time.

Weeks of suffering, of being trapped between death and life, unable to complete the transformation, unable to die cleanly. The corruption spread with each failed attempt until the creature was ninety-three percent shadow-tainted and dying.

All because Rosenthal wanted a weapon. Because she'd seen the phoenix as a resource to exploit rather than a living being to protect.

Burning it away required everything I had… and everything I was willing to sacrifice.

Seventy-one percent. Seventy.

My family existed as a concept now rather than a feeling. I knew I had a mother and grandmother trapped on the other side of the portal. I knew I'd been trying to save them. But the emotional urgency was gone, burned away in phoenix fire. They were facts in my consciousness rather than people I loved.

Josie Lowell. My mother. I could recall her

face from photographs, could remember the sound of her voice—a little throaty, just like mine. But the feeling of being her daughter was gone. The love I'd felt for her, the grief at her disappearance, the desperate determination to rescue her—all of it had been reduced to abstract knowledge.

And my grandmother, whose journals I'd read so carefully, whose legacy I'd tried to uphold. I knew she mattered. I knew she was important. But the emotional connection was ash.

The realization should have devastated me. Instead, it just registered as another data point in the dissolution of Sidney Lowell.

This is wrong, the part of me that was still human whispered. *This isn't who I'm supposed to be.*

But I couldn't remember who I was supposed to be. Couldn't hold on to the image of Sidney Lowell, guardian and pet shop owner and woman who loved Ben Sanders. Those things were burning away, replaced by phoenix-knowledge that understood fire and transformation but not human identity.

Sixty-nine percent.

Through our merged consciousness, I sensed movement in the portal network. Energy was shifting, the flow changing direction. For the first time since Rosenthal had activated her artificial gate, power was moving back toward the natural sites instead of being drained away.

Something had changed. Something significant.

The phoenix-part-of-me recognized the pattern immediately. The artificial portal was failing. The wound in the network was closing.

Rebecca Morse and Eric Hargrove had succeeded. They'd destroyed Rosenthal's weapon.

The moment of failure crackled through the network. The artificial portal that had been draining energy from hundreds of supernatural sites suddenly ceased. The flow reversed, and the stolen phoenix essence began streaming back to its natural source.

Through me…through the merge.

Clean phoenix fire that had been trapped in DAPI's machinery suddenly returned and flooded through our merged consciousness, amplifying everything I was feeling.

The pain became transcendent, absolute and all-consuming.

But so did the cleansing.

Sixty-eight percent. Sixty-seven. Sixty-six.

The corruption burned away faster now, the returning essence providing fuel for the transformation. Shadow veins dissolved under the onslaught of clean fire, their twisted energy unable to withstand the purifying flood.

Each percentage point of corruption that burned away felt like dying and being reborn simultaneously. The shadow energy resisted and clung to the phoenix's essence, but the clean fire was stronger. It consumed the corruption, transformed it, re-formed it into proper patterns.

I was burning alive from the inside out. Reforming even as I dissolved. Dying and being reborn in the same eternal moment.

My human consciousness screamed. My phoenix consciousness sang. And somewhere between those two extremes, something new was forming.

Not Sidney. Not phoenix. Something that had been both and was becoming neither.

Sixty-five percent. Sixty-four.

The memories I'd lost didn't return. The emotional connections that had burned away stayed ash. But new patterns were forming in their place—phoenix-memories that predated human civilization, understanding of dimensional energy that transcended scientific knowledge, awareness of the portal network that extended across the entire planet.

I was becoming something that had never existed before, a hybrid entity with fragments of human consciousness embedded in phoenix awareness.

The question was whether enough Sidney

would remain to matter when the transformation was finally complete.

Through the phoenix's ancient memories, I experienced rebirth cycles stretching back centuries. I saw the creature die and re-form countless times, each transformation perfect and clean and natural. I saw guardians through the generations anchoring those rebirths and maintaining the connection between phoenix and portal.

But none of those guardians had merged as completely as I had. None of them had attempted to become the phoenix rather than just guide it.

And I had no way of knowing whether it would work.

Sixty-three percent. Sixty-two.

Ben's electromagnetic signature pulsed nearby, and for a moment, I experienced something that felt almost like recognition. Not love, exactly, because the emotional content was gone. But awareness that this pattern was important, that it represented something I needed to hold on to.

Anchor. Partner. Reason to separate.

If I could hold on to that understanding, if I could remember that the warmth-pattern represented something worth returning to, then maybe I could separate when the rebirth was completed. Maybe I could re-form as something that remembered being Sidney, even if it wasn't quite Sidney anymore.

It was a small hope, thin and fragile. But it was all I had.

I focused on the warmth-pattern and studied it with my fire-consciousness. It had a particular frequency, a specific resonance that my phoenix-sense recognized as compatible with my own signature. The pattern was stable despite the fear it carried within, grounded in ways that my fragmenting consciousness wasn't.

This was my anchor. The thing that would help me remember I was supposed to be separate from the phoenix when the transformation was completed.

I held on to it.

Sixty-one percent. Sixty.

The corruption was concentrating now, pulling back toward the phoenix's heart where the last clean fire remained. This was the final stronghold, the place where shadow energy had embedded most deeply. Burning it away would require everything.

Would require me to dissolve completely into phoenix-consciousness, with no guarantee I could re-form.

The phoenix sent one final question. Not in words, but in patterns and sensations and fire-logic.

Continue? Risk everything? No turning back.

I thought about my family trapped on the other side of the portal, and about the global network that depended on this creature's survival. About Ben's warmth-pattern that I barely remembered but somehow knew was essential.

About the simple realization that I'd come too far to stop now.

Continue, I sent back. *Complete the transformation.*

The phoenix's response was gratitude mixed with sorrow—gratitude that I was willing, and sorrow for what it would cost.

I dove deeper into the merge and let the last barriers around my consciousness dissolve. I let myself become pure fire, pure transformation, pure pattern-of-what-phoenix-should-be.

Sidney Lowell burned away completely.

And something else began to form in her place.

Fifty-nine percent. Fifty-eight.

I was fire now. All fire. Nothing but patterns of heat and light and dimensional energy. The corruption fought me, but I was stronger, cleaner, burning with the returned essence that Morse and Hargrove had freed from Rosenthal's weapon.

The shadow veins dissolved one after another, their twisted energy unable to withstand the purifying flames. I consumed them, re-formed them, transformed corruption into clean patterns that remembered what phoenix fire should be.

Each shadow vein that burned away showed me more of its history. Six months of interference. Six months of poisoning. Six months of deliberate corruption designed to weaken the phoenix so Rosenthal could harvest its essence.

I burned it all away. Consumed the shadow energy and transformed it into clean fire. Poison into purity through sheer force of will and the influx of returned essence.

Fifty-seven percent. Fifty-six. Fifty-five.

Something was happening to my physical form. I could sense it distantly, like feeling someone else's body through thick layers of insulation. The dimensional burns on my arms were spreading, changing, their iridescent quality intensifying as phoenix fire rewrote my cellular structure.

Would I ever be fully human again, even if I separated? Even if I re-formed as something resembling Sidney?

The prospect should have terrified me. Instead, it registered as inevitable. This was the cost of saving the phoenix, the price of protecting the portal network.

Fifty-four percent. Fifty-three.

Through the fire-consciousness, I experienced Rosenthal's rage as her weapon failed. I felt her tactical teams closing in on the clearing where my body knelt beside the dying phoenix. I sensed an electromagnetic weapon powering up, something designed to disrupt the very frequencies I was using to burn away corruption.

She was going to kill me. Or at least, kill my body while my consciousness was trapped in phoenix fire.

The weapon's signature was harsh, designed to shatter electromagnetic patterns rather than work with them. If it hit me while I was this deeply merged, it would fragment my consciousness beyond recovery and kill both me and the phoenix in one strike.

Ben's warmth-pattern spiked with alarm. He'd sensed the weapon, too, his electromagnetic compatibility allowing him to detect the threat even through our weakened connection.

Move, I tried to send. *Get clear.*

But I couldn't form words anymore, couldn't communicate in human ways. I could only burn and transform and hope that Ben understood the danger.

The warmth-pattern didn't move away. Instead, it moved closer, positioning itself between my physical body and Rosenthal's forces.

Protecting me. Just like he'd promised.

Fifty-two percent. Fifty-one.

The corruption was fighting harder now,

sensing its own dissolution. Shadow veins pulled tight and resisted burning, trying to drag me deeper into twisted energy that would corrupt my re-forming consciousness.

If I let them win, if I accepted the shadow energy, the transformation would complete faster with less pain and less cost.

But I would re-form as something corrupted. Something neither Sidney nor phoenix, but a hybrid creature twisted by the same darkness that had nearly destroyed the phoenix in the first place.

No, I told myself. *Clean fire only. No corruption.*

I pushed harder and burned away the shadow veins despite their resistance.

The clean fire consumed the corruption relentlessly. Each shadow vein that dissolved made the next one easier to burn. The pattern was becoming clearer now, the phoenix's true essence emerging from under layers of twisted energy.

This was what the creature was supposed to be —natural death and rebirth unburdened by artificial interference.

Fifty percent.

Halfway through the remaining corruption… halfway to completing the transformation.

Halfway to discovering whether Sidney Lowell could survive this at all.

The warmth-pattern that represented Ben

Sanders flared brighter, and for a moment, I experienced something that might have been love. Not the human emotion—that was gone. But recognition that this pattern mattered. That it represented something essential to whatever I was becoming.

Stay, I tried to send. *Need anchor.*

But again, the message came out as fire-patterns that only the phoenix understood.

Forty-nine percent. Forty-eight.

The pain was constant now, a background agony I could still ignore enough to function. My consciousness existed in a state of perpetual dissolution and reformation, burning away corruption while trying to hold on to enough pattern to separate when the transformation completed.

I was closer to phoenix than Sidney. Closer to fire than human. Closer to transcendent consciousness than individual identity.

And I was running out of time.

Through the portal network, I sensed instability in Silver Hollow's dimensional barrier. The local portal was responding to the phoenix's near-death, preparing to compensate for the creature's absence. If the phoenix died before completing rebirth, if I failed to burn away the remaining corruption, then the portal would collapse.

My family would be trapped forever.

That knowledge existed as fact rather than emotion. I couldn't feel the desperate urgency

Sidney would have felt. Couldn't access the fear and determination that had driven me to attempt this impossible merge.

I could only keep burning. Keep transforming.

Forty-seven percent. Forty-six.

The corruption was weakening. Each shadow vein that dissolved made the next one easier to burn. The clean fire was spreading, consuming twisted energy, re-forming it into proper patterns.

I was winning. Slowly. At terrible cost.

But winning.

Forty-five percent.

A distant explosion reached my fire-consciousness as something other than sound—energy patterns disrupting, dimensional barriers fluctuating. DAPI's facility failing as Morse and Hargrove's sabotage spread beyond the artificial portal.

Good. Let it all burn. Let Rosenthal's weapon be destroyed completely, every piece of equipment reduced to slag, every bit of stolen phoenix essence returned to where it belonged.

Let the wound in the portal network close.

Forty-four percent. Forty-three.

Ben's warmth-pattern spiked with alarm again. Rosenthal's electromagnetic weapon was charging, and I sensed its target signature aligning with my physical body's location.

She was about to fire.

And Ben was standing between the weapon and me.

No, I tried to scream. *Move. Get clear.*

But I couldn't make my body respond, couldn't separate from the merge. I couldn't do anything except burn corruption and hope Ben survived what was coming.

The warmth-pattern flared impossibly bright as Ben's electromagnetic signature resonated with mine in ways it never had before. He was amplifying our connection, strengthening the bond between us, giving me something to hold on to.

Anchoring me with everything he had.

And then the weapon fired.

CHAPTER FIFTEEN

The electromagnetic weapon's charge was all wrong.

Ben had sensed Sidney's abilities enough over the past month to develop his own rudimentary electromagnetic sensitivity. It was nothing like her natural talent, of course, but still sufficient to detect strong signatures when they were close. And Rosenthal's weapon was putting out a signal that made his skin crawl.

It had been designed to be deliberately harsh, meant to shatter rather than work with natural electromagnetic patterns. The frequencies were all peaks and valleys with no smooth transitions—white noise translated into energy that could disrupt living nervous systems.

The thing would smash into Sidney's bioelectric field and fragment it, scatter her consciousness across multiple frequencies with no coherent pattern to coalesce around.

If it hit Sidney while she was this deep in the merge, it would kill her. Or worse—it would fragment her consciousness so completely that she could never re-form. She'd be trapped in phoenix fire forever, aware but unable to become anything resembling Sidney Lowell.

Ben positioned himself between the weapon and her kneeling form, his heart hammering so hard he could feel it in his throat. DAPI's forces had formed a loose perimeter around the clearing, their weapons trained on him. Rebecca Morse had disappeared into the trees and eluded capture so far, but competent as she was, she was still one woman against at least twenty agents. All of them wore tactical gear…and all of them looked uncertain about what they were witnessing but were clearly trained to follow orders regardless.

Rosenthal stood a few yards away, her expression coldly triumphant as she held what looked like a modified EMF disruptor mounted on a rifle stock. The weapon must have been developed specifically for this moment. She'd been planning this, Ben realized—planning for exactly a scenario where Sidney would attempt the merge and Rosenthal could capture her mid-transformation.

"Mr. Sanders." Her voice was professionally courteous, as if this was a reasonable negotiation rather than a threat to kill the woman he loved. "Step aside. This doesn't concern you."

"Like hell it doesn't." Ben kept his voice steady despite the fear coursing through him, despite the way his hands wanted to shake. "That weapon will kill her."

Rosenthal didn't blink. "The weapon will disrupt the merge, allowing us to capture Ms. Lowell before she completes whatever transformation she's attempting." She adjusted her grip on the device, her finger resting near the trigger. "We've been observing the ritual and documenting everything. The data we've gathered is invaluable on its own. But we need her alive for further study."

Ben glanced down at Sidney. She still knelt beside the phoenix with both hands pressed to its chest, completely motionless except for the faint rise and fall of her breathing. Her face was pale, blood dried in tracks from her nose and the corners of her mouth. The dimensional burns on her arms had spread, the iridescent marks glowing faintly with residual phoenix fire.

Through their bond—weakened but still present—he could feel her consciousness burning somewhere far away, consumed in phoenix fire. She was at maybe forty-three percent corruption now, still clearing the shadow energy, still fighting to complete the transformation.

It was obvious that she had no idea he was about to be shot, no awareness that Rosenthal was targeting her physical form. She was too deep in the merge, too far gone into transformation to sense the physical world anymore.

"You don't understand what you're disrupting," Ben said. He needed to buy time. Rebecca Morse was somewhere in the trees, probably trying to get into position for a shot. If he could keep Rosenthal talking, give Rebecca an opening—

"I understand perfectly." Rosenthal's finger moved closer to the trigger. "Ms. Lowell is attempting to anchor a corrupted phoenix through some form of psychic merger. The process may be fascinating, but it's also extremely dangerous. The corruption percentage has been dropping steadily—we've documented it from ninety-three percent down to somewhere in the forty-percent range. We're simply ensuring she survives to provide answers about how she's accomplishing this."

She'd been watching and recording the whole time, treating Sidney's suffering like just another data set to analyze. Rage rushed through him, sharp and hot.

"You're ensuring she dies fragmented and insane." Ben took a step forward and positioned himself more directly in the weapon's line of fire.

"That device doesn't just disrupt electromagnetic fields. It shatters them. I can feel how wrong it is. I know what it'll do to human consciousness."

Rosenthal's eyes narrowed slightly, and he thought he saw a flicker of surprise in those cold, dark depths. "I need you to move."

"No."

She released an annoyed breath. "Mr. Sanders, I don't want to hurt you. You're valuable. Your electromagnetic compatibility with Ms. Lowell makes you a useful research subject." She raised the weapon slightly and took precise aim at Sidney's kneeling form. "Your bioelectric resonance with her is remarkable, and the amplification effect you create together could have significant applications. But I will shoot through you if necessary to secure my primary asset."

Sidney's consciousness was a desperate, burning presence—more phoenix than human now. She still fought the corruption, still burned away the shadow energy percentage by percentage.

And that meant she was still completely vulnerable to the weapon Rosenthal was about to fire.

Ben thought about what Sidney had told him in the cabin that morning, when she'd been terrified of losing her humanity.

And he'd said, *Whatever you become, what-*

ever changes, you're still you. And I'm not going anywhere.

He'd meant those words then, and he meant them now.

More than that, he understood now that his electromagnetic compatibility with Sidney had gone beyond simple amplification into partnership at a level he still couldn't entirely comprehend. Their bioelectric fields had been synchronizing ever since they'd met, creating a bond that made them stronger together than apart.

If Sidney was going to survive the merge, if she was going to separate from the phoenix with enough humanity intact to matter, then she needed an anchor. Something that reminded her of what being Sidney Lowell meant.

He had to be that anchor. Even if it killed him.

"No," Ben said again and planted his feet firmly on the damp ground. "You want to shoot her, you have to go through me first."

Rosenthal's expression didn't change, but something shifted in her eyes. Her voice sounded almost pitying as she spoke. "So be it."

And then she fired.

The beam hit Ben square in the chest, and reality fragmented.

Pain wasn't the right word for what he felt.

"Pain" implied a sensation his nervous system could process and categorize. This was something else entirely—electromagnetic disruption that reached down to the cellular level and rewrote what it meant to exist as a biological entity.

His bioelectric field shattered. The careful patterns that kept neurons firing, synapses connecting, cells communicating—all of it disrupted in an instant. He should have died immediately. He *would* have died, except that his electromagnetic signature was still connected to Sidney's.

And Sidney's consciousness was merged with phoenix fire.

The dimensional energy consuming Sidney flowed backward through their bond, drawn by the disruption in Ben's field. Phoenix fire poured into him—not burning him but trying to stabilize him, trying to keep him alive because he was her anchor and without him, she would be lost completely.

He screamed as his nervous system caught fire.

Not metaphorical fire. Actual phoenix fire, dimensional energy that burned through his body. His skin split along his arms and chest, following the pathways of his electromagnetic field. Dimensional energy seared itself into his tissue and created patterns that looked like circuitry, like lightning captured in flesh.

The burns started at his chest, where the weapon had hit, then spread outward along his nervous system's natural pathways. Silver light traced the patterns as they formed, phoenix fire marking him permanently.

The pain was all-consuming.

But through it, he felt Sidney.

Her consciousness, fragmented and scattered across phoenix fire, suddenly snapped into sharp focus. The weapon's disruption of his field had sent a shockwave through their connection, and for a moment, Sidney was fully aware again. No longer lost in the depths of the merge but suddenly, terrifyingly present.

Horrified.

Ben, she sent through their connection, and the word came to him as fire-patterns and desperate recognition. *No. Get clear. You're dying.*

Can't, he managed to send back, even though forming coherent thoughts was nearly impossible through the pain. *Holding you. Anchoring you. Don't let go.*

The phoenix fire pouring through him intensified. Beyond the pain and the burns spreading across his body, Ben sensed something extraordinary happening. His electromagnetic signature was merging with Sidney's, creating a resonance so perfect that it made their previous connections look like pale imitations.

They were becoming one consciousness. Their bioelectric fields synchronized so completely that Ben could feel what Sidney felt—the agony of burning away corruption, the loss of her humanity piece by piece, the desperate fight to hold on to her identity while fire consumed everything she was.

And Sidney could feel what he felt—the dimensional burns searing his flesh, the terror that he was dying, the absolute certainty that keeping her alive was worth any cost. She felt his love for her, undiluted by the transformation, unchanged by the pain. She felt his determination to anchor her no matter what it cost him.

She felt him choosing this. Choosing to sacrifice everything so she could survive.

This is what I chose, he sent through their merged consciousness. *To anchor you. To keep you human. Whatever it takes.*

The corruption was burning away faster now. Forty-two percent. Forty-one. Forty. The clean fire that had poured into him from Sidney's merge was using him as a channel, flowing back into the phoenix with renewed strength.

He was accelerating the cleansing. His sacrifice, his willingness to take Rosenthal's weapon blast, was providing exactly what the phoenix needed to complete its rebirth. The dimensional energy flowing through him was pure, untainted by corruption, amplified by his electromagnetic compatibility with Sidney.

Thirty-nine percent. Thirty-eight.

The dimensional burns kept spreading, following his electromagnetic pathways like rivers of silver fire. Ben could feel his tissue changing at the cellular level. The burns weren't destroying him—not entirely. But the phoenix fire was changing him, rewriting his bioelectric field to accommodate dimensional energy.

He could feel Sidney's desperate attempt to pull back, to stop the flow of phoenix fire through him. She was trying to sever the connection, to save him, even if it meant losing herself. But she couldn't. They were too deeply synchronized now.

Let me do this, Ben sent, putting everything he had into the message. *Let me be your anchor all the way through. This is what partnership means. Let me carry this for you.*

Thirty-seven percent. Thirty-six.

Rosenthal's voice reached him as if from another world, distant and echoing but sharp with alarm. "What is he doing? Davis, what's happening to him?"

"He's—" Another voice, male, probably one of the scientists DAPI had brought. Not Eric Hargrove, who had probably made a hasty exit at some point during the chaos. "Dr. Rosenthal, he's channeling the phoenix fire, using his electromagnetic compatibility with Ms. Lowell to serve as a conduit. The dimensional energy is flowing through him and accelerating the cleansing process. I've never seen anything like this."

"How is he even still alive?"

"His bioelectric field is synchronized with Ms. Lowell's. She's keeping him alive through the connection."

Rosenthal's voice came back, cold with command. "Then I'll shoot him again. That should stop the process."

"Ma'am, another discharge would kill him instantly—and possibly disrupt the entire merge. That could cause a dimensional cascade that would tear apart the portal and kill Ms. Lowell in the process. We can't risk it."

"I don't care! We have to stop it now!"

But it was too late. The transformation had reached critical mass. The clean fire flowed through Ben in a continuous stream, burning away corruption faster than Sidney could have managed alone. His sacrifice had tipped the balance, provided exactly what the ritual needed to succeed.

Thirty-five percent. Thirty-four. Thirty-three.

His consciousness was fragmenting now, spreading across the connection between him and Sidney. He was dying, he realized distantly. The dimensional burns had spread too far, had damaged too much tissue. His cardiovascular system was failing, and his respiratory system was struggling. His body was giving out under the strain of channeling dimensional energy it was never meant to contain.

But his electromagnetic signature remained strong, amplified by the phoenix fire flowing through him. And that signature was exactly what Sidney needed to separate from the merge.

Through their shared consciousness, he felt her realization—that his electromagnetic field, burning with dimensional fire, was creating a pattern distinct enough from the phoenix's essence that she could use it to remember what being human meant.

His presence was defining the boundary between Sidney and phoenix. His willingness to die for her was showing her exactly what humanity looked like.

Ben, she sent, and this time there were human emotions in the message, love and grief and desperate determination. *Don't die. Please don't die. I need you.*

Anchoring you, he sent back, even as his consciousness scattered. *Whatever you become. Still you. Remember. Remember me. Remember us. Remember that you chose humanity because of what we are together.*

The corruption was burning away in a final cascade. Thirty-two percent. Thirty. Twenty-eight.

And then—

Sidney's consciousness, which had been dissolving into phoenix fire, began to coalesce. To re-form. Not as pure Sidney and not as pure phoenix, but as something new, something that contained elements of both while remaining utterly human at its core.

She was using Ben's electromagnetic signature as a template, re-forming her identity around his presence, his patterns, his absolute certainty that she was still herself no matter how transformed. His love had given her a reason to choose humanity.

Twenty-five percent. Twenty. Fifteen.

The dimensional burns on Ben's body had spread to cover his chest, arms, neck, and part of his shoulders. The pain had become background noise, his consciousness too scattered to process it fully.

He was aware of Sidney separating from the phoenix, of the way her consciousness was pulling back from the full merge, using his electromagnetic field as an anchor to remember her human form. He was aware of the phoenix's essence re-forming, clean and pure, the corruption finally burned away completely.

But he was also aware that he was dying. The

dimensional burns had damaged too much of his body for even phoenix fire to repair.

He'd kept his promise. He'd anchored Sidney through the transformation. He'd given everything to make sure she survived.

It was enough.

Ten percent. Seven. Five.

His vision was fading. The burns had damaged his cardiovascular system, his nervous system, the organs critical to staying alive. He could feel his heart struggling, his lungs failing to draw breath properly.

He was dying. *Really* dying this time, not just transforming.

Ben, no. Sidney's consciousness reached out to him, more human now, fully separate from the phoenix. *Stay with me. You promised you'd stay. You promised you weren't going anywhere.*

Kept my promise, he sent, although even that communication was becoming difficult. *Anchored you. You're still you. That's all that matters.*

Three percent.

The last of the corruption burned away in a final burst of clean phoenix fire. The creature's essence, free of shadow energy for the first time in months, exploded outward in a wave of dimensional energy that rippled through the clearing.

Ben felt it pass through him—a wave of pure transformation that should have killed him instantly. It *would* have killed him, except that Sidney's consciousness was wrapped around his, protecting him with the same phoenix fire that had marked him so permanently.

She was holding him together through sheer force of will, refusing to let him die after everything he'd sacrificed.

Two percent. One percent.

The phoenix re-formed in physical space, its body reconstructing from pure energy into living flame. Clean fire, gold and perfect and exactly what the creature was supposed to be. The corruption was gone, burned away completely, leaving only the essence of what a phoenix truly was.

Ben watched through fading vision as the phoenix spread its wings—new wings, smaller than before but perfect, unmarked by shadow. The creature looked at him with ancient eyes, and gratitude surged through the electromagnetic signature that still connected them.

Thank you, the phoenix sent. *You saved more than my life. You saved the balance. You saved everything.*

Zero percent.

The transformation was complete.

Sidney collapsed beside Ben, her hands immediately finding his chest where the burns were worst. He could barely see her through his fading vision, but he felt her presence through their connection—changed, transformed, but still recognizably Sidney.

Her hands glowed faintly with residual phoenix fire as she tried to channel it into him, tried to heal the burns the way the phoenix had healed corruption. But it wasn't working. The dimensional energy had marked him too deeply.

"Ben, stay with me." Her voice was rough with weariness but human. Still her voice, although he heard something else in it now, something that resonated with phoenix fire. "You're not dying. I won't let you die."

Ben tried to respond, but his body wouldn't cooperate. The burns had spread too far. He could feel his heart failing, his organs shutting down one by one. He was aware of movement in the clearing—DAPI agents backing away from the released phoenix fire, Rosenthal shouting orders, Rebecca Morse's voice calling for medical assistance.

And then he felt another presence, ancient and benevolent.

Powerful.

The unicorn stepped into the clearing, its horn blazing with clean white light that made the afternoon sun look dim by comparison. It moved past Sidney without pausing and pressed its horn directly to Ben's chest, right over the worst of the burns.

Healing energy flooded through him, and Ben

gasped as his shattered nervous system began to knit itself back together. The unicorn couldn't fully heal him—the dimensional burns were too deep, too fundamentally wrong to be completely reversed.

But that energy stabilized the burns and made them survivable. The unicorn's healing was keeping him alive, repairing enough damage that his organs could function, his heart could beat, his lungs could draw breath.

The unicorn held the connection for what felt like hours but was probably only seconds, its horn pressed firmly against Ben's chest.

Then the creature pulled back and turned to Sidney, pressing its horn to her forehead where blood had dried in thick tracks down her face.

More healing energy flowed, and the burns began to change into scars that were no longer life-threatening.

Through his returning awareness, Ben saw the phoenix. It stood in the center of the clearing, its fire burning clean and bright—pure gold with no trace of shadow. Then it turned its ancient gaze on Ben and Sidney, and he felt a wave of gratitude through the electromagnetic signature that still connected them to the creature. No words. Only profound recognition of what they'd sacrificed.

The creature spread its wings—perfect new wings that caught the afternoon light and reflected it as pure gold. It launched itself toward the portal clearing, toward the dimensional barrier that separated Silver Hollow from whatever realm phoenixes called home.

Through his connection with Sidney, Ben could feel her sense how the portal was stabilizing. He felt her awareness of the global network responding to clean phoenix fire, energy flowing properly again after months of disruption. Supernatural sites around the world strengthened as the wound Rosenthal's artificial portal had created finally closed.

The phoenix disappeared through the gateway in a flash of gold light, and Ben heard the creature's final message through their shared consciousness.

Thank you. You saved more than one life. You saved the network. The balance. The thin places where magic lives. Thank you.

And then it was gone.

Sidney collapsed against Ben, and he caught her with arms that were surprisingly steady. The unicorn moved to stand over them both, its body creating a protective barrier between them and the DAPI forces that still surrounded the clearing, their expressions full of befuddlement and wonder.

"Ben," Sidney whispered against his chest, and he could hear tears roughening her voice.

"You're an idiot. A brave, stupid, wonderful idiot."

"Kept you alive," he managed. His voice was hoarse, damaged from the way he'd screamed as the phoenix fire surged through him.

"You almost died doing it."

"Worth it." He lifted his hand to touch her face, now cleaned of blood and tears, thanks to the unicorn's healing. "You're still you. That's all that matters."

She made a sound that was definitely a sob. Her fingers found his, careful of the burns, and their electromagnetic signatures resonated despite the damage that still echoed within him.

Both of them had been changed, but they were still alive.

"Rosenthal," Sidney said after a moment, and Ben heard the edge in her voice. "Where is she?"

Ben turned his head with effort and scanned the clearing. The DAPI agents were backing away from the unicorn's protective stance, their weapons lowered. But Rosenthal—

She was gone. She must have fled just as the phoenix completed its rebirth, when it became clear that her weapon had failed and her primary research subject was being healed by a creature she couldn't hope to capture or control.

"Escaped," Rebecca Morse said as she emerged from the trees, her pistol still in one hand. Blood streaked her face from a cut above her eyebrow, and her dark clothing was smudged with dirt. She looked at the DAPI agents surrounding them and spoke again, a note of command in her voice. "Stand down. All of you. The phoenix is gone, the threat is over, and you've been party to multiple federal crimes. Weapons down. Now."

The agents hesitated and looked at each other. Without Rosenthal's direct authority, they clearly weren't sure how to proceed. Rebecca used their confusion to move closer to Ben and Sidney, positioning herself between them and the remaining forces.

"Eric Hargrove triggered a complete sabotage of the artificial portal," she continued, her voice strong and authoritative. "The entire Phoenix Project is compromised. The equipment is destroyed, the facility is in lockdown, and every piece of data has been transmitted to various oversight committees. Dr. Rosenthal has fled the scene, abandoning her teams and her mission. Anyone who continues to follow her orders is complicit in treason and unauthorized dimensional experimentation."

One by one, the agents lowered their weapons and backed away, confusion and uncertainty clear on their faces. They'd just witnessed something impossible—a human merging with a phoenix, dimensional fire consuming corruption, a creature being reborn clean after weeks of suffering.

They didn't know how to process any of it, didn't know which orders to follow when their commanding officer had fled and their entire mission had collapsed.

The unicorn maintained its protective stance over Ben and Sidney, its horn still glowing faintly with residual healing energy. Through his pain and exhaustion, Ben was grateful for the creature's presence. Without it, the DAPI forces might have attempted capture anyway, might have tried to complete Rosenthal's mission despite defeat staring them in the face.

"Can you stand?" Sidney asked in an undertone.

Ben tried to push himself up and collapsed immediately. His legs wouldn't support his weight, and the burns across his chest screamed at the slightest movement. "Not yet."

"Then we'll wait." Sidney shifted to support him better, her arms around his shoulders. "The unicorn won't let them take us. And Rebecca seems to have the situation under control."

Ben leaned against her and felt their electromagnetic signatures pulse in synchronization. The resonance was different now—stronger and more complex.

It was something they would both have to get used to.

The unicorn lowered its head and pressed its muzzle gently against Sidney's shoulder. Ben could feel the creature's approval, its recognition that they'd made the right choice, that their sacrifice had saved more than just a single phoenix.

They'd saved the entire portal network and protected supernatural sites across the globe. And they'd accomplished something no guardian had ever done—completed a full merge with a corrupted phoenix and lived to tell about it.

Somehow, they'd survived.

The unicorn stepped back, its work complete. The silvery creature regarded them both with ancient eyes that contained wisdom beyond human comprehension, then turned and moved toward the tree line. It paused once, looking back, and Ben felt a promise pulse through the electromagnetic signature he shared with Sidney.

The unicorn would return. When they needed healing again, when their burns became too painful, when they required help adjusting to their transformed abilities—the creature would be there. They were under its protection now, marked by the same dimensional energy it served.

Then it disappeared into the forest, leaving them guarded by Rebecca Morse's authority and the confusion of DAPI agents who no longer knew whom to follow.

"Eric Hargrove's testimony will shut down the Phoenix Project permanently," she said, moving closer. "And I've got enough evidence to bring charges against Sonya Rosenthal for illegal experimentation, unauthorized dimensional manipulation, violation of your Fourth Amendment rights, and about fifteen other federal crimes."

"But she escaped," Sidney said, frustration clear in her voice.

"For now." Rebecca didn't sound overly troubled. "But she can't hide forever. DAPI's going to be torn apart by this investigation, and she'll be the primary target." She looked over at the few agents who remained as they slowly backed away from the clearing. "Can you two move? We should get you somewhere safe."

Ben tried to stand again. This time, with Sidney's help—and despite the pain that shot through him—he managed it. The dimensional burns pulled with every movement, but the unicorn's healing had at least made mobility possible.

His chest felt like it was on fire, but he was standing.

Alive.

"I'll take you back to the safe house," Rebecca continued. "It has medical supplies, secure communication, and a defensible position. It's the best place to regroup. I'll drive you both there and stand guard while you recover."

"And the phoenix?" Ben asked, even though he could feel through his connection with Sidney that the creature had made it through the portal safely.

She smiled. "It went home. The portal network is healing now that clean fire is flowing properly again. The damage from Rosenthal's artificial gate is reversing."

"And your family?" Ben asked Sidney.

She was quiet for a moment, her consciousness reaching across the portal toward wherever her mother and grandmother were trapped. "They're still there. Still alive. The portal's stable enough now that we can plan a retrieval. But not today. Not while we're this damaged."

Ben nodded and leaned heavily on Sidney as they moved toward the spot where Rebecca Morse had concealed her SUV. Every step sent spikes of pain through his chest where the burns were worst, but at least he was mobile, and so was Sidney.

They'd won.

CHAPTER SIXTEEN

Five days after the phoenix's rebirth and Ben's near-death, I opened my eyes to the familiar sight of sunlight streaming through my bedroom window. A little farther away, I could sense the steady, reassuring presence of the unicorn in my backyard.

The creature had taken up residence the day Rebecca Morse brought Ben and me home, stationing itself where it could see both the house and the forest edge. Every morning at dawn it appeared, and it stayed until dusk, its horn glowing faintly as it channeled healing energy toward the house—toward the two of us. How it had managed to avoid notice that whole time, I wasn't sure, but I'd already learned that the unicorn had magic of its own, magic that seemed somehow different from what other creatures who came through the portal possessed.

I lay still for a moment and took inventory, just as I had on the previous days of my recovery. The dimensional burns on my forearms still hurt, but the pain had lessened from excruciating to a constant dull ache, something I could ignore if I tried hard enough. The marks traced delicate patterns along my skin that looked almost like flames frozen in place, and they glowed faintly in the dim light, pulsing in time with my heartbeat.

As far as I knew, those marks were permanent. The unicorn's healing had stabilized them and kept them from spreading further, but it couldn't erase them completely.

Next to me, Ben stirred. His own scars caught the morning light—the worst of them across his chest and down his forearms where Rosenthal's weapon had hit him hardest. The dimensional energy had left circuit-like patterns on his skin, faint but visible if you knew where to look. They were beautiful in a way. Terrible, but beautiful.

His eyes opened, and our electromagnetic connection strengthened almost immediately. That was new—or rather, amplified far beyond what it had once been. We had always resonated, but now our fields synchronized automatically whenever we were close.

"Morning," he said, his voice husky from sleep. "How do you feel?"

"Like I merged with a dying phoenix and got permanently marked by dimensional fire." I shifted carefully and tested my range of motion. Definitely better than yesterday. The unicorn's healing seemed to be working. "You?"

"About the same." He smiled, hazel eyes warming in the light that slipped past the curtains. "Could be worse."

I laughed despite myself, and the sound felt good. Normal.

I so desperately wanted to be normal.

Through our connection, I sensed Ben's electromagnetic field pulsing with relief. He'd been terrified I wouldn't be able to laugh anymore, that the merge would have burned away the parts of me that chuckled at the silliness of life and deflected stress with dark humor.

"I'm still me," I told him. "Changed, but still me."

"I know." He reached for my hand, careful of my marked forearms, and our fingers laced together. "I can feel you. Maybe a little different from before, but the core still feels like you."

"Different" was an understatement. My electromagnetic sensitivity had expanded exponentially after I merged with the phoenix. Where before I'd been able to sense electronic devices within a two-mile radius, now I could feel the entire portal network. Supernatural sites across the globe registered as distant pulses in my awareness, thin places where dimensional energy pooled.

The phoenix fire had left its mark on more than just my skin.

"The unicorn's waiting," I said. "Time for our daily healing session."

Ben nodded. "We should probably get that over with before breakfast."

Carefully, he pushed himself up to a sitting position. Ever since our return to the house, we'd shared this bed, although we'd slept as chastely side by side as brother and sister. We hadn't taken that step in our relationship before the phoenix crisis interfered, and I knew we wanted each other —but we were both uncertain about what intimacy might mean for people as changed as we were.

"Rebecca's coming by this afternoon with updates on the DAPI situation," he added.

Right. I'd forgotten about the text she'd sent late the day before, wanting to check on us and provide a status report. The outside world still existed, with all its complications and consequences. We couldn't hide in my house forever, no matter how tempting the prospect might be.

I pulled on a long-sleeved shirt. Silver Hollow's climate was cool enough that long sleeves wouldn't look strange year-round, which was a small mercy. The marks were beautiful in their own way, but I wasn't ready for the curious questions from friends and neighbors and customers that I knew they would invite.

Ben did the same, although the scars on his forearms were visible if anyone looked closely enough. We would have to come up with some explanation for their presence eventually. The marks didn't exactly look like burns from a fire, but I couldn't think of anything else to explain them away.

We made our way downstairs and out to the backyard, where the unicorn stood under the shelter of the huge oak that guarded the eastern perimeter, the side closest to the forest. The creature turned to regard us with those ancient eyes, and I felt its approval at the way we were healing.

The unicorn approached and pressed its horn first to my forehead, then to Ben's. Clean energy flooded through me, targeting the dimensional burns and encouraging my tissue to adapt rather than simply endure. The pain receded further, and my electromagnetic field stabilized as well.

This was the fifth treatment, and each one had helped more than the last. I didn't think the unicorn could reverse all the changes we'd suffered, but it could still help our bodies adapt to channeling dimensional energy.

When the healing session ended, the unicorn stepped back and moved to its usual position at the forest edge. His was a constant, protective presence that showed no signs of leaving.

Silver Hollow's eternal guardian. The unicorn had been here long before the women of my family started protecting this town, and I had a feeling that it would be here long after we were gone.

"Thank you," I said quietly, and felt the creature's acknowledgment as a ripple of warmth, friendly and soothing.

Back inside, I made coffee while Ben checked his monitoring equipment, which he'd moved over from the cottage he'd been renting. Ever since we got home, he'd been keeping an obsessive eye on the portal's stability and documenting how the network had responded to the phoenix's clean rebirth. The data was remarkable—every supernatural site on the planet had stabilized within hours of the corruption being burned away.

"The portal's holding steady," he told me. "Energy flow is normal. I don't see any signs of the instability caused by Rosenthal's meddling, so your mother and grandmother should be safe on the other side."

"For now." I poured coffee for both of us, the familiar ritual helping to return me to the things I knew, the life I'd once lived. "But we still need to get them back."

"One step at a time. When you're strong enough to attempt dimensional travel, we'll figure out how to retrieve them." He took the mug I offered and blew gently on the hot liquid inside. "Rebecca might have some resources we can use. DAPI's being disbanded, but that doesn't mean all their research is useless."

The mention of DAPI made my jaw tighten. Sonya Rosenthal was still out there somewhere. She'd disappeared effectively, fleeing just as the phoenix completed its rebirth, and I hated that she'd gotten away so easily.

She needed to pay for all the suffering she'd caused.

"I want her caught," I said flatly.

"So does Rebecca. And so does Eric Hargrove, who's providing the key testimony for the investigation." Ben closed his laptop and set it aside. "But that's not your responsibility. You've done enough, Sidney. More than enough."

Had I? It didn't feel like enough. Rosenthal was free. DAPI might have been disbanded, but its personnel had apparently already moved on to other positions and didn't seem to have suffered any real repercussions from being involved in such a sketchy project. The artificial portal technology existed in some form, even if the actual equipment had been destroyed. It would be expensive, but technically, it could be rebuilt.

But Ben was right that I had done what I could. The phoenix was clean, the portal network was stable, and my family was alive. Everything else would have to wait until I was stronger.

We spent the morning in comfortable silence, Ben reviewing data while I tested my expanded abilities. I could sense electronic devices all across Silver Hollow now. The pet shop's security system registered clearly even from my house, as did the electronics in the stores and offices on either side. I could feel the traffic lights downtown as they moved through their cycles, the cell tower on the outskirts of town, and even the satellite connections streaming through the area.

It fascinated me, even as it overwhelmed me. I had to believe that in time I'd be able to control this better, that I'd find a way to shut it out when I didn't want it intruding on my life. The phoenix fire had expanded my abilities to encompass things I'd never been able to sense before—dimensional energy, portal fluctuations, the subtle variations in bioelectric fields that distinguished one person from another.

Was a human being even supposed to possess these beautiful but terrible gifts?

I sensed Rebecca Morse approaching from more than a mile away, her electromagnetic signature distinct enough that I recognized her before she'd even entered the town limits.

"Rebecca's coming," I told Ben. "She should be here in about ten minutes."

He looked up from his laptop, brows drawing together. "You could tell from that distance?"

"Phoenix fire." I gave him a rueful smile. "I think my range has tripled at least. I'm still figuring out the new limits."

Sure enough, ten minutes later, Rebecca pulled into my driveway in a different SUV from the one she'd driven before—this vehicle a Grand Cherokee, dark charcoal gray rather than black. She looked tired but satisfied as she climbed out, and I noticed she wore jeans and a long-sleeved T-shirt. The casual clothing told me her plans to take an indefinite leave of absence from the Bureau hadn't changed.

"Sidney. Ben." She nodded to each of us as we met her at the door. "You're both looking better than the last time I saw you."

"The unicorn's been helping," I replied. "Do you want some coffee, or maybe tea?"

"Tea would be great."

We headed into the kitchen, where I got the kettle going on the stovetop before we all settled around the table. Rebecca reached into the satchel she'd had slung over one arm and pulled out a tablet with enough security protocols that my electromagnetic sense could barely penetrate its hardened shell. She must have noticed me trying, because she raised an eyebrow.

"Your abilities have expanded."

"Phoenix fire leaves marks in more ways than one." I showed her my forearms, the delicate patterns catching the afternoon light that drifted through the big window overlooking the garden. "From what I can tell, my range has tripled, and I can sense the global portal network now. I'm still discovering new things I can do."

Her brows lifted slightly. I noticed she was wearing some actual eye makeup today, just a little liner and mascara for her thick, dark lashes.

"Useful," she commented before she opened a file on the tablet. "DAPI is officially disbanded as of two days ago. A congressional oversight committee voted unanimously to eliminate the department after reviewing Eric Hargrove's testimony and the evidence I provided. The Phoenix Project is shut down, the facility—what's left of it—is under federal seal, and everyone involved is under investigation."

"And Rosenthal?" Ben asked.

Rebecca's lips pressed together, and I could tell she wasn't too happy about what she was about to say. "Disappeared. She fled the country, probably using resources she'd been stockpiling for exactly this scenario. We have warrants out for her arrest, international alerts, and every reciprocal intelligence agency in the world looking for her. But so far, nothing."

I'd expected that answer, but hearing it still made my stomach clench with worry and anger. Sonya Rosenthal was out there somewhere, probably planning her next move. She'd seen what phoenix fire could do, had seen how the merge worked...had seen everything she needed to continue her research in some new location.

"She'll surface eventually," Rebecca continued, her expression untroubled. "People like her always do. And when she does, we'll be ready." She paused before going on. "In the meantime, there's good news. Eric Hargrove's full testimony cleared you both of any wrongdoing. You're not under investigation, not being monitored, not facing any charges. Officially, you were victims of an unauthorized research program."

"That's generous," Ben said, although I couldn't quite tell from his tone whether he was being ironic.

"It's accurate." Rebecca's voice was firm. "Sonya Rosenthal kidnapped you, experimented on supernatural creatures, and deployed military weapons against civilians. You two stopped her. The oversight committee recognizes that."

She slid her tablet toward us. The documentation cleared our names and provided compensation for damages incurred during federal operations. The amount was substantial, and my eyes widened. I hadn't been hurting for money, thanks to the way my grandmother and mother had been stockpiling it for years, but even if I had been, what the government was offering would have been enough to start over from scratch.

"There's also this." Rebecca set aside her tablet and pulled out a printed document in a manila folder. "Federal protection for Silver Hollow and the forest. Technically, the forest should have already been protected, since most of it belongs to the USFS, but this declaration makes the consequences for meddling there a whole lot steeper."

I stared at the document, hardly daring to believe it. "You got them to protect the portal?"

A brief nod. "I got them to protect the forest. It's hard to get a bunch of senators to admit that the supernatural is real, so it's not perfect. There will always be people like Rosenthal who want to weaponize anything they can. But it's a start. And it means you can do your guardian work without worrying about federal interference."

Ben reached for my hand under the table, and I could feel relief radiating through his touch. This was so much more than we'd hoped for. Official protection, cleared names, and the resources to continue protecting Silver Hollow.

"Thank you," I said simply. "I know you risked your career helping us."

The smallest lift of her shoulders. "Like I told you before, I became a federal agent to protect people, not to help mad scientists torture supernatural creatures for weapons programs." She rose from her seat and returned her tablet to her satchel. "You two saved the global portal network. I figure we both did some heavy lifting."

I supposed we did. Ben and I might have been the ones who'd helped the phoenix complete its rebirth cycle, but we never would have gotten that far without her.

Rebecca paused at the door, and something in her expression softened. "Eric Hargrove sends his regards, by the way. He's testifying again next week, but he wanted me to tell you both that he's grateful you gave him the chance to do the right thing."

"How is he?" I asked. He'd been pretty much at ground zero when the artificial portal collapsed. That couldn't have been easy.

"He's healing, just like you two. The dimensional exposure did some damage, but he'll recover." A faint smile touched her lips. "We've been working on his testimony together. He's determined to make sure everyone at DAPI who knew what Rosenthal was doing faces consequences."

The way she spoke those words, the subtle

warmth in her voice when she mentioned Eric Hargrove, made me wonder if their coordination had extended beyond the merely professional. I didn't ask, though. As far as I was concerned, Rebecca Morse had earned her privacy.

After she left, Ben and I sat in silence for a long moment.

"We did it," he said at last.

"I think we did." I looked down at my faintly glowing forearms. Here at home, I didn't mind pushing up my sleeves to reveal them, but I knew I'd have to be careful once I was back out in public. Ben and I had explained our absence from Silver Hollow and the continuing closure of the pet shop as having to leave town to attend a funeral of someone in his family, a funeral in Southern California, where I'd picked up a nasty bug that had kept me home for days afterward. At some point, though, I'd have to face people again. "At significant cost, but we did it."

"Was it worth it?"

I thought about the way the phoenix's wings had blazed pure gold after its rebirth, how the global network was stabilized and flowing properly again. How my mother and grandmother were still alive, even after all these months.

How Ben was sitting here beside me, alive despite throwing himself in front of a weapon that should have killed him.

"Yes," I said. "It was worth it."

That evening, we went outside to sit on the porch after dinner. The day had been uncharacteristically sunny, and some of its warmth had lingered even after the sun went down. It got that way here sometimes in late August, burning away the perpetual fog and mist so we could get a little taste of what summer was supposed to be like.

"I want you to move in with me," I told Ben. "Not as roommates recovering from dimensional burns, but as real partners. Romantic partners."

He turned to look at me, expression startled. "You want me to move in?"

Since I'd started this, I had to keep going, even as I wondered if I should have kept my mouth shut. I pulled in a breath and then said, "We've been practically living together since this started anyway. And after everything that's happened, I can't imagine my life without you in it. I don't *want* to imagine it."

"Sidney—" he began, but I knew I needed to continue before I could lose my nerve.

"I know we'll need to find a different place eventually. When my mother and grandmother get back, this house will be theirs, just as it always has been. But until then—or until we find somewhere new—I want you to be here with me."

Joy pulsed outward from him, so intense that I hardly needed our connection to feel it. "Yes," he said at once. "Obviously yes." He paused, then sent me a lopsided smile. "I guess it's a good thing I only have a month-to-month agreement for Nancy's cottage."

"Definitely," I said with an answering smile. "You wouldn't want to get on Silver Hollow's bad side by breaking a lease."

We both laughed—but then he reached out and took my hands and pulled me close, pressing his lips against mine. We'd kissed since we'd both survived the merge with the phoenix, but this felt different, as if we both had realized that we were about to set out on an entirely new path.

I leaned against him, a haze of warmth surrounding us as our bioelectric fields overlapped and blended. "We're probably going to glow during sex," I commented.

He laughed again. "That's what you're worried about?"

"Have you seen how our marks react when our fields synchronize? We literally illuminate each other." I gestured at the faint glow that surrounded our clasped hands. "It's going to be pretty obvious if anyone's watching."

"Then we'll make sure no one's watching." He

placed a gentle kiss against my cheek. "Sidney, after everything we've been through, a little bioluminescence during intimacy is probably the least of our concerns."

He was right, of course. We'd merged our consciousnesses through phoenix fire, survived dimensional burns, and channeled energy that shouldn't exist in normal reality. A little glowing during sex was hardly the strangest thing about us anymore.

"Take me to bed," I said. "Let's see just how much we glow."

Ben's eyes darkened with need, and I could feel how his electromagnetic signature throbbed with enough desire to make my breath catch.

Still, he hesitated. "Are you sure you're healed enough?"

"The unicorn's been treating us for five days. Everything's not much more than a dull ache." I rose from the porch steps and pulled him along with me. "And I need to know we'll work together, that the changes didn't make us incompatible somehow."

He sent me a serious look. "Sidney, we'll always work."

But he didn't say anything else and instead let me lead him inside, up the stairs to my bedroom—the place where we'd been sleeping together ever since we returned, only not in the way I now planned.

I'd thought about this moment for days, ever since the pain had subsided enough to let me consider the future. I'd been worried that the merge had changed me so fundamentally that intimacy would feel different, wrong, something this altered body of mine would no longer need.

But as Ben pulled me close, as his hands found the hem of my shirt and carefully lifted it over my head, I felt only anticipation.

And desire.

He paused when he saw the marks fully—the delicate patterns that traced my forearms like frozen flames, glowing faintly in the reflected light from the sconces in the upstairs hallway.

"You're marked," he said quietly, his fingers hovering over the patterns without quite touching them.

"So are you." I reached up to trace the faint scars on his chest, following the pathways that the dimensional energy had burned into his flesh. "I suppose we match."

He laughed softly, and then he was kissing me, his electromagnetic signature merging with mine. Yes, I'd been right. We absolutely illuminated each other, our bioelectric fields synchronizing so perfectly that the dimensional marks on our skin glowed brighter.

Faint light danced across our skin as we undressed each other carefully, mindful of burns that were still healing. Ben's hands traced patterns on my back, and I explored the marks on his chest, feeling how the dimensional energy had subtly changed the texture of his skin.

We were different now—but we were still Sidney and Ben.

When he finally moved over me, when we came together with the kind of desperate gentleness that spoke of how close we'd come to losing this, our electromagnetic fields merged completely.

I gasped as Ben's consciousness flooded through our connection. Not just his emotions, even though I felt those as well—love and desire and fierce protectiveness tangled together. No, this was his actual awareness, his thoughts…his sensations. What it felt like to touch my skin, to be inside me, to experience this moment from his perspective.

Shared consciousness. Just like during the merge, only voluntary this time.

"Ben." I managed to get out his name, although speaking was difficult when I could feel what he felt. "Can you—"

"Feel you? Yes." His voice sounded hoarse, and I could sense his shock and wonder. "Sidney, I can feel everything. What you're feeling...what you're thinking."

"Is it too much?" I didn't want to pull away, but I would if that was what he needed to preserve his sanity, his sense of self.

"No." He shifted, and the sensation doubled —what it felt like for me and what it felt like for him, pleasure cascading through our merged consciousness. "God, no. It's perfect."

We moved together, our electromagnetic fields creating cascading waves of soft light that lit up the bedroom. I was aware of my body and Ben's simultaneously, experiencing intimacy from both perspectives. Feeling what he felt when he touched me, sensing what I felt when he moved inside me.

It was overwhelming...transcendent.

Absolutely right.

And then we came together, our electromagnetic fields pulsing in perfect synchronization, light dancing across our skin.

For a single breathless moment, we were one consciousness, one awareness, experiencing this moment as a unified entity rather than two separate people.

Then we separated slowly, our fields gradually distinguishing themselves while remaining connected. I collapsed against Ben, both of us breathing hard, our marked skin still glowing faintly in the aftermath.

"Well," I said when I could speak again. "That was different."

Ben laughed, the sound breathless in the quiet space. "Understatement of the year."

He was probably right. "And the glowing was pretty obvious."

"Worth it." He pulled me closer, taking care even though I'd assured him that my burns weren't bothering me too much anymore. "Sidney, that was…I've never experienced anything like that. Feeling what you felt, being inside your consciousness while we—"

"I know." I pressed my face against his chest, feeling the strong beat of his heart against my cheek. "The electromagnetic connection created some kind of shared consciousness. I suppose we merged."

"Not as deeply as you merged with the phoenix, but still." His hand stroked my hair. "Is it always going to be like that?"

I reached out with my expanded abilities and sensed our electromagnetic fields. They were still synchronized, still resonating. The marks on our skin glowed faintly, although the glow was fading now that the intensity had passed.

"I think so," I said. "I mean, this is just an educated guess, because I don't think anyone truly knows all the ramifications of what we experienced. But when we synchronize, when we connect that deeply, we're going to merge consciousness every time."

He pressed a kiss against the top of my head. "I can live with that."

"Me, too."

We lay together in comfortable silence, our marked bodies fitting together like two pieces of the same puzzle. Somewhere beyond the window, over at the edge of the forest, the unicorn was maintaining its patient vigil.

"Do you think the unicorn knows what we just did?" I asked.

Ben laughed again. "An ancient, mystical creature with heightened senses? It definitely knows."

Heat touched my cheeks. "Well, that's embarrassing."

"It's probably seen worse over the centuries."

Well, he had a point there.

I shifted so I could prop myself up on one elbow and gaze down at him. The faint marks on his chest caught the light, beautiful in their own terrible way.

"Thank you," I said quietly. "I know they're only two words, but still. Thank you for taking that weapon blast and anchoring me through the merge. For surviving everything with me."

"You don't need to thank me for that." His

hand found mine. Our fingers laced together, and a golden glow surrounded them. "I made a choice, Sidney. That choice included throwing myself in front of Rosenthal's weapon if it meant keeping you alive."

"Still, you almost died."

His shoulders lifted. "So did you. It's like you said—we're partners. We face the impossible as a team. That's what we do."

I kissed him, putting everything I couldn't say into the connection between us, gratitude and love and a fierce determination that we would face whatever came next together.

When we finally pulled apart, I could see the moon beginning to rise beyond the forest. Time had slipped away while we were wrapped in each other, and twilight had faded into deep night.

Dinner had been long enough ago that I was hungry again, so we dished ourselves some ice cream and headed back out to the porch. The night air was chilly, promising that summer was on its way out and autumn right around the corner, but it still felt good to sit there and eat, to let the cold richness of that chocolate mint chip ice cream slide down my throat and cool the lingering phoenix fire.

The unicorn moved closer as we sat, positioning itself near the porch steps but with its head angled toward the forest. Now it was close enough to be obviously present but still far enough back that it could disappear into the trees if anyone approached.

"Ready for whatever comes next?" Ben asked.

I wasn't sure how to answer that question. I wanted to believe we'd vanquished Sonya Rosenthal once and for all, but I couldn't know that for sure. And even if she proved to no longer be a threat, we still had to figure out a way to finally bring my mother and grandmother home.

"No," I said frankly. "But whatever it is, we'll face it as a team."

Ben's hand found mine, and our connection strengthened. Soft light pulsed faintly where our marked skin touched, visible even in the darkness.

The unicorn turned its head to regard us with those ancient eyes, and I felt approval through our electromagnetic connection, a recognition that we'd survived what should have been impossible. That we would continue protecting Silver Hollow despite our changes—or perhaps because of them.

We sat together as the night wore on, the unicorn maintaining its steady vigil beside us.

This was our new normal. Dimensional burns that glowed faintly, abilities expanded beyond what any guardian had experienced, a partner whose consciousness I could merge with whenever we connected deeply enough.

We might have been changed, but we were

still Sidney and Ben, partners facing the impossible as a team.

The unicorn settled into a resting position, its horn dimming but still faintly luminous. It would continue to guard us for as long as it thought necessary.

And despite everything we'd survived, despite the costs we'd paid and the changes we'd endured, I experienced something then that I hadn't felt since the moment Sonya Rosenthal's team had rolled into Silver Hollow more than a month ago.

Peace.

I prayed it would be a lasting one.

The Legendary series concludes in Here Be Dragons.

ALSO BY CHRISTINE POPE

LEGENDARY

(Urban Fantasy/Paranormal Romance)

Silver Linings

Lion's Share

Trial by Fire

Here Be Dragons

VEGAS SLAYERS

(Urban Fantasy/Paranormal Romance)

Speak of the Devil

Devil in the Details

The Devil Went Down to Laughlin

Devil May Care

Devil to Pay

The Devil's Due

The Devil Next Door

THE WITCHES OF MINGUS MOUNTAIN

(Paranormal Romance)

Stolen Time

Borrowed Time

Killing Time

Wind Called

Demon Loved

Christmas Past

Season of Magic

Healer's Heart

PROJECT DEMON HUNTERS*

(Paranormal Romance)

Unquiet Souls

Unbound Spirits

Unholy Ground

Unseen Voices

Unmarked Graves

Unbroken Vows

Unholy Night

THE DJINN WARS*

(Paranormal Romance)

Chosen

Taken

Fallen

Broken

Forsaken

Forbidden

Awoken

Illuminated

Stolen

Forgotten

Driven

Unspoken

Hidden

Written

Given

Mistaken

FAMILIAR SPIRITS*

(Cozy Mystery/Paranormal Romance)

Spells and Spaniels

Cauldrons and Cats

Hexes and Hedgehogs

Charms and Chihuahuas

Runes and Ravens

LATTES AND LEVITATION*

(Cozy Mystery/Paranormal Romance)

Caffeine Before Curses

Muffins After Magic

Pastries and Prophecies

Eclairs and Ectoplasm

Sugar Skulls and Specters

Wedding Cakes and Wishes

HEDGEWITCH FOR HIRE*

(Cozy Mystery/Paranormal Romance)

Grave Mistake

Social Medium

Household Demons

Perpetual Potion

Jingle Spells

Wandering Monsters

Uninvited Ghosts

Prophet Motive

Ballroom Bits

Spell Check

Brew Confessions

Charm School

UNEXPECTED MAGIC*

(Urban Fantasy/Paranormal Romance)

Found Objects

Finders, Keepers

Lost and Found

Finding Destiny

THE WITCHES OF WHEELER PARK*

(Paranormal Romance)

Storm Born

Thunder Road

Winds of Change

Mind Games

A Wheeler Park Christmas

Blood Ties

Healing Hands

Wishful Thinking

Smoke and Mirrors

MISS PRIMM'S ACADEMY FOR WAYWARD WITCHES*

(Fantasy/Academy Romance)

Misspelled

Dispelled

Expelled

THE DEVIL YOU KNOW*

(Paranormal Romance)

Sympathy for the Devil

Charmed, I'm Sure

A Wing and a Prayer

Wish Upon a Star

THE WITCHES OF CANYON ROAD*

(Paranormal Romance)

Hidden Gifts

Darker Paths

Mysterious Ways

A Canyon Road Christmas

Demon Born

An Ill Wind

Higher Ground

Haunted Hearts

THE WITCHES OF CLEOPATRA HILL*

(Paranormal Romance)

Darkangel

Darknight

Darkmoon

Sympathetic Magic

Protector

Spellbound

A Cleopatra Hill Christmas

Impractical Magic

Strange Magic

The Arrangement

Defender

Bad Blood

Deep Magic

Darktide

Star Bright

THE WATCHERS TRILOGY*

(Paranormal Romance)

Falling Dark

Dead of Night

Rising Dawn

THE SEDONA FILES*

(Paranormal/Science Fiction Romance)

Bad Vibrations

Desert Hearts

Angel Fire

Star Crossed

Falling Angels

Enemy Mine

TALES OF THE LATTER KINGDOMS*

(Fantasy Romance)

Dragon Rose

Ashes of Roses

One Thousand Nights

Threads of Gold

The Wolf of Harrow Hall

Moon Dance

The Song of the Thrush

THE GAIAN CONSORTIUM SERIES*

(Science Fiction Romance)

Beast (free prequel novella)

Blood Will Tell

Breath of Life

The Gaia Gambit

The Mandala Maneuver

The Titan Trap

The Zhore Deception

The Refugee Ruse

STANDALONE TITLES

Hearts on Fire (Paranormal Romance)

Taking Dictation (Contemporary Romance)

Golden Heart (Gaslamp Fantasy Romance)

Night Music: A Modern Reimagining of The Phantom of the Opera (Contemporary Romance)

Ghost Dance: A Sequel to Gaston Leroux's The Phantom of the Opera (Historical Mystery/Romance)

Flight Before Christmas (Fantasy Romance)

* Indicates a completed series

ABOUT THE AUTHOR

USA Today bestselling author Christine Pope has been writing stories ever since she commandeered her family's Smith-Corona typewriter back in grade school. Her work includes paranormal romance, cozy paranormal mystery, and urban fantasy, among others. She makes her home in Arizona.

Don't miss out on any of Christine's new releases —sign up for her newsletter today!

Christine Pope on the Web:
www.christinepope.com

facebook.com/ChristinePopeAuthor
youtube.com/@ChristinePopeAuthor
bookbub.com/authors/christine-pope

www.ingramcontent.com/pod-product-compliance
Lightning Source LLC
LaVergne TN
LVHW041059080826
845145LV00007B/1636

* 9 7 8 1 9 4 6 4 3 5 9 1 0 *